The Captain's Door

C·S· Houghton

The Captain's Door is dedicated to my mother.

THE CAPTAIN'S DOOR

Printed in the United States of America
First Printing 2013
ISBN 978-1482689921

Cover and book design by C.S. Houghton
Special thanks to the endlessly supportive copy-editing team of my mother Karen and my wife Sonia.

www.minaparadis.com

1

It is comfortable to lie naked in the dark on the netting underneath the bowsprit. I hung there in the widow's net, counting each fall of the ship back into the sea while whitecaps passed beneath me like flashes of reflected fish silver. Mist collected like perspiration along the length of my body until I shivered, but I fixed my attention on the endless dark below. I flew like that, fastened by hand-spans of wet hemp that ran too tightly across my legs, brow, wrists, shoulders, and stomach while my toes pushed idly past a spray softened section of rope.

I licked my lips and rubbed the salt from my tongue along the ridge of my palette. After a time, I rolled slowly onto my back, feeling the rope peel away and leave me embossed with the form of the braided lines. My head turned last, following my body reluctantly. The stars coming into view looked like scales washed off into a pool of water, but unlike the way the moon shimmers across the serrated edge of a wave, those points of light above could actually be counted and recounted. I supposed that would not be true if years passed like seconds; a night sky like that would be a roiling and unknowable mirror of the sea.

Still, I could think only of putting out those stars. I wanted to extinguish every point of light until it became a matter of habit, a conditioned response to any kindling flicker. Maybe then I'd be able to snuff out the torch that waited for me within my chambers. Maybe my hand on the screw at the base of the torch would move as though it were mechanized, and I finally could kill that little, lesser, star. I closed my eyes and tried not to think about the damned flame. After all, it was the thought of tomorrow's run into Pomin, not the torch, that drove me out to the widow's net. I was doing it again, obsessing over the torch.

The parted sea collected on my shoulders, running in streams down to the small of my back. Even though it was a hot night, the wind bit hard. Struggling to put that chill out of mind made it a little easier to give up all thoughts and lose myself. I tried to focus only on my own inner warmth and the consistency of each prolonged breath. The wall of noise created by the clipper cutting through the water helped me submerge my senses in the sea as I deliberately relaxed each limb and digit in turn. Time passed in waves, unbroken but also unsteady and deep.

When I finally sat up, I first twisted around to look in the direction we sailed. No light. It would be at least two hours before we hit the navigation channels, but sooner than that we would see an unnatural star, Pomin's island-bound lighthouse sweeping its beacon arm to the west as we tacked eastward.

Arrival would be near daybreak, but I didn't plan to wait above deck for the sunrise. Aside from some kind of useless modesty, I felt renewed by the water and eager to get the day's tasks over with. After tunneling back into my nightshirt, I climbed the rough jute pull-line over the bulwarks to the empty forecastle deck. If anyone had been watching, they didn't stick around. Besides, I sometimes jumped into the water with the men while they bathed and no one ever seemed pay any mind.

Ships get noisy at night. They flap sails and crack lines. Hulls creak. The belly of the ship sounds-out a hollow thud whenever it falls back on the body of the water. But, in all of that, at those hours there are fewer birds or men likely to interrupt one's thoughts. As a girl, I had fantasized about having control over day and night, just to quiet the world. That's a lot of tampering for some peace — it's so much simpler to just cross through my door.

I passed the foremast and counted my steps. The Transcendent was small for a trading clipper, and with my eyes closed I brushed against the main mast at only twenty steps, as always. Three more paces and I took the quarterdeck step where I opened my eyes. The silhouette at the wheel mouthed an extinguished pipe. If it had been lit earlier, I hadn't smelled it downwind.

"Evening, Captain."

I nodded in return to seaman Haggard, but I wasn't sure if he saw it. Able seaman, I corrected myself — he had been promoted from seaman to able seaman before departure from New Liguria. I hadn't seen him for at least the past week. Of course, I must not have spent more than a half hour a day out on the ship during the entire voyage. Yet even as I greeted him I pursed my lips and caught myself nervously touching my collarbone. I wanted only to slip by unnoticed and disappear off of the ship and into the door. Instead, I planted my feet broadly and watched my posture.

"It's a beautiful night, isn't it?" asked Haggard.

"Yes, although I think it's morning."

"Well, that's true." Haggard put his pipe back to his lips.

I supposed that was enough banter. I turned without comment and dropped down the nine steep steps to the galley, my bare feet hardly grazing each stair. Across the length of the Transcendent's only enclosed deck, I saw a sailor turning to ascend the forecastle stairs. Maybe he'd been waiting for me to leave the widow's net. The stooped man stood at attention when he noticed me. I returned his salute, although the whole affair wasn't really necessary. It looked like Crane. He was relatively new. Most of the crew had served with me for more than a decade, something for which I was very thankful.

I walked on the balls of my feet past the mates quarters to the louvered doors at the aft end of the ship. I lost count of my steps only as I passed into the cramped captain's quarters and locked the door.

The room was dark and smelled like vanilla. Moonlight through the row of small windows at the back of the quarters cast long milky shadows. The comfortable scent of the space came from the extinguished votive candle set on the table by the bed. It was a gift to me from Crocodile. I had left it burning there in the captain's quarters all night and a day while I was actually far off within my door. The timing of the veteran sailor's odd present probably coincided with some Quiripi holiday. I felt a little guilty that I hadn't thought to ask. In any case, he explained that he'd cooked the gift himself in the steward's pot from candle ends. I suspected that the vanilla pods were likely the same ones that had been rattling loose around in the hold for several years.

The linen of the cabin bed felt chilly as I smoothed it with my hand. I had never slept in the bed, although it was mine by issue and station. Instead of crawling onto the mattress, or remaining on the ship at all, I crouched down to the row of cabinets underneath the bed and removed a panel. Behind that facade I had hung my door. When doors like mine were more plentiful in the world, they had been called captain's doors, whether they were found on a ship or not. I simply called it *my* door.

The iron bolt underneath released with a sharp click and the small door opened to me. The cloth under my wet knees stuck to the tunnel floor as I passed from the ship to the stone passage within. At the end of the narrow, square corridor waited a slice of light that poured from the open crack of the heavier inner door. More light filled the entrance tunnel when I pushed that hatch-like door open. I rose from my hands and knees into the warm antechamber beyond. There, the gentle rocking of the ship could not be felt. It was probably thousands of miles away — I didn't know for sure. All within was stone and steady as the bedrock from which the chambers had likely been carved. I spun the iron wheel attached to the round bulkhead hatch to seal the entrance.

I always loved the sound of my own bare feet slapping against the cold stone floor when I crossed the foyer. The echo would ricochet off of the pillars and the alcove above and down the three main halls and all the way back to me again. I pushed aside the ultramarine blue curtains dividing the foyer from the living areas beyond and slipped between the folds, intentionally letting the velvet sweep across my cheek. I pulled off my damp nightshirt under the tall arches of the wide hall. After stepping out of my pantalettes, I threw the clothes into the basket I kept by the entrance arch — there was no reason to wear anything within the door, so I rarely did. Slippers were the exception, and I hurried to get off of the stone floor and into my favorite pair.

Although I knew I should have rushed to the torch before I lost my nerve, I looked away from the task and towards the washroom. I unpinned my braids and stepped up onto the stool I used to reach the sink. In front of the big lead mirror I inspected each braid, welcoming the possibility of having to take them out if they needed to be washed and combed — anything to distract myself from another useless, thankless tomorrow wasted in the service of madame secretary. I shushed myself out loud. Nothing mattered, and I knew it. Unless, of course, I did put out the torch.

The braids were fine, although the longest, a butterfly braid that reached my waist, had begun to fray towards the end. If the occasional ritual combing weren't so calming, I probably would have chopped it all off and spent eternity passing as a boy.

I stepped down and tucked my well-worn slippers between the tightly-fisted lion's claw feet of the stool, turning them around toe-first as I always did. Without looking, I reached for a fresh towel hanging from the rack and laid it across the edge of the tub where I liked to sit with my feet dangling into the empty granite basin.

After pulling one of the tasseled chains, I waited for the sound of gurgling within the wall. Preceded by a rush of warm air, water poured from the square opening in the stone and splashed into the basin several feet below. I kicked my toes lazily in the heated stream. It escaped down the tub drain nearly as quickly as it filled, but I didn't set the stopper. Instead, I stepped into the deliciously warm, shallow pool. The drain had grown slower over the decades and enough water accumulated to cover my ankles. Using a cup dipped into the flowing stream, I washed the salt off my body.

The water running through my hands beaded up on my legs and reminded me of the sea spray. In turn, that reminded me of the lights I had seen reflected in the under-dark of the ocean below the net. And, while it should not have, all of that reminded me of the torch. Like an external thought cast against the mind's eye by an intruding projectionist, I saw the green flame. I tried to put it out of my head, but I could hear the hum of it over the trickling water. The idea of the torch resonated at a pitch that made my head ache. If I wasn't under contract, if I'd never even seen one of those torches, I could be headed for Pomin on holiday, not some ridiculous political errand.

After bathing, I walked into the bedroom where I made myself as comfortable I could, sitting on the edge of the bed and picking at the ends of my hair. I would go to the torch when I was ready. And, this time I would put it out. Or, could I hear it already? Yes. I could put it out, or I could cradle it. My own cowardice gave me goosebumps.

I reminded myself that there were two more coordinates I had not plotted — I shouldn't forget to do that, but how could I concentrate on a map while the torch wouldn't shut up? And, I had noticed earlier that the outer jib was tearing where it was last stitched, again. I pinched a split end between my nervously bitten nails. I also needed to have Bosun show the greenhands again how to mend a staysail properly. A sound, not unlike a ringing in the ear grew and subsided.

In frustration, I walked to the library and climbed the cascading outer stair to my study. After crossing behind my desk I dug my feet into the thick, felted rug. The big desk stood between me and the cabinet embedded into the mural wall at the other end of the room. Whatever I did, it would be more than ninety years too late. I moved the desk chair with one foot and sat down. With my arms crossed on the desk blotter, I rested my head and avoided looking towards the cabinet. My eyes drifted through the desk clutter and settled on the long speaker. I picked it up. It was actually a small thing, but they were still called long speakers anyway. Some called them Kirkland tubes, but the man never actually invented them; he just came up with a clever way to link any two regular old brass speaking tubes by connecting them the same way my door connects to the ship.

I wished the speaker would sound. If someone was trying to contact me I could pull myself from the study and away from my task. It wasn't likely. I looked up to the cabinet dead-across from me. Maybe I would go get a shirt instead. It felt colder in the study than I liked it. The chain that I used to increase the temperature in the library and study had not worked for a long while.

I sighed and met the inward-projecting gaze of the torch. The cabinet doors hid it from view, but it could be seen with something that was akin to sight. I suppose I imagined it. Still, I maintained that matched stare and crossed the room. My hands closed comfortably around the pulls of the cabinet doors.

Although the torch flamed within the cabinet, it needed no chimney. In fact, the cabinet wasn't much larger than the lamp, stem, and flame. It didn't matter. I pulled at each of the half doors. Light opened across my chest. The nearly transparent hair of my stomach cast slivered hints of shadows against my skin while that light shining from the opening doors painted the flesh in an unhealthy jaundice. That verdigris beam cutting and dividing me lengthwise widened as I opened the doors. I looked into the carved space of the wall-set cabinet. Whoever carved the space into the living rock had certainly not planned on having a lamp set there, but I had stored it inside those doors ever since I discovered my captain's door and the chambers within.

Within the cowry-like hollow of the torches glass base I could see plenty of copper. I called it copper, but the lamp was filled with a quicksilver-like syrup, not unlike a cool but molten copper. A metal-wet wick coiled up through the lamps narrow neck until its path was obscured by a black obsidian-like glass sheath. The smokeless green flame itself issued from the lamps tulip-petal shaped black neck. It burned as a neatly formed almond shaped head of nearly opaque fire. The head barely moved, rippling more than flickering. It was also not truly green — the parted neck of the lamp fed a whiter throat of fire that opened up into a cool sage green. That green body then yellowed towards the dancing head of the flame which itself closed down to a tiny point that moved like a tortured and twisting grain of singularly beautiful flax.

I let my eyelids fall, and with some effort brought my hand to the cold brass dial hidden behind the ornately scaled base of the lamp. My fingers slipped along the ridges of the small dial until I applied more pressure and the knob began to turn. It was then that I noticed how easily the light of the torch could still be seen through closed eyes — it burned a warm summer green, even more enticing than when seen plainly. The flame's glow diminished as I started to turn the knob. Yet there was something wrong with keeping one's eyes closed through such a task. It seemed disrespectful not to watch the flame expire, like I owed it more than this after so many years.

If the neck of the wick were to shrink into the body of the black lamp, the fire would gasp and die. It wouldn't be like a candle, which kindles the tiniest red heart of a flame in its wick for seconds. When you put out a candle, the red body of it persists in the wick, at least until it smokes and goes dark. I recalled mother speaking of that to Aunt Phyll.

"Phyll," my mother had said. "A lit candle is so bright, but an extinguished candle is light itself. You can see its red body. Watch. Look at this one on the table." At that point my mother had walked the room, putting all the other candles out with a long-necked snuffer that had a squeaky hinge. After some dramatic pause, she put out the final candle at the center of the table. I remembered the way my mother stared at her sister in the near-dark before the candle fully died. I don't think they knew I was watching, but wasn't not sure. "Look at the glowing wick. It's a crumpled little worm, isn't it? It even wriggles a little bit. The wick wasn't just the last of the body — it *was* the flame body made visible, the vital stuff. Well, it's really out now, isn't it?"

While I stood in front of the cabinet staring at the torch, I considered exactly when it was that I first considered the possibility that my mother had ordered my aunt killed. That odd speech had been delivered by Mother to Aunt Phyll the night before she in died in a barn fire.

Thoughts of my own torch returned and I opened my eyes. My hand had drifted from the knob at the back of the torch lamp. Look at it, I thought. I would kill that flame with no more consideration than one might afford a candle. I brought both hands to the flame, forming a loose cup.

The memory of what I had come to do left me and was replaced by a kind of physical relief. Bridges of thread-thin sparks twisted and wormed from the flame to my palms and fingers. A familiar tingle traveled down my arms and settled in my chest. Gently, it spread across my back and moved through me as if it would pass into the floor like water seeking the center of the earth. I shivered comfortably.

After some time I withdrew from the torch, first turning the dimmer abruptly back to where it had been just a few minutes earlier. The flame grew to its full size. The light floated above the neck like a swollen and worthless gem might hang from the neck of a street peddler who just tricked you out of your only coin using nothing but three cups and a wide smile. That damned torch. How could I not have put it out?

I closed the cabinet and went downstairs where I paced a while before curling up on braided throw rug. I had nearly made it through another night without sleeping. All sleeping did is bring on the next day a little faster. I hated sleeping.

2

The long speaker woke me up before I had a chance to dream, or if I had been dreaming, it was only of an endless, dark tunnel. If it were possible to ignore the long speaker, I would have, but the whistle is a scream when heard within the absolute silence of the door. I gained my footing and ran down the hall through the curtains to the long speaker that I kept in the foyer. After flipping the whistle-cap backwards, I spoke into the tube. "I'm here."

"Captain, we have sighted the signal light."

"Isn't Allan available? Wake him. He should be making arrangements with the ship Zephyr."

"Aye, Captain."

It was difficult to identify the speaker by the tinny and too quiet voice, but I suspected it was seaman Crane. I didn't recall him ever having used the long speaker. He likely held the mouthpiece too far from his lips — through the tube, I could hear the ambient sounds of the ship nearly as well as the sailor.

I replaced the whistling cap. It must have been seaman Crane. The other night, the former accountant turned enlisted sailor had lowered his head when I announced that most of the crew would not be able to go ashore in Pomin. It was difficult for any of the men to sail uninterrupted for nearly a month and take no leave while moored at a large port like Pomin. Second and third mates Rohad and Allan would have business on shore, but that would be work. We all had orders. It didn't much matter what anyone wanted.

I hurried back through the blue curtain and into my bedroom, stopping under the adjoining archway that lead to the wardrobe. After enjoying the quiet dark for a few minutes, I pulled a match from the tin hanging on the wall and struck it against the box. I brought the flame to the hanging lamp. It leapt from the match to the fragile gas mantle as I opened the valve. The gas lines were new; I had sweated, joined, bent, and installed all of the piping and fixtures myself during the brief leave we had enjoyed before disembarking from the capital. It was wonderful not having to prime the lamp, but I wished I was still off in the capital learning about gas liquefaction.

I looked over the shelf lined wardrobe and tried to quiet my mind by concentrating fully on the simple task of dressing. I laid out stockings, a simple chemise, my favorite corded stay, an empty holster, and my least favorite pantalettes, the long fancy ones. They weren't my favorite, but they were the right ones for the job. I rolled my stockings up high and strapped the holster to my thigh, tightening it until it wouldn't budge. The small pistol I secured had been a gift from a former first mate. The scrimshaw ship on the handle of the gun had been his own work. The etching was of the Alkyd, the ship we'd sailed in together before his passing. I kept dressing, reminding myself not to dwell on people lost decades ago.

I didn't tie the stay too snug. In addition to not caring too much about the aesthetics of lower-body strangulation, I planned to actually move. Still, it was the only part of the outfit I appreciated, if only for the thin leather-enclosed chain cloth I'd sewn into the lining. Thoroughly annoyed by having to fiddle with the clips for my tights, I sat down on the bench to open the boxed petticoat and dress. Both of them were presented to me before I left the capital. Mother assured me that they were very much appropriate for the peculiar fashions of Pomin, although I knew she'd never visited the city herself.

The joke of a petticoat ballooned where the hips would be and then pulled inward towards my feet, like an upside-down droplet. I held up the dress. With do-nothing laces and false gathers it looked only garish and childish. The sleeves, which I had to slide on past my elbows, were puffy. I bet I could hide a length of rope or a garrote in the poof.

With some effort, I laced the dress behind my back in front of the two opposing mirrors at the far end of the closet. The further one walked into the wardrobe, the older many of the dresses and skirts were. Things moved so quickly in and out of style. I shrugged at the idea that it might be worth the effort of throwing them out. Last time I did that it was only because I had run out of room. I found it a little funny that I had more clothes than my sister Charlotte. She actually liked playing dress-up.

I practiced drawing my revolver several times. It wasn't easy to fish it out through the narrowed bell of the dress. Already frustrated, I realized that I hadn't even attached the binding cloth, but instead of fetching the binder, I opened a long sliding drawer, originally made for printing press paper. Without focusing too hard on any one item, I scanned the rows of rings, brooches, and bracelets — most had a story of some kind and not all were pleasant. As I usually did, I picked out the bloodstone choker. Charlotte's gift felt good around my neck, if a little tight.

The low boots were of my own design, although not of my making. Another old friend had cobbled them. I often thought of him when lacing the boots. They fit me incredibly well and were made to flex for running. When wearing the light boots I could sprint faster than I could even when barefoot.

I leaped from foot to foot, turned, and drew my pistol. After replacing the gun, I moved forward in a low crouch, unfastening a long thin knife while I advanced. I tucked into a roll and tumbled through the closet arch, thrusting the dagger as I came to my feet. Before returning to the wardrobe to select a bag, I practiced some kicks in the open hall. The new dress moved well enough. I temporarily lost a couple of stocking clips, but I was satisfied. At least I'd be able to move until I put the binder in place.

* * * * *

I sat down on the quarterdeck bulwark. The railing was still a little damp with morning condensation, but I doubted it would ruin the already awful bell of the dress. I feigned a stab at tall Lasko with my umbrella, and the sailor dodged like a plucked rubber band, moving his midsection as if his feet had been glued to the deck. I swept the umbrella out in front of me in a wide arc and he avoided that too, also without moving his feet. He'd probably learned to keep his footing while clinging to crosstrees and lines long before taking his first steps. I remembered that Lasko told me he'd actually been born on a ship while his mother fled war in Macedonia. Most of the crew had spent most of their adult lives on a ship and the better part of those lives serving on one of my vessels.

Bosun joined Lasko on the deck. He wiped his machine greased hands on a rag which he always kept half-submerged in his back pocket. Other men followed. Emery and Crocodile climbed down the shrouds but hung there waiting. Brand sat upon one of the cannons, raising his bushy black eyebrows. We were all waiting around for the same thing.

Stake emerged from the galley ladder. "Rohad is almost done, with makeup." The steward gestured to his own face with both hands as if he was holding a powder puff. The men laughed.

The crew had loosely arranged themselves in a semi-circle

before the quarterdeck. They laughed and talked while I looked to the shore where the sun had risen above the forests beyond Pomin. The entire pillar city looked much like one single misshapen and pockmarked building. The local style of construction consisted of many wooden beams running between regularly spaced pillars, forming an irregular grid that framed most of the buildings. Very few structures were entirely freestanding and traffic mostly passed above, almost entirely on foot and never on the backs of animals.

"It looks like a tent," Stake said, pointing across the harbor as he joined me. He gesticulated like he was setting up camp himself on the deck. "But," Stake finished. "It fell apart." He was a short Patagonian with big hands. In the twenty years I had known him, I'd never met another person, on board or elsewhere, that could speak the old steward's native tongue.

I nodded in agreement. If I had not once visited one of the rural villages outside Pomin, the inspiration for the structure of the city would be lost on me. In the outlying communities there are sometimes groves of very slow-growing straight trees, well suited for mast making. Where they grow in abundance, village centers are constructed by weaving smaller trees and branches into a grid across the larger standing trees. Various types of walls are then built using that upper framework, walls that couldn't stand on their own. In some cases, planks would be laid upon the beams. These were then used to enter many of the dwellings from above. However, that was all the work of the indigenous people and not the colonists. I had absolutely no idea why the Genoans modeled the city after native fashion.

"How do I look?" Rohad asked. The men all saluted and cheered as he walked backward up the ladder, engaging the small crowd before even setting foot on the weather deck. He moved to the center of the circle and bowed in all directions. The last was for me, and he finished by removing his leather tall-cap.

"I don't see it." I joked. "Did you change something?" With his hair and short sideburns always so well trimmed and his uniform nearly always immaculate, the tailored pinstriped jacket and pants actually suited him well enough.

The men catcalled and applauded. Crocodile whistled with two fingers in his wide mouth.

I withdrew and considered Pomin while the men laughed. I barely understood what I was expected to accomplish in the city. It was the fourth assignment in what had become a long voyage spent carrying out the business of the court.

"All right," I said and clapped a few times. "Allan, see that the boat is ready. Emery, I want the fore stunsail boom irons replaced while we are away. Bosun should have them ready."

"They are." Bosun nodded and ran a still greasy hand through his wild, bushy gray hair.

"Anderson, please see to the staysail again and let the greenies watch closer this time. Keep watch, all. If anyone comes aboard, there's not a one of you that knows the language, no matter what they are speaking. Just shake your head and send them along to Allan. All right. Back at it." The men dispersed, except for Rohad and Kant. Seaman Kant seemed entranced by the sun coming over the city and the fog of the bay. I said nothing, but Rohad broke Kant's reverie with a gesture and the sailor hustled off.

When the quarterdeck cleared, Rohad lifted his cane and raised his eyebrows expectantly. I shrugged in reply.

"Be ready then." With that, I rushed him, swinging my umbrella overhead and quickly sweeping it low like I had with Lasko.

Rohad leapt over the strike. I swung the weapon around for a second pass. As he regained his footing he planted his cane on the deck. My umbrella struck the steadied cane. Fanning my face with my free hand, I staggered back.

"Okay, fop. You've won the privilege of escorting me."

"An honor, Captain."

"Then, with honors, please tie the binder?" I held a long silk ribbon out to him. The length of cloth, as wide as a hand, was embroidered with pastel flowers and what looked like little maidens carrying baskets.

"Certainly." He took the fabric and extended it to length with his arms spread. "I really have no idea how to tie this."

"Didn't you live in Pomin for a bit?"

"Yes, but I didn't wear a lot of day dresses."

"I guess you were unpopular with the women then?"

"Well, I've seen a few binders in my time." He wrapped the cord around my legs, passing it through several loops hanging from the dress. His face tightened with concentration as he tied the knot behind me and cinched the cord. "I think that's right."

"It can't be that tight," I said as I sidestepped like a hobbled crab. I couldn't take more than a three-quarter step. "I didn't expect it to be this tight. Don't take any offense, but I am going to re-tie this with a reef knot."

"Perhaps you'll set a trend." Rohad adjusted his collar and shirt.

Allan stepped behind Rohad and placed his arms akimbo. "The boat is ready." He spoke to the deck in front of us and kept his eyes down. The third mate was about the same age as Rohad, but he'd prematurely weathered his brow by constantly screwing his face into a frown.

"Allan, you have the ship," I said. "Be prepared to meet anyone who rows out. They are too curious in this city, and I'll have none of that."

He squinted instead of answering. I ignored it and crossed the deck with short awkward, bound steps. It didn't look as if I could even make the climb over the side in the dress. With effort, I lifted myself up to sit on the bulwark and turned around to face the bay. The dinghy below sat low in the fog. Crocodile was already in the boat, his legs lost to the mist like some kind of titan. He easily let me down from the Transcendent with a hand under each shoulder. While I was lost in the cloud, the angle of the morning light was such that one nearly could pick out individual sunlit motes of floating water vapor. It was a beautiful morning.

Crocodile and Rohad pulled the three of us across the windless harbor. Calm water has a sound not unlike cold soup when it is stirred by an oar. I say cold because hot soup has an altogether different sound. When we neared the more populated area of the marina, Rohad and I laid flat on the aft bench, each leaning to our side so we crossed one another while Crocodile continued rowing. I watched the giant pull while enjoying the comfortable warmth of Rohad. It is curious to observe someone row when the water is hidden by your perspective; it is somewhat comical, like a ridiculous dance. We were rowing towards the Zephyr, a luxurious passenger frigate moored on the other side of the marina. Per our instructions, the captain of that vessel was to anchor her away from most of the traffic. After ten or twenty minutes the mast of the ship came into view.

Only Rohad and I switched to one of the Zephyr's own dinghies. The transfer was somewhat difficult to manage in the binder — it felt a bit odd to again be lifted like a sack, but Rohad raised me from the waist and carefully set me on the passenger's step of the small but fancy boat. The seat planks on the craft were even covered in padded canvas.

Crocodile began the return trip to the Transcendent while the two crewman of the Zephyr rowed Rohad and I past the keel of the Zephyr so that we emerged on the opposite side of the ultramarine blue ship. If anyone was watching it should look as if the two of us had simply disembarked from the frigate. The two rowing sailors said nothing. Setting aside the odd circumstances of our transfer to the Zephyr's boat, I imagined the men were used to ferrying people in such formal silence.

"Father?" I asked of Rohad.

"Yes?"

I could tell he was already suppressing a smile. "Will there be fish?" I opened the umbrella over the water and twirled it to watch the spokes.

"Fish?"

"I would like to eat fish."

"Of course there will be fish."

"I don't like river fish. I want sea fish."

"I am sure they will have many fish." Rohad tilted his head and looked upwards momentarily. "It is sturgeon you do not like. I remember now."

"No, sturgeon are not river fish. They are anadromous."

"What?"

"They live in the sea, but they return to fresh water only to breed. It is river fish I do not like. Although, I do not like sturgeon either."

"Did you learn that in school?"

"You told me I wasn't allowed to go anymore."

"Oh, yes. Your mother's idea."

"She is a bore. You should leave her."

"I have a mistress."

"Is she pretty?"

"No." Rohad couldn't wholly keep a poker face.

"Well, if we are to have fish, I would rather sea fish. It would be a terrible shame to visit a port city and not eat sea fish."

"Very well, my dear."

* * * * *

We entered the city through a small wharf known as the wood dock. A lot of timber passed through the African colony, and portion of that valuable wood left by ship. However, most of it passed through transatlantic doors to the other Genoan colonies that comprised Liguria. I saw the doors of Pomin once, five miles outside of the city within a thick-walled fort. There was a time when France, England, and even Spain linked cities overseas, but nothing could make a more attractive military target; large ocean-leaping doors rarely persisted for long. Still, the Genoans owed their empire to the doors. At the expense of their own immediate expansion, they had concentrated all military and diplomatic efforts to the ongoing defense of their doors while the larger European powers perpetually distracted themselves with old feuds and territorial squabbles that left their own portals vulnerable to theft and destruction. Now, even a door as small as mine, if anyone knew of it, would attract some real unwanted attention.

Rohad stood aside and let me pass first up a narrow rock-carved stair to the city proper. Before and above us the multi-floored grid of Pomin lay like a single endless half-gutted building. It looked as if we were about to walk into the hold of a great ship.

The two of us passed up another larger set of smooth foot-worn wooden steps. From the new height, I could see the pillars and great platforms of the city. The eclectic ramble stretched out in every direction, save for the sea. I could only follow the patterns with my eyes until thick humid air reduced the shapes to a colorless wash. At the far horizon lay an indistinct black line of jungle. It was a cool day for the area, but it was still humid. I'd rather not be out of my door at all, but still, I was glad to see some blue sky showing through the cloud cover.

We entered a third story open-air market where native men and women sold local treasures like dark violet African pears, round braided breads made from cocoyams, and spices spread out on squares of unfolded cloth. Most vendors sold out of small handcarts as no one was permitted to bring animals up to the higher levels of the city. Down on the ground there were plenty of donkeys, traditional shops, and European staples. In another life I would have stopped and looked around.

The market itself was set on a large wooden planked platform supported by enormous timbers held in place by hollows in the ubiquitous concrete obelisk-like pillars. It's said that those ivied pillars flow out from the capitol tower in 34 clockwise and 21 counter-clockwise Bernoulli spirals. Perhaps someday I would have time enough to commission a balloon so that I could see the true form of the city from above.

For now, it was the high catwalks radiating out from the center of the city like the spokes of a wheel that demanded my immediate attention, particularly the black and white uniformed sentries that passed along those spokes. The city guard looked much too well organized.

It was easy enough to get lost in any city, but the many layered colony of Pomin was a labyrinthine puzzle. Most travelers crossed upon the high level, just below the catwalks, on the platforms and connecting elevated wooden foot roads that allowed residents to pass over whole neighborhoods of large buildings, estates, and dwellings one or two floors below them, on what Pomin citizens called ground level. Still, most of the structures down there used part of the communal hatch-work to support a wall or supply a roof. And, even below that I knew that there was still a lower layer used mostly for drainage — the city was continually at war with mosquitoes and that meant tight control over standing water. It occurred to me then that they must have won that war because I hadn't seen, felt, or heard a single pest.

Rohad broke the long silence. "We received a communication earlier this morning from Dillon."

"The news?"

"No changes. He is still waiting for some package."

We passed under what was marked as the sixteenth high level walkway. The area did not seem to have any railings, just a foot and a half wide board nailed to the borders.

I looked back to Rohad, who was rubbing the back of his neck. "Two months now?"

"It is three."

"Three then." I said. "I don't even know what he is to receive."

"I didn't realize."

"You wouldn't. The order to leave him there came directly from the secretary."

"Your mother's request then?"

"Yes." I noticed a runner moving along a distant catwalk. The man was nearly sprinting along the thin line of rope and board.

"Long time to wait."

"Yeah."

"I imagine he doesn't know what he is waiting for either?" asked Rohad after a time.

"No, I don't think so."

The Ligurian flag at the top of the enormous capitol building grew increasingly clear in the haze. None of the other smaller towers were capped in such a way. I suppose that the Genoans had simply run out of cloth after making the first one. The thing was grotesquely large. The flag began as the standard white field crossed by red, but the horizontal red bar continued a hundred yards beyond the rest of the flag, narrowing into a thin flame-tongued runner that moved in the breeze with enough force to crack a man in half.

We continued mostly in silence. I couldn't speak much because I was memorizing our path to the tower. I did this using a mnemonic device called a memory palace. The particular memory palace where I stored the landmarks of that trip happened to be a familiar garden drawn out in my mind. I had reused that same mental storage place scores of times to briefly recall passages through other cities.

In my mind's eye, I placed a notable something of some sort at each preset station within that imaginary garden. Each image represented a real location, corner, street, or landmark I had just passed. A merchant stand selling mutton on sticks became a lamb chained to a spear, and I stationed that image within the memory palace garden. The fat reed vendor I stored as a comically plump cobra rising out of a wicker basket. I would then need only to walk through my garden backwards to know which marker to look for next. The more ridiculous the images were, the more likely it was that I would be to recall them.

In Pomin, the sheer number of stands selling mutton on a stick did present a challenge. Much of the city looked the same to me as the rest of it. Since there wasn't anything else notable at the next intersection, I memorized that mutton stall by odor. There was enough smoked curry in the air to make me choke. So, that vendor became a sheep's head stuffed with little flame-yellow peppers. I had eaten a pepper like that when I was living in the blue gardens of Heath. I had eaten it without asking, not ignorant of hot peppers, but unfamiliar with that variety. It had made me very sick. After eating the pepper an old gardener had led me away, insisting that we find my mother. Of course, I had actually left Tremont and gone to Heath just to be rid of her.

"Did you have an opportunity to read The Voyage of the Green Knight?" Rohad interrupted.

"Yes!" I smiled.

That seemed to please him. He had nice hazel eyes when he smiled.

"I'd almost forgotten that it was from you. I enjoyed it very much. I could hardly believe the main character survived all of that. I mean, I'm not sure I do at all. He even returned to the self-same prison where he was interred."

"He was in disguise."

"Yeah, but that was a stretch. The so-called knight saw a 'flicker of recollection' in at least ten men's eyes."

"True."

"And, men don't simply flicker about like that. So, I think it unlikely that the author was ever there at all. I bet he found the man some other way. Maybe he just asked around until he found someone that knew the man. It's easier to do that than one might assume."

"That could be."

I could hear the snap of the flag at the top of the capitol building. I realized that I had been hearing it every few minutes for the last few platforms. "Excellent tale though. Thanks for lending it."

"Good. I'm glad you almost liked it."

That smile again, like he wanted me to keep up the conversation. I realized I was doing the same. I stopped. I had to concentrate.

By the time we reached the capitol complex there were at least two stories between us and ground level. The structures below, visible over the edge of the railings and through the slats of the platforms, were constructed of rich woods handled in Pomish style. That same style of unfinished bark-stripped hardwood had spread throughout Liguria, including their New World colonies.

I noticed that the further we traveled inward, the more often I saw women wrapped in a binding cloth. I also noticed that the closer we came to the center of the city, the more fruit remained unscavenged on the pillar ivy. Not all Genoans were rich. Or, perhaps the further one went into the wealthier inner rings of the city the worse the berries tasted.

"Okay." I said. "Have the paper?"

"Right here." He motioned to his jacket pocket.

"You'll need to lead for a while. Good luck with your Ligurian."

Rohad laughed.

3

I watched Rohad withdraw the invitation slowly from the long pocket of his silk jacket. He unfolded the paper. It looked a lot like a bank note, except I could see the signature I'd forged at the bottom. I didn't mind doing the forgery. I was rather good at it. What I minded was entering a capitol building to carry out someone else's will for the sake of some unknown. Pomin was just another city where I was expected to walk in and blindly carry out her orders. I felt myself again tugging against that familiar blindfold. All was service at the pleasure of Madame Secretary. The wooden spars at the mouth of the lifted tower gate may as well have been my own mother's teeth. The entrance seemed to grin as we walked through.

Rohad handed the invitation to a garishly festooned man with a long twirled mustache. He looked more like a doorman than a sentry. To either side of him stood a guard armed with a long pike. Rifles hung in a glass locker near the man on my right. I smiled politely at that guard, deliberately casting my eyes down for a moment only to meet his again and shyly look away. I took Rohad's hand.

"Write your name here. Sign here. And, describe your business there." The doorman instructed Rohad in Ligurian. Over the course of my lifetime, the Genoan dialect of Ligurian had grown in prominence. It had been years since I had heard any other sort of Ligurian. The doorman turned towards me and stared. "Is this your daughter? She's quite little beauty."

"Yes." Rohad patted me below my neck.

"Impressive building isn't it?" The doorman motioned to the unremarkable foyer surrounding him and looked at me expectantly.

"She's curious of nearly everything."

"What?"

Rohad repeated himself to the doorman, stumbling over the unfamiliar words.

The doorman switched to Italian. "If that includes congress, then she's probably a little too curious for her own good."

"Yes. It seems to." Rohad replied.

I nodded enthusiastically. I decided also to speak in Italian, trying my best to match Rohad's, possibly unintentional, Roman accent. "It is all very important. Does anyone live here or do they only work here?"

"They only work here, but senators keep long hours."

The guest book was of a peculiar shape, perhaps nine inches by a foot and a half with a wide green binding. A forked red tongue of a bookmark lay across the center. I leaned in close, pulling myself up slightly over the edge of the table. When I looked up at the doorman he half-waved at me. I looked back to the book. It smelled like leather. If closed, it would be perhaps four inches thick. They wouldn't store the completed books by the guard station for long — they were too large and cumbersome not to bear away after completion.

While doing my best to feign disinterest, I thumbed the stack of previous pages, scanning for dates while letting the pages fall away in chunks. At least halfway through the volume the entries were still no more than a month old.

"Are trials held here?" I asked. It was a silly question.

"No. Trials are held in the red tower."

"Is there a library?" I tried to look absently bored and then interested, raising my eyebrows as I said 'library.'

"Yes."

"My uncle is a lawyer. I love libraries and his is excellent. He also has maps. Some of them are real sea charts too." The real kind -- that may have been too much.

"Brynn. You forget yourself," Rohad said, calling me by our arranged name. He waved his hand. "She is something of an explorer."

"It is fine. I have a daughter too, sir." The doorman turned and bowed slightly as another man walked past the guard station. That man didn't pause to sign or return the greeting -- probably a senator.

The doorman gave Rohad directions to his appointment and then took my umbrella and hat. I asked if I could keep the hat and he returned it happily. I doubted anyone would recognize me, but I'd always been too cautious for my own good. The two of us passed through the foyer, towards a large cylindrical chamber with polished walls of black Marquina marble. There, the floor broke from the smooth banded granite of the entranceway to an enormous mosaic sealed within a transparent layer of what looked like poured glass. The mosaic was decorative and dizzying, with a repetitive pattern curving into the center of the hall. I counted three doors on that level. The central stair, wider than I expected, rose freely in an arc to the wall of the tower and then spiraled upwards in a white corkscrew. I stopped walking.

"Captain, I'm not even sure what we're looking at." Rohad's beardless chin jut out from his craned neck. We were both staring upwards.

The inner expanse of tower above us seemed to open up without an end. I felt sure the hall was capped with a mirror, but that didn't ruin the illusion. The wide 500 foot tower appeared as if it were at least three times that height. At a glance, the rising white spiral stair that clung to the glassy black walls seemed to rise into a star filled night sky. The effect was nearly dizzying. I half-desired to run back outside and again look at the top of the building. Maybe it was taller than I recalled. Did it end in a peak or a platform?

We ascended slowly at first, still taking in the scene. I realized there was not simply a mirror far above — lights had been placed behind the mirror glass, adding some stars to the impossibly high ceiling. As was often the case, I only felt at ease with something once I understood how it worked. Were it not for the binder and the task at hand, I would have bound up the stairs until I could actually touch that ceiling.

A red-faced portly man passed us on his descent. He held both of his pant legs up with his fingertips as he dropped stair to stair. I wondered how the man had managed to climb that high.

Rohad paused for a moment. He was breathing a little heavy. "There are 12 more offices to go. Need to rest?"

I shook my head, and we continued climbing until we reached a black door marked 81 in red paint. "Knock," I said.

Rohad knocked.

"Now, wait a moment, wave and enter. I will meet you here in under an hour. If I haven't returned, just inquire for me with the doorman. This shouldn't be all that difficult."

Rohad opened the door and pretended to wave into the empty window-lit office beyond the cracked door.

"That's it. See you soon." I curtsied and descended casually. I was glad the office was unlocked. Our only trustworthy contact within the Pomin capitol was a custodian who worked in the tower, and I had not even been the one to make the arrangements. Relieved, I focused on the beautiful spiral as I circled back down eight stories. At a certain pace, it looked as if I were simply walking forward while the entire star-lined building rotating around me like a rolling barrel.

At the bottom of the stairs several suited men with braided beards slowed my descent, but they were loud and distracting, so I followed them across the mosaic for a ways until I needed to break to the right and walk past two guards posted at the entrance to the side hall. I kept the brim of my hat low. It was hardly going to hide me, but I didn't want to have to work any harder than necessary to avoid making eye contact. The guards did not hold pole arms. They looked to be of the more practical sort. I preferred the ceremonial guards that may as well be empty suits of antique armor.

"Can we help you find someone?" A voice rolled out into the hall after I had already cleared the guards by a few feet. I slowed to nearly a stop and looked back.

"My father has sent me to the library to get him a book. Am I going the wrong way?"

"No, that's correct. It's on your right after the hall curves a bit there. Let me show you."

"You're too kind," I said, running off. My binder threatened to unravel as I rushed. I slowed. Sharp steps behind me on the marble told of the guards rather casual pursuit. I approached the double doors on my right, hesitating to give the men a chance to gain. "Here, yes?"

"Yes."

I slipped through the heavy doors, opening them just wide enough for me to squeeze through. They led into another hall, one with an open ceiling and erratic walls. The uneven walls were actually bookshelves. The hall was like a street of books. The stacks there were nearly fifteen feet tall and stretched without interruption for twenty yards. At the end of the corridor waited a desk where a man sat reading. He was a blond guard wearing reading glasses and staring down at an open book. I glanced back at the lighted double doors. For whatever reason, the back of the helmet of the guard who escorted me remained mounted to the door window like a framed subject hung on a wall.

I looked up and down the stacks with genuine interest as I advanced down the corridor towards the library. Most of the books there were old. I could smell it. It was in the air. It was not a mold or a rot, but rather the smell was a suspension of pages diffused into the atmosphere of the library. It was a thick and nearly volatile air. I wanted badly not to be visiting the capitol building solely to run an errand. The city government in Pomin had become a model for the rest of the Ligurian government. And, since the founding of this particular colony in Cameroon and the incorporation of Pomin, more than 200 years had passed. Politically, little had changed during that time. Progressive at the time of inception, it remained so. So, during that time a wealth of knowledge and books had accumulated, much of it stored in this capitol library. The venerable stacks looked to me as if a single spark, or perhaps a matter of a misplaced word or two, might set the entire place ablaze.

The blond guard at the desk looked up and started a bit when he saw me. Perhaps he was knocked awake by something he read, or maybe it was my boots on the floor. In either case, I was certain he had not noticed me until that moment. He stood. Taking his glasses off slowly, he set them upon the table. The man took the time necessary to carefully fold them, although his gaze seemed fixed on my boots. I wondered if they were entirely wrong, like someone shoveling pig shit in slippers. In any case, they were clean enough, and they fit and moved like none other I had owned.

The guard placed his arms akimbo as a slight smile crept into the edges of his mouth. I considered smiling in return but decided against the idea. The man's nostrils flared wider as I approached the desk. Either direction looked good enough — I lowered my head and then broke to the left. Left again. There, a clearing stood with several empty tables and some wooden chairs. I turned to the right and then right again. I looked upwards. The ceiling was larger there and domed, a stretched grid with blue panels. Alternate panels in the ceiling held small rectangular and dirty windows; if there was sky above, it was hidden by the grime. The pattern was simple and very darkened. I suppose the dull yellow had probably once been a gold shimmer.

Ahead of me a white bearded man with a silver watch around his neck watched me approach. He held a short pile of books in his joined hands. The stack neared the tip of his beard, which said more for the beard than the books. I looked upwards again at the man then kept my head down and tried to pass.

He cleared his throat loudly.

I turned around.

The man looked at me, and his brow gathered up in the middle between his narrowing eyes.

I smiled like I had figured it all out. "I apologize, sir." I took off my hat and dipped my shoulders in the little shrug that passed for a curtsy in that hemisphere. That done, I continued on my way, pretending that I supposed a little courtesy was all he wanted. A few more turns through the maze brought me to the edge of the massive room. I then began to circle around the perimeter, darting my eyes casually to each side and occasionally stopping to read a title or two with a tilted head. It would probably not do well to ask a librarian where they stored their confidential records.

I passed a marked supply closet, an arch into some kind of study room, and an empty hall with stacked chairs. To my right the man watched me through a vacant place on a shelf. I pretended not to see him and continued following the outer wall. A yellowed globe the size of a small elephant sat in my path. I set my search aside long enough to see if the globe was as incredibly inaccurate as it was large. It was. Terra Australis looked like a lopsided and wrinkled lemon. I wished I had some time to look at the rest of the globe; old maps were good fun.

The next door I came to was also locked. It had a small window, but it was too high for me to look through. I leaped up with my hands on the pane to help me gain some height. Books covered the shelves that stretched to the ceiling. There were a few tables and a long leather couch. I jumped again. A wall of dark green tall books capped the far end of the room. They were there. I was not certain, but those tall green books looked likely enough. It had been difficult to see as the only light within the locked room came from tall half-shuttered windows. The door lock looked a little too tidy to pick; I preferred antiques. Without any further hesitation, I resumed my apparent wandering while repressing a sigh. If I had known of the windows I wouldn't have shoved myself into the dress and walked through the front gate. The next few doors were marked as offices.

I felt at a loss for a way into the records room. However, I reminded myself that everything is cured by walking and then I doubled back through the stacks, counting my steps and considering the goal. Slowing to a lazy mope, I made the return trip through a large central aisle. My bearded pursuer was there. He stepped directly into my path and crossed his arms.

"Girl, what are you doing?"

Almost authentically, I stopped and sighed with a short shrug. "I suppose I'm pretty turned around."

"What are you looking for?"

"I told my father I would bring him a book."

"Well then. Who is your father?"

"The thing is, I kind of lied. I only told them all that because I was so sick of the talking. All the talking. They never stop talking."

"We owe the country to that talking, don't we?"

"I don't know. I guess I just hoped I could hide myself for a while and take a nap."

"Oh." He looked at me without speaking for a full breath and then straightened. "This is no lounge. And, I am sure you will be missed. Come on with you." He turned and began to walk towards the fore, looking back several times to be sure I was following.

"When I was little," I began as an idea unfolded. "And, my father used to study a lot, I remember that he slept in the library all the time. So, I think it is all right." I watched the back of the librarian's balding head bob.

He said nothing.

"I won't disturb anyone." We continued walking. "And, I don't snore. Not at all. I know because I would wake myself up. You see, I am an especially light sleeper."

He slowed.

"I also do like libraries. I especially enjoy natural history. I'm just tired."

"All right," he said. "These chairs are more comfortable over here. You should probably take a book. I think that would be more proper. This is not a boarding house."

I nodded and beamed my very best at the librarian. I grabbed a smaller book at random and thanked him. As I sat I yawned big with an uncovered and wholly uncivilized noise. Once settled into the wooden chair I let my wide-brimmed hat fall forward. It was easy enough to see through the loose white basket weave. Some time passed while the man crossed the corridors, intermittently disappearing and returning for a new pile of books. Whenever I thought he would be in view, I shifted or rolled my neck and moved my shoulders or arched my back or fidgeted restlessly. All of my yawns closed with an unhappy groan.

Finally, he stopped to watch me. I went limp in discomfort and raised my head. He was still watching, crumpling his lips in some kind of empathetic gesture.

"I am so tired, but it's too bright."

He approached.

"I'm really sleepy, but there's too much light and this chair is terrible. It's not even midday, and we came so early."

He only watched me and turned his hands up.

"I just want a little nap. I can't sleep in the office, the stairs are so cold, and everywhere is too loud. I hate it here."

"Come with me."

I followed him through some stacks. We turned towards the wall and then followed it. We approached my target, the locked door, but rather unfortunately, did not stop. I followed it with my eyes. How many couches could they possibly have? "Where are we going?"

"My assistant is not in today, but you can nap a little at his desk if you like. He has my old chair, and it was always so comfortable."

"But I want to stretch out. Can't I stretch out somewhere?"

"There's nowhere like that here, girl. You can find quarter elsewhere if you need it so badly."

"I am sorry. A chair will do if there is no couch."

He pulled a small but full key ring from his belt and unlocked the first of three doors labeled *Office*. The man drew the shutters closed and adjusted the padding of the desk chair like a gentle grandparent. He smiled at me. "There you are. I will check on you shortly. And, don't poke around or you'll have me in trouble. Agreed?"

"I just want a nap." I entered the stuffy closet office and situated myself at the small desk. After fussing down into the chair, I tried to use the blotter and my arm as a pillow. I set the sun hat on the desk beside me. When I looked up the librarian was still standing there. "Begging your pardon," I said.

"Yes, Of course." He pulled the door a foot near to closed and left hastily.

I rose immediately and went to the door to check for the man. The office wasn't what I was hoping for, but it was something. I pulled each of the drawers of the desk and checked every shelf, careful not to upset any of the contents. The red jacket hanging on the backside of the door looked likely but contained no keys. A ring left on a pile of books at the bottom of a shelf seemed promising at first, but they weren't right at all. The keys looked like they would fit a Grommel and Taylor or perhaps a Bastion, but I recalled that the lock on the records room was a Cooper and Son. I looked to my left and then my right and again. Books. Anything. Nothing.

I opened the shutters. The view to either direction was ideal; a tall uniform wall about ten feet from the window filled my field of vision, providing reasonably good cover. I fiddled with the latch and pulled the windows open. Floors below, a narrow cobbled path snaked through a garden alley. At my level there were windows to the left and also twenty feet to the right where I saw the particular window I wanted. The windows themselves had decent ledges, but except for some rough bricks, there was nothing between me and the next window ledge. I felt along the exposed edges of the bricks with my fingers. The crevices would have to be deep enough.

Within the office desk I found a short length of old twine. I tied that to the window latch with a good hitch and swung my purse over my shoulder and around my chest. Once I was out the window and on the ledge, I closed both inner shutters and one window. After carefully laying the latch twine so I could open the window back up from the other side, I shut the remaining pane. If the man returned, I would rather not have him assume I flew out the window.

I dug my fingers and the edges of my boot soles into the narrow grooves along the cut stones of the wall to my right. I moved carefully, half expecting that the decision to leave the binder in place would be the death of me, but if I could make it, why bother? There is caution in old age, but there is also a recklessness that amused me nearly daily. I scurried across. Thirty-six shifts and the ledge was underfoot. I checked the window. It was locked, so I turned around and leaned forward, bunching up my dress between my knees and pressing it close against the lower glass. I counted in for three and held for three and breathed out for another three. I struck the window between my legs with my palm and a fistful of dress, withdrawing with a snap. After shaking my dress out, I turned around to kick in the remaining shards. I then had only to unlatch the window and enter. To cover the broken window from view I closed the left shutter.

I moved immediately to the shelves where I had seen the green books. As hoped, they were the entrance door records. I traveled in time across the guest books until reaching the penultimate volume, which seemed to be about right. Using a sharp small foldout knife from my purse, I cut out a particular section of pages spanning about a week. I replaced the book and retreated to a corner where I untied the back of my dress and let it hang to my waist. With some effort I pulled up my camisole and then worked the folded papers into the space between my corset and the full pantalettes underneath. I stuffed the camisole back down as best I could and laced the dress back up.

I tried the door, but it wouldn't open from within. Knowing the trip had already taken too long, I swiftly returned to the window. I was pulling myself back up onto the ledge when I noticed I a uniformed man walking along the tall wall on the other side of the garden alley. I waited for him to round the corner of the building and then began the frustratingly slow return trip across the bricks, weighing the likelihood of his return against the chance of the librarian catching me out of the office. By the time I made it back to the office ledge and the blood returned to my sore fingers, I noticed that several of them were scuffed enough to bleed.

At the corner of my vision I caught sight of the patrolling guard returning to the wall. I flattened myself against the window but realized at once how ridiculous it would be to try to hide while my dress fluttered into the alley like a sail. I bent down and pulled the latch string as quickly as I was able without breaking it. The window opened, and I jumped to the carpet. After sealing and shuttering the window, I returned to the desk and resumed my original posture at the desk blotter.

My hat was gone.

I stood and hurried to the door, which was half ajar. Further down the hall another office door was also open, and there was a hand on that door frame. Two men were speaking. I walked softly from the office to the next break in the stacks. Once out of sight, a pull on the exposed string of the binder unraveled the knot and the ribbon hung loosely in the dress loops. I sprinted across the library. My speed fell off to a natural walk just before exiting the exposed end of the book-lined corridor. I reached the desk of the guard and the way out. The blond man was still reading.

"Have a good day," I said.

"Lady, your cord is untied."

"It fell off. I'm on my way to have my father tie it." I continued past the desk.

"Nonsense, I can tie it. Here."

"No, thank you."

"I insist." He trotted to me with his glasses still on his face.

I started guiding the loose ribbon through the missing loops like a seamstress might thread a needle. He bent before me and took the ends. He tied a remarkably good bow. "There."

"Oh. Thank you."

"Your dress is filthy. Were you climbing the shelves?"

"I guess you have daughters?"

"Yeah, four."

I thanked him again and shuffled out of the library double doors into an empty hall. I wasted no time in climbing the stairs of the mirrored tower, although it was more difficult now to move in the binder. It was hard to see from so far below, but I still took the time to wonder at what point the stairs terminated. Did they simply hit the ceiling? Would some bald senator strike his head there? However, I did do my best not to look behind me, concentrating on reaching the 81st office.

At the dark door I knocked and held my breath. I heard the door unlock from within and I entered. The office was dark except for louvered window light. Rohad stood ready. I gestured, and we hastened back down the stairs.

"And now?" was all that Rohad asked.

"It's all done. We leave."

"I'm glad it worked out," he said. "Whatever it may have been."

We exited the stairs and were crossing the glassy mosaic when several uniformed men near the entry station advanced toward us. My face fell slack when I noticed that the librarian was standing by the main gate.

"What is this?" Rohad asked me.

"At the most, a broken window. Take it from my allowance if you must."

"Hallo," called Rohad to the men.

"Wait, sir."

Rohad paused and smiled stupidly.

"You forgot your hat," said the smiling guard to me. He pointed towards the librarian.

"Oh, thank you." I moved quickly as I could to the librarian while gesturing an apology with my open hands. Rohad stayed back and massaged the back of his own neck while he spoke to the guard.

"I thought you flew away, little bird," the librarian said me.

"I'm sorry. I ran off when I woke. I thought my father would be worried."

"Yes, I thought you might have."

"Thanks again." I waved and walked away.

"Oh. Did you fall?"

"What?"

"Your dress is torn there. Dirty too. I thought you may have fallen."

"Yes. It's this binder. I'm not used to it."

"I thought you had a bit of an accent. Where are you from?"

"My dear," called Rohad. "We will be late for dinner."

"We are just visiting the city. It was a pleasure meeting you." I curtsied hastily and rejoined Rohad.

We marched through the exit. I traveled with Rohad in hand until we were in the thick of the crowds advancing along the capitol street.

"I think we are fine," I said and led Rohad back through our path, retracing the locations I had stationed in my memory palace. The snap of the great flag soon lessened in intensity. The covered ground began to encourage me, to ease the agony I felt over having forgotten the hat, over having to break a window, and over generally failing to plan carefully enough. I'd been so distracted. More than that, I simply didn't want any of this. It made it so difficult to stay on task, and that was not fair to Rohad. It wasn't fair to any of the men.

"Were you bleeding?"

"No." I answered too quickly.

"Your dress is bleeding then."

"Oh." I pulled at the side of the skirt. "That's from my fingers. I didn't realize."

"I thought maybe it belonged to someone else."

"Not today."

"Thank god."

"What do you mean?" I regretted asking when he squinted slightly and brought a hand to his chin.

"I worry, what else? That's all. You locked me up in the tower; if things went bad I wouldn't have been around."

"For what? It was safer that way."

"You don't know that."

"Don't I?" The concern seemed ridiculous. I persisted while my crew mates died. They moved on. They died on my ship or some other. The lucky ones got old and expired in their sleep. One clawed at the side of his head while a stroke took his sight. Another went away for twenty years and then showed up coughing blood into a handkerchief. Others turned into drunks, went to prison, or fattened up and faded away to manage the books at a job they didn't want anyway. None of them stayed.

"Well, why do you have to do so much of it alone? We want to help."

"It's my part. There are a lot of things only I can get away with."

"I get that, but if you do anything long enough it'll catch up."

"I know it. But what else?" I knew he wouldn't understand the question. It had something to do with how little I'd care if the boards of the walk below us opened up and swallowed me. "Exactly how much longer do you think I expect to stay alive?"

"Well, I think you should care about it."

"I do care." I tried to sound convincing.

"So do I," said Rohad. He spoke to me directly, hardly seeming to watch his way through the crowd. "We care about you, Mina."

"Why are there so many posted men in this city?"

Rohad ignored the question and we walked quietly for a time. The upper left edge of my lip began to tremble. It did that when I became upset enough. I tried counting our footfalls but realized that I took nearly two paces for each of his. Most people walk in step, but ours would never line up.

"I wouldn't worry so much if you were a little taller, you know." Rohad said it with awkward lightness.

"It would suit you if I put on a few years?"

"Very much."

"How many?"

He looked at me for a while. "Maybe ten more. I can almost see it."

"Would it matter so much?"

"Oh, I bet." He laughed.

"What's that supposed to mean?" I really did want to know.

"I'll tell you when you're older."

I wanted to laugh, should have laughed. Instead, I thought about ten years and then twenty. I thought about crows feet on Rohad's face and gray hair growing out to the tips. I thought of myself as a child beside his grave, thankful for the time we'd spent together but too aware of all the time we didn't, everything from which I'd been shut out. Also, the sentries up above began to worry me.

"Is everything well?" asked Rohad. "I apologize if I upset you."

"Did that guard ask you anything?" I pushed past his question.

"Actually, they scolded me, Captain." He returned to the formality, even if he said it with a tinge of irony.

"For what?"

"For letting you run around the building. I told them I could hardly keep you."

"Because I am so curious, of nearly everything?" I smiled up at him.

"Yes, that. And, because when you've stared at the pillar all your life, it's hard not to want to explore it."

"Ah. You told them that? We were not from here. We were visiting."

"That's true. I did say that."

"I wouldn't think much would come of it, but it's looking like those runners on the beam up there have been following us."

"I don't think that guard paid it much mind. They didn't appear so suspicious as that."

"You're probably right, but it really does look like we're being followed." When one runner broke off another took his place at the next large pillar; the series of relays appeared to be keeping up with us. In this way they were a chain of crows passing an alarm along a typing line. "See the lamb spit vendor up there?"

"Yes."

"When we reach it, you will need to take a left."

Rohad put up a hand as if to protest, but I continued. "Follow that until you reach the small red brick building with sunflowers planted in front. Take another left there, where the road forks. Right at the tea house. When you get to the center with the large stair, take that down and follow it east until you reach the docks. So, left then left at the sunflowers. Left at the fork. Right at the tea house. Beyond that point just make for the water. Meet Allan in the Whistler as planned, but don't delay there or enter dressed as you are."

Before Rohad could argue I veered to the right at the lamb tent while he kept to the left with most of the foot traffic, just another man in stripes. In case it helped, I stepped to the side of a solitary stranger in a dark suit, smiling stupidly at him. After a few minutes, during which the man cast a few curious glances my way, I pulled the binder bow, although it took more fidgeting to loosen it than it had the first time. The cord then pulled out smoothly from th loops, and I took it in hand along with my hat.

I sprinted down the elevated street, artfully dodging and squeezing-by as I moved through and over everyone and each other thing along the road. I ran like there were people pursuing, although I did not look back to see if it were true. While I trusted my ability to run like that and keep it up, I also knew that trained men would always catch up to me on a clear path. My legs were just too short. However, that's not the same thing as actually apprehending me. I threw the hat and binder off of the platform once I found myself close enough to an edge.

In the hope that the honeycomb of catwalk runners above might lose sight of me in the lower levels, I threw myself off of a platform onto a staircase. I descended to the bottom, holding the railing loosely and only contacting the stairs once. I crossed lengthwise across the cell-like ground area. A white tented cluster of dwellings hung above me, suspended by cables from the platform above. A grooved footpath through scraggly and intermittent patches of grass took me through a smithy and past a group of capped men face-down in prayer. I crossed up another stair and continued once again on the high level until the next stair, which I threw myself down again. Despite my efforts, I repeatedly found myself forced to regain the high road sooner than I liked. It was difficult to move from one area of the comb to another without returning briefly to the upper level.

Giving in to the structure of the city, I decided to continue the marathon on the upper level. Within moments I heard heavy pursuing boots. I wasn't certain where the runner came from, but he was fast. I reminded myself that it was their city — I was only there to do as I pleased, or, really, what the court pleased. Even as I considered whether I could manage any more speed, I became frustrated again at having no real way to judge how crucial the mission in the capital building had been. So what if I didn't return with the papers. Did it matter? I had no idea. Mine were orders issued in the darkness, and I played only the role of the automaton that couldn't dare to break its master's geas. How long had I been sleepwalking like that? How long has that lamp been burning? I made a terrible soldier. He was close. The man's labored breath sounded louder than my own panting.

I tore sharply towards the right and leaped, throwing my arm around a lamp post. The world spun, and I fell into a controlled roll on the planks. I recovered into a crouch, with the man now in front of me; he was turning back as quickly as he could manage. I reached into my dress without looking down. The uniformed sentry had such thick black hair. His eyes were like that too. Black — and narrowing white. I wished I could take him with a bullet in the hollow of the right shoulder and still make it out of the crowd without a chance of being seized. Or, perhaps the dark-haired man was a mute and I could wiggle out of any forming crowd before he shouted at them to grab the girl. But, that was all fantasy. I shot him in the chest before he closed half the distance between us.

I holstered the gun securely, patiently, before rising and giving voice to a low scream of help. Men and women were advancing and retreating on the platform. Some turned towards me. Several rushed to the man, whose chest was emptying onto the platform. Since it didn't hurt to try, I turned behind me and pointed. "There he goes!" While screwing my face up into an expression of terror, I backed away from the already dead man with my hands up at my ears. I noticed a woman with a sack slung over her shoulder pointing towards me. As a frightened child might, I ran off. Once I was out of the gathering crowd, I ran like my life depended on it.

Guessing that I was still probably running into the arms of the next man sent to intercept me, I kept close to the edges and kept glancing down to the city below. It was thick and seemingly impassable, but it was also rich with hiding places. I considered another possibility but kept running.

I found my opportunity waving at me from within a food tent. After slowing to a stop just past that square tent, I circled behind it into the space between the outer platform railing and the canvas. I crawled through the entrance slit in the back.

A boy faced the street through the opening at the tent counter. He waved a paper genovino in the air and called out to passersby. The spit of lamb beside the boy stood taller than him by a foot. I grabbed the back of his shirt with two hands and pulled him to the floor. He came down as if he were swinging his legs out in front of himself to sit upon a soft bed. I swung him down and immobilized him on his back by pinning one arm to his side and pinning his shoulder under my folded arm. Although I was careful not to push too hard on any pressure points, the move had been solid and probably jarring.

With my free hand I covered his mouth. "Shh." I let my eyes go wild with desperation. "You have to promise not to yell."

The boy screamed into my hand.

"You have to promise. Please, it's important." I relaxed my hold on his arm and withdrew tentatively. "I need your help."

The child was immediately sweating and breathing hard. I waited a moment until he stopped trying to speak.

"There are guards after me. They are going to force me to marry."

"Who are you?" He spoke into my lifting hand.

"My father is a senator. He sold me. In a game of cards no less." I cautiously spoke Ligurian using my best Genoan accent. I sat up at his side, withdrawing my hands and placing one upon my chest. "I must escape, or I'll be married off to a balding fat man. Please, tell me you will help."

"What would I do?" said the boy. Breathing heavily, he shuffled back along the floor. "You hurt my arm!"

"You don't have to do anything but stay hidden, for at least an hour. Take off your pants and shirt. Do you have a hat?" The boy did not move. I began unbuttoning my dress until I remembered the gun and the knife under the petticoat. "Well, turn around."

"Is this a joke? I am going to be so mad if this is a joke."

I stopped and opened my purse. Within I found three silver crowns and tossed them towards the boy. They were probably worth more than he or his father would make for a week at the spit. "Hurry, turn around."

The boy turned to face the canvas wall. "I'm not going to put on your dress. If that's what you want, you can just go marry the fat guy because I am not doing it."

"Don't turn around. Give me your pants, belt, and shirt. Keep your shoes. Do you have a hat?"

"No."

I put the clothes on over my corset and pantalettes. The pants were fortunately big enough to accommodate the knife and gun. They were big on him and they were downright baggy on me, but they worked. His belt was nothing more than a hemp rope. As I finished adjusting everything I saw the boy, sitting there in his breeches, staring at my dress.

"What am I supposed to wear?"

"I don't know. Hand me that sack," I ordered him.

"You still don't look like a boy."

"Give me that bag there," I said. I fastened my belt tighter and moved to a crouch. Some general commotion seemed to be forming outside.

"It has potatoes in it."

"Dump them out."

"No. I can't carry them without the bag."

"Look at the coins again and give me the bag." Grudgingly, he upended the bag and handed it to me while I laced my boots.

"Listen, please." I brought my hands together as I began shoving my things into the sack. "You can't tell anyone, or they will find me. I will meet you again here in three days. If you promise to help me I will be in debt forever."

"I will. I promise."

"No lies?"

"I don't lie."

I withheld a great breath of air at the sound of that. Those were once my own words. I looked out the flap at the rear of the tent. "If you wanted no one to see you, how would you get as far from here as you could?"

"I can show you."

"No, you can't, certainly not like that." When the boy only shrugged, I stood to leave.

"I would go below," he offered. "You can just drop here. There's a canvas awning nearly under us. I do it a lot. And, I would follow under the beam. You can get pretty far that way, but then there are some larger buildings that cross the path. The first you can go over easy, and then there's one you can't go over, but you can go around it if you sneak under the fence. And then, there's a cobbler and you have to go pretty far around that too because there are houses. But, that's pretty far away."

"Follow under the beam?" I assumed that beam referred to any given leg of the upper structure.

"Yeah, there's a cart road there for a while, and then there's just junk, but you won't get stuck."

"Thank you!" Before leaving I fished out another coin and placed it in the boy's outstretching palm.

I dropped off the side of the platform to a sloped canvas roof and wall. As he said, it was directly behind the shop and a simple drop. The fabric was dirty with boot marks, probably from the boy. I began to run down the damp stretch of empty land under the length of the beam. I drew some stares but did not return them.

4

"16:15 Edward Berilee — visiting Mr. Paul on invitation. 16:17 Jerald Butcher — petitioning Mr. Graith for services." The voice of third mate Allan came off the pages like that and was lost into the narrow long speaker set upon the boatswain's table. The box was iron but the tube was brass and Bosun kept it well-polished enough to capture a reflection. The side of the black box bore the striped symbol of the court, although some of the white paint was flaking. Allan held it tightly against the table, as if the universe would only remain stitched through his constant, tight vigilance. "17:10 Percy Mann — business with Speaker Paul."

I walked out of the cramped space and crossed the galley. After a moment I returned. I crossed my arms and waited. What would I feel like if I had put it out? A night older? Perhaps. Would my limbs feel stretched? Maybe my teeth would ache, having grown a little over the night. I laughed at the image of my wisdom teeth suddenly descending out of pent-up eagerness to split my gums open.

Failing to put out the torch had become something of a foot-draggingly tedious nightly ritual. It seemed unlikely that I ever could summon the courage. Yet, so long as that was on my mind, it felt like a betrayal to distract myself with some new activity or study. The result was a dull apathy born of procrastination. I could hardly bear it.

"Allan," I said. "Stop, please." I moved beside him and held the end of the tube as he withdrew, frowning. "I know lady secretary is available. Try again to fetch her. We will withhold the remainder of the list until she speaks herself."

Silence. Allan shrugged at me. He thumbed through some pages.

I wondered briefly if I shouldn't have someone else take over the primary responsibility of communicating with the court.

"Please, continue," spoke the voice issuing from the tube. "This is your second warning."

"Warning? At what risk?"

After a time the tube sounded again. "Insubordination will be met with full reprimands for the crew."

"Well, then. She must certainly be there. Put the secretary on or I will burn the pages and take a holiday." I waited. The tube was silent for the time while Allan fidgeted like a restless boy.

"Captain Paradis, please hold for lady secretary." Unless I imagined it, the man sounded slightly relieved.

"Mina." My mother's voice sounded sincere and upbeat. "How are you making along there?"

"Mother, stay there." I'd been trying for at least an hour. I gestured for Allan to leave. Holding tight to the box I drew a deep breath before speaking. "Mother, I will do nothing. I will supply nothing. I will quit this immediately. You don't know to what ends I have reached inside. Please, tell me you have some good news." I could hear my words fall out of me like a sigh. "There is just no fuel left in me."

"You are putting me in an awful place," replied my mother in the diplomatic tone I thought of as her secretary's voice. "Just awful. If it matters that much I will tell you to what purpose that list is needed. But, you must stop talking like that."

"I am not speaking only of the damned list. Yes, I want to know about that too, but I am not asking about that. I am not speaking of just this mission or whatever else it is you have dreamed up for me to do next. No, I am talking of some plan for getting out of all this. Tell me you have made some progress."

"Oh, Mina. Why do you hate me? I'm not alone here. Are you to embarrass me as well? Is it all a joke to you?" The words tumbled out of the tube in airy puffs. It sounded as if my mother was cupping her hands around the mouthpiece. The air from the tube was warm and smelled like chewing mint. "There's progress. But, it is slow, and it isn't looking good. You have a contract and there are obligations to consider."

"I can meet those obligations in other ways."

"If you quit this, you quit me. You quit your sister. You're talking about growing tired? You're too tired? You are bored? It doesn't even make sense. Besides, they will cut you off." My mother grew louder with each word.

"I don't care about that. I just want to be left alone." I meant it.

"Why do you threaten me with your own death? Why do you do this." She screamed the words and the tube vibrated visibly.

"There must be a way to break the contract. There has to be some end to it."

"The magistrate…"

"Mother, you do realize I know you have been sleeping with him for years?" I had assumed by that point that my mother was presently alone or else she wouldn't be screaming.

"Don't speak of things you don't understand."

"There must be a way."

"You will get no lamp oil. I know they will cut you off."

"If it comes to that."

"Oh, why do you do it? You would murder my child? I realize that you are fine with growing old for want of oil, but it won't come to that. They will hunt you long before that happens. It is a broken contract with the court — it is treason besides." My mother's accent slipped, not into any foreign tongue but an older antiquated affectation. When she was upset enough she would sometimes use words or pronunciations most considered long-dead. I supposed it was a symptom of extended life. I'd caught myself doing it sometimes as well.

"I can't, mother. I can't anymore. I can't even bear to look up. I only leave my cabin when I must. There's nothing left of me."

"And, of us? What will be left when you leave? How can I possibly hold this position without you? You know this court is a den of serpents. What will your sister do?"

Silence.

"Mina? My beloved. Please, just let me pull the strings. It feels as if you are ripping my heart from me, but I am trying to do what you ask. I am trying. If there is a way out then you will have it. Please, will you stay with me a while longer?"

"Yes. Yes, a while longer — for Charlotte. But, please try."

I left the galley and entered the captain's cabin. Looking through a veiled blur of watery eyes, I crawled into my door. Upon entering the foyer I collapsed sobbing upon the stone. Later, when Allan signaled me using the Transcendent's other long speaker, the one connected to the speaker I kept in my foyer, I dragged myself to my feet and reluctantly returned to the ship. Back in the boatswain's workroom, I listen out of pledged obligation to a low voice describing my next task. I hated the voice at the other end of the iron box. I'd heard a hundred different men reading my mother's communications through that speaker, but it was all really the same voice, the unbeatable voice that gives you what you'll get. After returning to my door I went to the torch, cupped the flame and lost myself in the glow.

* * * * *

I knew I was procrastinating, but that didn't help. I was to prepare a small package — I didn't want to. Realizing that I had been standing idly in the source room, I really wanted to try and recall why I had come in there. But instead of even trying to remember, I enjoyed the warmth of the nearby copper piping. It is pleasant to place one's cheek on a hot water pipe, at least for a few moments. I suspected that all of the heat within the door was controlled by that hot water moving through the system, rather than some warmth emanating from the stone walls themselves. But really, I didn't know.

Pressing my ear to the pipe and trying to forget why I had come into the room, I thought I could hear water flowing. I suspected that the water came from a hot spring. I imagined it traveled miles from a subterranean lake. Perhaps if there were people there, they would be a slow and deliberate folk. Perhaps they saw change, but they saw it on a scale most people would not understand. They would have to avoid stalactites forming as they walked — they were that slow. Maybe if I banged on the pipes I could make contact with them. Or, perhaps the entire complex was built out of my own imagination and it didn't matter where the water came from at all. That was nearly as likely.

I allowed my back to rest against the pipes. The cold ones were on the other side of the room. They were not nearly so pleasant to lean against. I followed one of the pipes to the wash basin. The sight of the clothes sink reminded me why I'd come down to the source room. I'd planned to wash the clothes the boy gave me. I wouldn't wash them though. At first I had been worried that they couldn't survive a wash. Then, I realized I'd actually been thinking of returning them to the boy, as if I hadn't only made that promise to smooth things along during the moment. Really, the best reason to leave them dirty was that the threadbare cloth would be much more useful to me filthy. With a hat to hide my hair, I could get far in the rags, if someone didn't hook my ear first and tell me to get back to work in some stand.

After placing a jar of cleaning powder back on the wooden shelf above the sink, I ambled about the room. Even though I used it as a laundry room and a work area of sorts, the walls there were no less masterfully cut than those of the other chambers within my door. The mundane ceramic wash basin and mops and bins seemed incongruous with the elegant and eternal stone walls.

I browsed the tool shelves, running the corner of a fingernail across the blade of a plane. Behind a rack of Japanese hand saws, I noticed a small crack in the granite wall. As with the others I had found, it had been filled in by some other occupant long before my arrival. There was no one to thank. The chambers may as well be made of magic, although I was certain they were not.

And, how deep was the place buried? On what world? That last question I could answer. There was a certain shift of temperature between the day and the night within. I had plotted those changes and found what I believed to be a reasonable approximation of the latitude. The chambers lay somewhere near the north 45th. I had a working guess for the continent too, mostly from the geology after bringing a chipped-off sample to an old friend back home in Tremont.

I continued staring at the wall duct. The constant breeze that blew from the vents was nearly always dry. My papers had never once curled. During the winter months, of the northern hemisphere, the air could sometimes be called cool, but it was never cold. My best guess was that the area was dug into a foothill of a remote mountain in the Italian alps, probably by some Genoans.

After idling walking back to the library, I realized I had forgotten my slippers in the source room. I passed barefoot back to the artificer's hall and retrieved them from the source room. I had left the lights burning, but I had more pressurized gas than I could reasonable burn through in a year. Without turning them off, I walked back to the library and sat on the large faded red checkerboard floor rug. I let my head fall back onto a stack of books I had assembled to read. The desire to read them was not lacking. I just knew I shouldn't. There were a lot of things I wanted to do. On my workbench down the hall sat a stained glass window I had nearly finished. My lute called to me, even if I didn't play very well. In the pantry I had been drying herbs, and they were ready to be added to some oils. I had a poem in need of revision on my desk. I had a painting I was ready to send by carrier to my first mate Dillon.

In any case, none of those things would be done. I refused to let myself think of them. Instead, I had to prepare a small package, an awful package. My next and only task was then to fasten a mechanism to that package. Although I had made such a thing before, it was never for the purpose at hand. Once I built a small actuating arm that would respond to the smallest vibrations, certainly those of careless feet crossing a wooden floor. That other, similar design had been constructed to ring a bell, but now it would serve another purpose, although not one of my choosing. And, to what end?

I considered a possible design for the device. There was a certain delight in the industry of making a thing, even if you don't want it to exist. I loved good tools. I liked sitting in the workroom and peering through a mounted magnifier. Even the smell of solder could be enjoyable. Rising to my feet, I made a list in my head of what I would need. I ran off down the hall to gather the tools. The drawing spline would be useful, as would the screw jig and braided coils. I reminded myself to look for the spring bender, even though it had a bad arm and often cut me. Oh, and I could wear the new lab gloves.

Many times a passing excitement of the same sort had moved me to act, to realize some goal I didn't want to move towards.

Once, I had constructed a fluid delivery system that I used to burn down a man's house, although I hadn't realized how it would be used.

I remembered my mother's voice. "I do not ask you to do anything dishonorable. I never have. I wouldn't, but stop, please. Stop all of this hateful doubting. Do you think me a monster? My purposes are your own. I hold to principles. We do it together. Were you to question everything seven questions deep, you would still never understand. These are orders, for our sake and everyone's."

In that particular farmer's accidental death by the fire I had set, my mother called me back to the burned-out property to show me the exposed tunnels that ran from the blackened basement to the city walls. There were shackles too. My mother explained that the man had been a slaver. His home was a holding station for the unfortunate wretches that passed from his care to brothels in Tisimo.

Later, I learned that while the man was a smuggler of people and deserved his death, the trafficker had been in the protection of one of my mother's rivals; she only had me dispatch him to settle some petty political dispute. A perceived slight had precipitated the action and not any concern for the women involved. I had heard the complete tale from the boatswain on my first command. That boatswain, Gould, would spit at the mention of the secretary. I remembered Gould for a moment. He used to call me the endless child.

To put out the thoughts of my mother I drew a slow breath inward and held it. I counted until I forgot to keep counting. Then I built the box. When I was done, I painted a knotted branch across the device's wooden lid in thinned India ink, leaving room to dab vermilion flowers.

Tired, of nothing really, I sunk into the couch in the library and hung my head over the back cushion so that I stared upwards at the domed ceiling. I began to count the full 324 white stars arranged on the 18 wheeled sections of the mural above me. I'd painted that night sky long ago, adding a star each time I lost someone I cared for deeply. Every star bore a name, and I called out each aloud as I counted.

I always took loss hard, but after a hard cry, the immediacy of the pain would be gone. Within a day or so, their memory would barely move me to sigh. Of course, I didn't only mourn death; loss mustn't always include death. I've never even really understood the fascination so many have with death. That part didn't much matter to me. I saw little difference in a dead friend or one who had simply moved on to retire in another country. What I mourned was the loss of them in my own life, and once I did, I felt very little, even if I ran into them again.

The exception, which I could feel creeping back up my arms and into my chest was this: whenever some unrelated sadness opened me back up again, the desire to have my lost companions near would crawl again into my consciousness. By the time I nearly finished calling out the stars, I had curled up on the cushions and begun pulling their names from my memory. I was crying too hard to see the ceiling.

Rohad. What did he mean when he said it would suit him if I put on a few years? What if I did? Nothing. It would mean nothing, not to him, not to anyone. I knew he would move on, and I would be crawling up the ladder to paint another star on the ceiling. Forget it all. I'd feel the part of the mourner for an evening or two, but then I would lose his memory in all but name. The image of Rohad young and smiling would mercifully dim.

If you leave a cyanotype near a lighted window it will fade. Yet some time in the dark will bring it back, mostly. So it would be with Rohad. Years from now I would sit under the painted stars, crying over someone else, and then, in that darkness, the picture of Rohad would return. I knew too what I would feel, regret for never being present all the time he sailed with me, regret for never having had the courage to join him on his mortal journey.

I sat apart in my door, naked and sobbing and ageless. I had nothing to do with Rohad or anyone else out there who bore the knowledge that each year, each minute, brought them closer to death. They spoke with their friends like they knew the value of the moment. They lived like they knew they would die. They loved each other like they knew that they were all they had, all they would ever have. Here in my door, I hadn't much reason to lift my head for any friend. Won't there be another? They come and they go. I cry for a while and then go on. My family remains. The door persists. Another star alights upon a dead spot in the night sky.

When the torch called to me, I answered, but I cried out even as I cupped the flame.

* * * * *

"Captain?"

"Thanks, Allan. These look excellent." I laid his neatly drawn map flat on the galley table. Allan had an excellent hand for map making. I wondered if he sketched. Many of his thick bold lines passed unbroken into little razor cuts that rounded corners. I knew how long it took to develop that skill. It had taken me much longer than I had ever expected. The map was entirely too well executed to stand as a throwaway, although that was the only purpose of the thing.

"Thank you, captain." Allan crossed his arms and held his head visibly higher. He always sat uncommonly straight, perhaps even straighter because his thin wool jacket was too small for him by at least a size. "The lack of detail beyond the apartments was unavoidable due to time constraints."

I glanced at the map and then at Allan. He looked as he usually did, as if he expected to be rapped on the knuckles. The expression that I had once interpreted as a smug sense of righteousness was actually that of a grinning submissive dog waiting to be pinned by an aggressive pack leader. I tried to treat each man appropriately, but if Allan needed senseless reprimanding and intermittent cruelty in order to feel secure, he would never get used to the Transcendent. Perhaps I should ask him if he wanted me to schedule a regimen of well-ordered beatings. I returned to the map. It was very well done. "What is this here?" I asked.

"A hazard." He pointed to the legend in the corner. The symbol was a small cross.

"I see, but what is it?"

"A posted man."

"Oh. What sort?"

"A proper watchman."

"Was he armed?"

"No."

"Was he a city man?"

"No, captain."

"What then?"

"A civilian."

"Did he have big arms? Was his jaw a great steel thing that you couldn't kick without breaking something?" I smiled. "What would I see?"

"He was a fat man. He sat on a stool and there was a spittoon too. Mind you, I wasn't there long enough to see a shift change." Allan's face reddened.

I nodded and studied the map.

"Captain?"

"Yes?"

"There was a lot of talk."

He was a slow speak, but he was also an accurate one. And, the way he drew out his vowels gave him a certain music. He had been recommended to me as an exceptional watchman. I had certainly never seen anyone drill a crew so frequently. Each week he repeated the same lessons as if everything the crew had learned fell out of their heads with the rolling of the sea. Maybe it did. I imagined that Allan had even rehearsed this encounter. "What did they talk about?"

"About a killing." He accepted a previously extended invitation from me and sat at the table. "About a guard that had been killed."

"Talk of the town? This was in the Whistler?" The dark eyes of the guard I murdered had never really left my thoughts. For me, he still walked across the town, clutching an unstaunched chest wound. I imagined him telling everyone he saw that he only wanted to catch the girl and ask if she had lost her hat. It did not help much to know that to have spared him would have meant likely capture and certain imprisonment. There were too many who knew me in Pomin. Someone would find the guest book pages. I didn't know where that would lead them, but it would not have been good.

"There, yes, but also on the street. I overheard it."

"Is that all?" I asked, sitting a little too straight myself. I wanted to roll the map up and return to the door. "Let me guess. They said a little girl in a dress shot him dead?" Or, I thought, they said a girl knelt before the guard and held a scale out, and she pronounced the man's heart too heavy, but we all knew she had her finger on the rim of the bowl. It didn't really matter what they said. I knew what happened, what had happened the last time I was in that situation and what would happen again next time. I wasn't annoyed at all with Allan, but I was annoyed. There are some level individuals who feel strong emotions all the time, they've simply learned to control them. There are others who have the pleasure of going through life without often encountering those same emotions. I suspect I have always been in the latter group. They may run deep, but I rarely find myself swimming in them, and, when I do, I had a tendency to flounder.

"It was suspected that the shot came from her father."

"Oh. Has Rohad heard he is famous, and a father no less?" A terrible knot continued to move within me like a twisted thing unraveling.

"I have not informed the second mate."

"Well, tomorrow I will probably find myself murdering a fat man who spits tobacco, just because he'll ask me where I am going." What I disliked so intensely in the previous encounter was that the dark-haired man had not advanced into harm's way knowing it could cost him his life. He wasn't charging for the sake of a god, king, or an idea. The man was just trying to apprehend what he considered a harmless child. "I'm sorry I shouldn't say such a thing."

"Captain?" Allan craned his neck expectantly.

"Return to your post and tell Rohad to come down. Unless there is an emergency, I would like privacy within my cabin until tomorrow. I will require a ship and two oars. Drop them at 6:00. I will be going alone."

5

The doorman's bushy sideburns made the fantastically stocky man's head appear even larger. Allan's description was too kind. The man's lips were beet-red and swollen with the mars root that puffed out his left cheek. Drops of semi-opaque carmine had dried in the corners of his mouth, others were fresh and glossy. Beside him sat a little copper spittoon painted pale green by time. When I walked past the giant I could smell the old spit and fermented root juice in the bucket. Once I was in the lit hall beyond, I let my smile fall into a grimace.

"Wait, girl. Come back here."

I walked only halfway back to the man. "I apologize. How rude of me." Holding out my plain day dress, I curtsied. It occurred to me that it was probably a bit late in the evening to be wearing such a thing. I scolded myself for not selecting something less noticeable. I didn't feel much like myself.

"A pleasure. Where are you off to?" The man could hardly twist his head back far enough to see me. It would take more than an errant visitor to get him out of his seat.

"I am taking these things to my mother's cousin." I held up a small round sack. In my other hand I waved a crumpled swatch of linen with some writing upon it. Some of the ink had bled onto my hand after having been held too tightly during the trek to the apartments. I pretended to read from the note. "It is apartment 36. The Biminey's"

"Second floor and all the way to the end. It's on the left." He moved his head as if he was caught in a net but wanted to shake free slowly. The copper pot rang when he spat.

"Thank you." I climbed the broad stairs, gradually easing my steps until even I couldn't hear them. With the linen swatch in hand, I walked on down the hall. I moved my eyes from side to side as if I were scanning for my cousin's place. Upon reaching apartment 36, on my left, I turned to the right. I inserted the key Bosun had cast for me from Allan's wax imprint. The door opened. I slipped inside the dark apartment and locked the door behind me.

I bent and lit my small mantle lamp in the dark with a match and a few pumps of the fuel well. The lamp base had been filled with my best whale oil. The spermaceti burned with little odor, save the scent lingering in the air from the Lucifer's match. I advanced to a small thin-limbed desk, careful to keep the tiny directional lamp beam from shining out through the two large windows of the apartment. My eyes moved across the papers strewn upon the desk. I checked the pen in the holder and then tried looking for something like a wax press. Upon an envelope buried deep in a pigeon hole I found what I had been looking for, confirmation of name. Having discovered some proof that the apartment belonged to the right victim, I kept the light low and crawled into the adjoining room without leaving a crouch.

A narrow space between the bed and the wall opposite the street windows provided a private place to change. It was a small apartment, and a rope-laced bed frame took up most of the room. The mattress was a size too small for the metal frame, so it hung in the web of lines. As a matter of practiced precaution in anticipation of my later egress, I undressed there beside the bed, exchanging my girl clothes for the breeches and shirt I had lied my way into owning. I also brought a hat with me, a high-crowned cap that covered my braids. It had been in my closet for years, but I had never worn it. To age the cap a bit, I had scuffed it up against the gravel at the end of the pier. Only one item remained in the bag, a small box encased in blue and green tissue paper. A ribbon too large for the small cube cascaded over the sides of the wrapped box, just in case I needed to pass it off as a present. I had learned to tie that particular bow from my sister. We'd spent all night carving little animals out of soap. When we were too tired to carve any more, we put them all into an old gift-box and wrapped them in violet paper, our mother's favorite color.

Still leaning over the bag, I unwrapped the package. The cedar cube within had a cut-and-hinge lid and no adornments, outside of the entirely useless branch I painted on top. I opened it and stared at the little winder. That part was actually a doll's winder that I had long ago pulled from one of my own toys. As a child I'd always enjoyed disassembling dolls and other useless things, something I never grew out of. I was less fond of putting them all back together. Somehow that old winder had found its way to a spare parts container within my workshop.

The soft light coming in through the windows appeared to grow as I turned the gas mantle lamp down to a blue flicker. I stared into the darkest corner of the room and allowed my eyes to adjust. While the moon was new and cast no light, pipe-fed gas lanterns burned along the street outside. Nothing in the room struck me as very remarkable. The place certainly belonged to someone. Like any private place, the area was an extension of some specific individual. There wasn't much order to the room, and the possessions themselves were not so remarkable, but I could, for the sake of example, see that the man had accumulated about forty years worth of books. I saw too that the beech handle of his blossomed badger-hair shaving brush had been polished smooth by time and pressure. On the side of the dresser the man had set an urn. The way the area around the urn had been cleared spoke to the importance of the object. I thought that urns made awful gifts. Perhaps the remains of the man's mother were there in the room with me. If so, the ashes had nothing to say. Only the man's possessions spoke for him, and they didn't do that very loudly.

I saw no obvious evidence of any real pastimes. He was not a game hunter. It was unlikely that the man carved, for who would stop him from leaving shavings on the floor? His mother? Outside of some dust and loose hair on the braided throw rug, the floor was clean. No cards, playing chips, or house tokens piled up on the dresser. The bed had been left unmade. It occurred to me that I hadn't made my own bed either, not since I was a young officer. Within the man's closet hung a line of suits. Each one of those little soldiers was gray. The man had also placed two pairs of empty shoes neatly in the open closet. Both pairs were gray, a warm gray.

I walked to the other side of the bed and pulled the thin blanket up to near the headboard. After lifting and adjusting the pillow I set it back down and under the blanket. With some care I tucked in each corner. After I made his bed, I sat upon it while the little box I had brought lay neglected on the floor by my dangling feet. Remembering then that something had indeed been forgotten in the sack, I reached inside the bag and removed a fragment torn from one of the guest book pages. The scrap had the man's name on it, along with the rest of the text from a guest entry left behind by his visit to the capitol. Apparently, the man had traveled in a party of three. On that day, not long ago, he had visited the central tower on some business I knew nothing of and now a young boy who was not a boy and who was not young was placing a fragment from a torn page upon his pillow. The man would probably find it after the incident. Perhaps he might ask someone else to read it to him. Once the device triggers, the man would have no choice but to ask someone else to read the note for him. When that stuff hits your eyes it works so fast.

When Allen had first conveyed the long speaker orders to me, I had wanted to burn the page upon which Allan had written my mother's wishes. Instead, I had marched back into my door. It mean nothing that I wanted desperately to burn up those orders in the torch's fire. For one thing, I didn't. For another, that fire was incapable of actually setting anything aflame. What a coward. I may as well have dared myself to eat a peach.

I placed the little box on the man's dresser and flipped open the hinged lid. The thing was set uncomfortably close to the urn, although I dismissed that consideration. I found that the winder turned more smoothly than expected. It spun into the capping layer of gray clay, clearing a wiggling cavity into the substance, much like a struggling leg might do when stuck in the mud. By the eighteenth rotation I felt certain that the small button within must be fully depressed. Once the winder made a full return to its original position, the box would be armed, a coiled thing waiting for some clumsy vibrations to run up the dresser from the floor planks. If the man's steps didn't set it off, a curious touch certainly would.

By the time I gathered my things and left the apartment, it was likely that the eighteenth counter-rotation had passed. However, I was too far from the box to trip the trigger device. I started down the hall after quietly locking the door behind me. From the top of the stairs, I spied a man in a circular derby standing at the base of the steps below. He was speaking to the doorman in a conversational tone. There was nothing remarkable about him. In fact, I specifically noticed how perfectly unremarkable the man appeared. At that realization I must have made a sound of some kind, perhaps a draw of air because the man in the gray suit and those warm gray shoes looked up. He didn't look past me. Rather, his eyes caught mine for a brief and impolite moment before he turned back to his conversation with the doorman.

I thought of the row of suits I'd seen measured out. What did they measure? Were they days? Were they hours? Will he still prefer to buy only gray after the pressurized sphere bursts the wooden box? Will he understand why he'd been attacked? Will he end up blind or blind and half-deaf?

I wasn't sure. My head began to throb. It hurt as if the form of it were swelling and yielding and swelling again. By the time I retreated back down the hall, I found it difficult to draw breath. My throat felt tight. To keep myself from falling to the floor, I had to steady myself with a hand against the wall. How long was the interim between each rise and fall of my chest? I couldn't think of anything but the man and the phrase 'unremarkable man.' Those words punctuated my thoughts like a forced mantra.

There would be time. I could get to the box and set it off harmlessly. Even if I only threw a blanket over the thing, no one would suffer. The idea was foolish, but I ran the rest of the way down the hall anyhow.

Standing in front of the apartment door beside my bag, I held the key out from my body as if I were showing it to the lock. My left hand tugged at my shirt, clutching at the bloodstone pendant through the dirty garment I had taken from the boy. I felt as though I could see the red-flecked green stone through the hand at my chest. The imagined light of that stone seemed not unlike the torch that so often shined in my mind's eye. What was that hand to me? Did it ever act on my own behalf? I saw my wants, my families for me, and the unbeatable machine on the dresser all turning like clockwork to mechanize my every action. The limbs moved, but my head lived elsewhere, perhaps within my door. After picking up my bag from the floor, I backed away from the door. Halfway down the hall I found myself too dizzy to stand. I wasn't certain if I was caught in a crying fit or having a heart attack. For a moment, I thought I saw the man in the gray suit walking towards me from down the hall, but then he was no longer there.

It had never really occurred to me that at the end of ones gray days, when you've eaten everyone else's shit for more years than you can hold in your head at once, there would be something else. Not really. I mean, I'd longed for that, but one can wish for a thing without expecting it. What if there was something to see at the end of that gray sequence. The unremarkable man would miss it, I felt sure of that.

There was a hand on my shoulder, but I wasn't sure when it had been placed there. Perhaps hours ago. The hand appeared to belong to the gray-suited man who crouched beside me.

"Are you all right?" he asked.

"I don't have a choice."

"A choice in what? Is someone upset with you?" The man patted my shoulder.

"I promised them. I never had a choice." I sobbed and the words burst out in fits and stops.

"I'm sure everything is alright. I was a kid once too, and I've been in trouble before. More than a few times, actually." The man reached into his pocket.

I realized where I was and what was happening. The horror of it came to me again in abbreviated intakes of air and tears that wouldn't end. Although I tried, I couldn't speak.

"Here, take this." He put something in my hands, and I held it tightly like a young child might in reflex. The man had placed a handkerchief in my left hand and had begun moving my fingers so that I wiped my own cheeks. "It's OK. It's clean. I have a lot of them. Actually, you can have it."

I nodded and took over the task, pressing the smooth and warm cloth against my eyes. Knowing that I might pass out if I couldn't control my breath, I forced myself to exhale to a count of at least two.

The man stood. "Well, run along to your parents. Nothing

could ever be so bad." He walked down the hall casually.

The black linen handkerchief left in my hands had been embossed with the characters AEA in thin gold script. Clutching the gift, I ran out of the building and past the fat man and did not stop running until I reached the dinghy I had left tied up at the pier. The night air blew cold against my drying cheeks. I spoke to no one when I reached the Transcendent and the boat was lifted to the deck.

6

I woke and sat up immediately. That sound again. The torch was screaming. That's what I called it. It was a hum really. The call built up in my head like sympathetically resonating glass. It was a sound one could feel. At first the noise would be tolerable, but the force of it would grow. The lamp would hum like that until I returned to it. As a child, I had been told by mother that if I didn't return the noise would keep getting louder until it killed me. I knew that wasn't true since I once went a week without returning and found only that the call ebbed after screaming for a few days. Of course, no one else could hear it. In that sense the sound is best compared to a primitive urge like hunger or thirst.

I wondered how much fuel was left in the torch. Mine had never been out. In fact, I didn't even know how to light it. Several people, my dead Aunt Phyll included, had whispered to me that the lighting involved a lengthy ritual. She half-covered her mouth when she told me that once something went wrong and the torch lighters died in a hungry green fire that swallowed up their building. I did know of some who had died, but not as a matter of withdrawal or lighting. The use of the torch — it's more of a lamp, really — was a contract with country and court, and those in power have killed to uphold that contract. All torches were in the possession of New England, and the court not only guarded them greedily, they made good use of those that were bound.

Tailors, torches, pens, knives, and pots; despite the common names for each of these things, they were all irreplaceable artifacts. Perhaps the simple names helped keep them secret. Some things are too valuable to flaunt or show off. Tailors, before they all ran out of fuel, were used to cut doors, like my small door or the end of the small tube in a long speaker. Sometimes they were called stitchers because of the way they joined two places. I didn't know what pens were for, or pots, but they were part of the original cache. Supposedly the knives never worked. Torches I knew well enough. There is also sun cloth, but it's not a device. It was a bolt of material that has since been cut up and used for a myriad of purposes. I doubted there was anything left, but rumors suggested that some of the uncut cloth remained in France.

I rested my head against the wooden rim of the library couch. My break down last night had not been a dream. I had fallen asleep in the boy's clothes. Feeling that there was as much sense in sleeping as there was in rising, I closed my eyes for a time, but I couldn't return. Leaving the library without glancing towards my office and the torch within, I entered the washroom and let the cold water run. My nostrils flared and I inhaled sharply as I cupped my hands and doused my face. Still dripping, I walked to the foyer and looked at the wall-mounted chronometer. 3:06 in the morning.

The first torch I had ever heard hum was the one in my mother's hidden chamber, the one through the window that was not a window and opened like a door. Within that sepulcher-like closet, it not only hummed, it rattled. What was it my sister had said? "It's like the lamp wanted us to find it." I thought it was our mother, not the lamp, that wanted us to find the green flame.

I walked from the area of my door that I called the hall of being to the hall of keeping. Although I carried a gas mantle, I lit the three wall ensconced gaslights as I moved down the hall and around a bend, but the area within the last door on my left was far too large to illuminate with my small lantern.

Shelves that stretched to the ceiling, where they were braced to the rock, filled most of the warehouse. Other areas held barrels that I had assembled myself, as nothing could be brought within that would not fit through the front door. I proceeded to the row of closets against the back wall and entered the door near the far corner where I hung my lamp on a hook.

The cedar closet was a four by four foot room lined with fragrant cedar planks. The odor was unmistakable and familiar. The closet was filled with coats and delicate, but rarely touched, garments. There was no real space to stand within the cramped closet, and I had to push myself into the mass until I was surrounded. I could almost lift my legs without the hanging coats allowing me to fall. The pressure and the smell of cedar had often helped me forget myself and the torch, for a time.

With some effort, I pressed further into the closet until I reached the back wall. I put my fingers to the narrow edge of a wall panel and pulled. The wood separated where I had cut a square cache into the granite behind the cedar planks. From within the hideaway, I withdrew a small unmarked corked bottle. I swirled the contents in the bottom. There was only about an inch left, but that would be enough to keep the lamp burning for at least four months. Like a coppery quicksilver, the liquid moved as molten metal does. When swirled it clung to the sides of the bottle and receded in smooth high-walled rivulets that beaded into a stream. When undisturbed, even for a moment, a pale milky green skin would creep over the top until it covered the copper surface like a film.

I left the cache open and swam back through the coats. Keeping a firm grip on the bottle, I walked to the hall of being through the blue curtain off of the foyer and entered the library where I wound my way up the stairs into my office. After carefully setting the syrup-like fuel down on the desk, I sat down into the soft leather chair. Even with the lamp humming, the room still felt right. It was so exclusively mine. And, that torch? It belonged to me too, but in a way I felt like I was sharing the room with the lamp. While it felt good to be in the office, or anywhere within the door, was I ever really alone there? I wondered what it would be like to live within, safe and separate but also free of that flame.

I crossed my arms on the blotter and rested my head on the sleeve of the boy's shirt. The mottled beige had probably once been white. I thought of that boy. He was probably still expecting me to return. Perhaps he had been told what it was that the girl did and why she was actually running from the sentries. He probably still waited anyway, not really believing it.

And, why shouldn't he expect it? I had lied. I killed the guard with the dark eyes and then I lied. I tore off the shirt and threw it against the wall near the torch enclosure. Knocking the chair back against the wall as I stood, I pulled off the rest of the boy's clothes and threw them down violently. I pushed the chair over to the floor. For a few moments I tried to let my breath fume slowly out from my nose until I calmed.

The black handkerchief given to me by the man the night before caught my eye; a portion of the fabric stuck out of the pants pocket. Feeling immediately ashamed at my outburst, I righted the chair and pulled the handkerchief from the pants. I held the square of cloth against my belly and crumpled against the back of the cool seat.

The torch still called to me. It was eager for copper. Through my closed eyes I felt I could see it on the other side of the louvered cabinet doors. Was it not the sight of that thing that kept me from putting it out the other day? I wished I'd extinguished the thing almost a hundred years ago. Most likely I would be thirty years dead, but so what. Within the span of the extra days afforded to me by the lamp, I'd existed only as a prisoner making the best of the time. I'd lived nearly 104 years, although the last birthday I celebrated was my 10th.

I wondered what it would be like to age, personally. I knew what it looked like from a distance. Old age had killed off so many of my friends and crew-mates — it was a patient and reliable assassin. But, the idea of it, of aging, seemed to run counter to my nature. I disliked changing ships. I even had difficulty setting my tea to the left side of my plate. How would I feel about watching my *body* actually change? I wasn't sure how anyone could bear that. Imagining my legs growing out into long stems unsteadied my mind. Would I grow pimples and the other irritations of an adolescence long-delayed? How long until I grew breasts? How uselessly awful. I could accept a shove off in a death raft amongst an ice-flow, but to have to live a life in an ever-changing corporeal form after having been without that for so long... The idea of it scared and somewhat delighted me. A little taller, as Rohad had joked.

The slight smile in the corners of my mouth left when I looked at the gifted handkerchief in my hand. Did that poor man scream when he realized the world would never come back into focus? The lamp must be put out.

I had interrupted so many nights with thoughts of what-if and then failed to complete the task. Like a villain in a serial novel that the hero occasionally throttles and releases to fight again next episode, I had let the torch persist for too long. But, there was that burn. Not the burn one felt when near it, for, if anything, that felt mostly a pleasant tingle. No, it was the burn of the image of the flame on the back of the eye, on the wall of the mind, that most concerned me. The actual sight of thing had stopped me too many times.

Even as an argument against putting out the torch rose in me again, I considered the second part of the orders I had received from the secretary's office through Allan. I was to prepare a team that would attach a sink line to the threatened — more like blinded — man's ship. The order held two assumptions. One was that my box worked. The other was that the man would be leaving Pomin by ship. The assumptions were certainly made by my mother herself. The woman excelled at predicting behavior, especially when someone was under stress. We'd both been trained for years on Ichazoian behavioral studies, with me being the first to apply the system to the now-popular crowned enneagon, but my mother was a natural.

Once the sink line was attached, the Transcendent had orders to tail the lined ship at a distance of at least forty miles while regularly communicating the course to the court. The last time I did that, the tailed ship was intercepted by two New England frigates setting out from Quinnipiac. They destroyed the vessel and all survivors were shot where they swam. I don't actually know if all of the passengers were a target that day or if it was just one worth the life of all the others.

I walked from the desk and stood facing the cabinet. I mimed in the air in front of me what I planned to do. Opening one door of the cabinet, I would reach around the side of the torch base and dim the lamp key until it was over. I practiced the knob-turning motion with two fingers. There was no need to consider the death of the torch, I would only be moving my fingers, the simple and mundane motion of a finger on a knob at the back of a lamp.

Keeping my eyes shut, I opened one of the cabinet doors. That light. Was something wrong with the light? It was too bright, especially through my closed eyes. Concern seized me. There was something wrong. I backed away and opened my eyes. The lamp was fine.

After a moment, I realized that my attempt had ended before I even reached the lamp. That would be it. I would spend another ten centuries carrying out the courts will, my mother's will.

I looked at the handkerchief on the desk. It was not remarkable. It wasn't any more impenetrable than my palm. In fact, it was far less so. I tied it around my eyes anyway and secured it with a knot behind my head. While I knew I could be killed for putting the lamp out, or at least for not agreeing to a relighting, perhaps I really could find a way to make myself and the crew safe before the court ever even learned of the darkened torch. It didn't have to be a death sentence.

Blindfolded by the unremarkable man's gift, I returned to the lamp. The hum nearly hurt. Why should the damned thing have any will? It was all me. It burned. It crackled. It gave me long life, of sorts. But, if the torch seemed to cry out for its own life, that was of my own imagining. Of course, the mind can create a very solid pearl after turning over an idea long enough.

I opened both doors. I would not see a light. There was no green light. There was only the man's unremarkable blindfold. I felt along the body of the lamp as sparks unseen crackled along my fingertips. As soon as my fingers found the knob, I began to turn it, mechanically. I had only to wait until the knob could turn no further or began to spin freely — I didn't know which. My fingers were the animated clockwork manipulators of a mad craftsman's golem. They were dumb machines performing an unknowable task. There were something unstoppable set to roll downhill. The knob stopped spinning as if I had struck a wall.

I pulled up the handkerchief and opened my eyes. The lamp was out. It did not flicker or sputter. I stepped back. For the first time in my life, I found myself looking at the extinguished head of the torch. No matter how low I'd ever set the flame, I had never seen the wick of the thing. The wick-less lamp head looked for all the world like a tiny thumb-sized mummified skull caught in an immortal scream. I followed the tiny strands of hair on the tiny head with my eyes, darting back and forth to each. After backing into the desk, I slumped down to the floor, banging my arm and head as I did. Moved by an overwhelming feeling of disgust, I ripped my sister's bloodstone necklace off of my bare neck, breaking the clasp. I rose to my feet and threw the stone. It struck the monstrous head and the top of the little terror cracked off, just above the nose. The upper half of the macabre ornament clinked somewhere against the back of the cabinet.

Drawn by morbid curiosity, I inspected what was left of the head. The thing was hollow but not hollow. In the exposed cavity I saw the irregular maze of the human sinus. I could even see some matter shriveled near the back of what looked like vertebrae. The ornament wasn't a decorative piece. It was a true skull with a little spinal column stuck into a metal tube. How many times had I lovingly cupped that flame? The little hairs of the dead man or woman must have tickled my palms.

I shut the cabinet doors and walked out of the office. I felt too light on my feet. Nausea built within me, and I found it difficult to hold my breath. I walked to my bath and sat within while it filled. The movement of my fingers along my scalp felt surreal as I took out my braid. Numb and out of my own body, I shut off the water and sank to my nose. I watched my hair float on the surface. Several times I sank underneath and rose again, wiping the water from my face and clearing my eyes.

And when would the consequences come and to whom? I needed to get word to Dillon to warn him. My mother could be terrible. No, she was terrible. I knew there was nothing I could do to protect my sister from her, but I did hope that Mother needed my sister as much as she relied on my own services, if not perhaps in the same way. At least the crew was in no immediate danger.

When my head calmed a bit, I thought I already felt a few moments older, as if I was moving along the path of a circle that had been cut and set into a straight line.

7

It took Rosso, the unremarkable man, two days to show up at the docks. I had posted a watch of six men, nearly half the crew, to cover points around the dock. Able seaman Emery was the first to spot him. The man was recognizable because his eyes were wrapped in a bandage; he traveled with assistance and probably always would.

Shortly after Rosso purchased passage on a ship called the Glorious, Crocodile swam out and attached the sink line. The attachment was Crocodile's first task of that sort. It never took long for a sailor to understand that The Transcendent was not an ordinary navy-commissioned vessel; the lack of regalia and uniforms made that clear, but it was another thing entirely when a sailor became responsible for some of the more delicate tasks, tasks that had little to do with sailing.

I knew that Crocodile was a strong swimmer, but swimming out undetected to a moored ship at night is a dangerous task. He did a fine job. I had followed his return through the watch glass. The sink line stained the water with a yellow glow that could only be seen through the glass. As he had been swimming in water stained by the sink line, Crocodile himself looked stained with yellow, at least when viewed through the lens.

The glass was another one of the rare things, although much more common than were the remaining doors. The eyepiece of the watch glass was covered with a circle cut from sun cloth. However, the sink lines were simple enough. A rough ball of a silicate mixture was formed by binding the powders with gum. The minerals in the ball were selected because they happened to glow in false color when viewed through sun cloth. Lots of substances glowed when viewed through sun cloth. Engineers then placed the ball inside a melon-sized iron cage which hung from a length of grease-blackened rope. The ball would dissolve very slowly as it trailed in the water behind a ship, making it possible for someone with a watch glass — or anything else that used some of the sun cloth — to follow at a distance.

By free-diving after a quiet row as near to the Glorious as he had dared navigate, Crocodile had attached such a line to the underside of Rosso's ship near the fore using a sharp catch screw. With each dive he tightened the screw further. Crocodile had said he made six such dives, and he still returned to us without being noticed.

I promised him a bottle of good brandy to share with the crew, something I did often. Although I'd never done more than sip some wine, I had enough casks and bottles of spirits aging within the door to bathe in the stuff. I kept them in the coolest of the storage areas.

Sliding off my slippers, I pulled opened the bulk head doors that led to the root cellar. In short doses, I actually liked the floor in the cold storage area. All floors within the door were cold, but down there one would probably die of exposure if one were to try and take a nap on the stone. The granite pulled the blood warmth from the pads of my feet and toes as I descended the carved steps. I decided to get two bottles of brandy from the racks within.

I didn't mind the dark, but sometimes I would remember that other people were afraid, especially of very dark places like the root cellar. Of course, I was probably a quarter mile under the earth and the cellar was really no darker than any other room. And, although I wasn't afraid, lanterns do cast awful shadows in cluttered places. Within the cramped room there were several aisles of wine and liquor. Light and color projected against the wall as I moved my lantern across the transparent bottles. The walls were of the same polished stuff as the rest of the door, so very little within received light that did not also reflect it.

I took a moment to look over the empty shelf space. Again, I regretted that we were not going to spend more time in port. A good store of food in the cellar provided no small amount of comfort and insurance, especially on long voyages. Often, I would periodically refill the shelves in the Transcendent's larder with foodstuffs from within the door, but as no one other than me should know of the door, we still relied primarily on the stock within the ship. Steward Stake never asked where the extra food came from, just as he never asked where it went when I took from the pantry to store in the root cellar. He simply restocked when able.

Most of the crew were old hands. Certainly some recalled a southern passage of one uninterrupted year with no chance of port, during which they enjoyed yams ten months into the voyage. Being a topsail schooner, the clipper did not have much in the way of holds, but the crew never openly questioned the supplies, even during that long trip. They simply enjoyed the squash, potatoes, turnips, and carrots. Of course, I also kept aisles of jarred goods in the larger storage area above. I reminded myself to later take inventory there as well.

I carried the bottles under my arm and left them in the foyer. I couldn't leave my door without wearing something, so I put on my sailing clothes. The outfit was a scaled facsimile of the suits worn by the men. While no one wore the New England uniform, we maintained the same standards of appearance that would be expected on any reputable merchant ship. The Transcendent sailed, to all eyes, as a private vessel, and we kept a good assortment of national flags on board to help tailor that image to the objective at hand.

I belted my blue breeches and put on my rigging boots, which had also been crafted by my cobbler friend. The high-laced boots were ideal for keeping tread on the deck and for climbing the shrouds and yards. I straightened the collar of my heavy white shirt in front of the full-length mirror. Did I look a little older? I played with my cheeks while squinting slightly. If I saw my mother in approximately two months, surely the woman would notice something. Two months in the face of a child you have known for a century... She would know.

Just above where my braid formed I secured the brim of a canvas hat. I had my hair braided double-back, where it wove down one way and then back into the same braid as it climbed the ladder. That kept it off of my head and shoulders. What if the crew noticed me aging? I had known some of them for the better part of their lives. Even as I dismissed the idea, I still checked my shirt for any changes. After shaking my head in slight self-admonition, I left the closet and returned to the ship beyond my door.

The air smelled rich with open water. I climbed up on the bed in the captain's quarters to look out the small aft portholes at the sky and the endless stretch of ocean behind us. I hoped the fine weather held. We were a day out from Pomin and following Rosso. For a moment, I wondered if I'd left enough fuel in the torch. Then I remembered that there was no torch, although that memory brought the image of the terrible shrunken face to mind. That horror had been left in the cabinet, but it took real effort for me to put it out of my head. I concentrated on the smell of the sea air — I wanted to stay in the moment. There was much to be done. I wasn't exactly sure what, but somehow the two months it would take before reaching port did not seem like nearly enough time to prepare.

According to some of the sailors from the Zephyr, Rosso's passenger vessel, the Glorious, was originally to leave for Spain, but they had made a sudden change of plans. Rumor had it that the captain of the Glorious withheld the new destination from his men. Emery had observed that only three passengers, counting Rosso, had boarded the ship before departure and all of them did so before daybreak. Whatever the destination, the Transcendent had been ordered to pursue via the sink line.

I closed my eyes and readied myself to exit the captain's cabin. After setting the bottles down, I covered my face with both hands. I flexed my mouth and moved the muscles in my face. My smile stretched and then relaxed as I put on my good-natured but unflappable captain's face. I could hear feet in the galley and maybe in the mate's quarters as well. After picking up the brandy bottles, I walked out into my ship.

* * * * *

What is the color of something that moves in the light but is still in the darkness? I wasn't sure. The odd question had occurred to me while securing the jib halyard. I had spent nearly the entire day above deck. Unless preoccupied, my mind often spun such nonsense. Outside of some time spent assisting with navigation, I mostly lost myself in the others. When the afternoon came and the winds were steady and the men were sleeping off the brandy, I had taken a nap too. Upon waking, I spent a full half hour watching Lasko shave. He had renewed the lather using a cheap horse-hair brush three times while I reclined on the deck, resting my body and head against the stack of sandbags where I had awoken after the nap.

"With the grain. Then, against the grain. And then you go across the grain and you are clean," explained Lasko.

That last bit I heard as 'free.' I wasn't sure if the blame fell on his thick accent or my own head. Everything Lasko said sounded like the word porridge. I fell back asleep where I lay and woke up in my cabin — someone must have carried me inside. I guessed that it was Rohad, but it could have been anyone. Since I looked like a child, I suppose it was easy enough for them to forget that I was rather old and somewhat stuffy about being moved around.

The cabin still smelled like vanilla. After lying there comfortably for a few minutes, I went into my door only to wash up and gather some of my navigational equipment. Within the unfamiliar setting of the captain's quarters I later did some charting, but I spent much of the day above deck. I also began to take over the use of the watch glass, leaving the artifact hung around my neck after noticing Allan keeping a peculiarly close eye on it. I reminded myself that it was usually his duty to keep watch. Even when we were not pursuing a sink line, the glasses provided contrast and false coloring to assist with watch duties at any hour.

While in the captain's quarters, I left the chambered door open to the galley beyond. Several men came to visit me throughout the day, simply to talk. I was all right with that. With my future so uncertain, it didn't matter quite as much if I engaged in idle conversation. I felt almost as if I had just retired. There were times when I had taken breaks, but I doubted if I had ever considered my future to be anything approaching unwritten. When you already know where you are heading, it is all just idleness if you're not making forward progress. That evening, before I again fell asleep in the captain's bed, I decided I would throw the remains of the torch overboard in the morning.

Instead, the clear cloudless day found me eating a good breakfast with the mates. They all seemed pleased to have me. I missed my private rituals, but something about heading back into the door displeased me even more than that loss. It may have been that tiny head. What man died to make that ornament? Was it swift? Did they pull his guts out with a hook? When I was little, my sister Charlotte had told me that traitors were killed in such a manner, that once she had seen it herself when Mother took her to an execution as a form of punishment. That poor man was forced to look upon his own intestines.

"Captain? Would you like any?" Allan asked. He offered me some of the cotto salami.

"No, thank you." I thought it was too spicy. I also didn't eat any of the roasted peppers or the onions, although the officers seemed to enjoy all of it.

"There was a red moon seen over Tremont last night," Rohad said.

"Oh?" I asked.

"Allan heard it from the long speaker."

"I imagine that idiots threw chickens into pits across the capital?"

"Yes. Tradition," replied Rohad.

"Disgusting superstition is what it is," I said. Rohad nodded to me in agreement.

"Peace is held in such ways," Allan said. Rohad and I both looked up at him. The third mate shrugged. "I just don't buy the idea that it's so harmful, harmful to society. If a tradition brought us this far, it would be foolish to drop it so quickly. I just don't think it matters why. It worked, and that's enough."

"It is disgusting," said Rohad. "I don't know if you have actually seen it, but it's awful. I can't think of it as anything but what it is, the murder of dumb animals for sport."

Allan shrugged again. I noticed that he never fully unfurled his brow.

After breakfast I climbed up into the rigging and sat upon the topsail yard in the shade to digest and look out at the sea. Within minutes I was joined by seaman Brand who took a line in hand and sat himself on the yard beside me, as if preparing to stay. The young sailor blinked repeatedly, either from nervousness or failure to squint into the apparent wind.

"Captain, permission to ask a question."

"Go ahead."

"You're up in the rigging."

"Yes, but that's not a question." I had to speak over the wind. Shouting tends to engender brevity. It was true that I had recently spent a lot of time above and much of it had been spent off of the deck. Earlier, a number of dolphins had accompanied the ship. From above I had been able to marvel at the organized movements of the pod.

"This is my first voyage with you. It's not common for a captain to be up here so much."

I doubted that any time spent in the rigging prompted the question. It was my presence. I could have emerged and paced the deck, and he would have said something similar, just not about the hours passed on a crosstree. It was doubtful that I had spent more than an hour a day out of my door during the entire voyage prior to leaving Pomin. It had been that way for at least a year, probably more. I thought about his comment some more and then answered. "I think I'd just like to see where we are going."

He didn't ask for clarification. Instead, he nodded. The man seemed to spend a lot of time up there himself. It probably made good sense to him. I then wondered why I was actually up there. Everything felt so open at the moment. Beyond a stop in Tremont, my path felt incredibly open. I probably did simply want to know where the hell I was headed.

My gaze fell on distant clouds, not dark, but of some height. They were not a threat. I began to think of the weather, but I found myself pulled back out of my head by Brand adjusting his posture and then sighing loudly.

I wanted to break away from the sailor. I hadn't expected anyone to sit so close. It was already one thing to be out of the door. I realized I couldn't remember what I had been thinking before he sat down. There was no room to consider anything with someone hanging five feet from me chewing spruce gum. I nodded politely and climbed higher.

I reached the topgallant, but I wished I could raise myself above the vessel, wanting to take in the totality of the world before deciding anything. I wanted to rise high enough to see my ship from a distance so great that I could see Tremont and the torch shared by my mother and sister. Their shared torch was probably still hidden in that room behind the wall where Charlotte and I had found it a lifetime ago. I also needed to see Dillon. I wanted all points drawn out before me as if they were placed upon a map or an intricate model of the world scaled to a table.

So far as I had decided, I would take my sister with me. Our mother would be beyond reason so I wouldn't bother speaking to her. Perhaps I would have to scatter the remaining crew by putting in a letter for their release. Then I could book passage with my sister on a private ship. And, my door. It had been a long time since I had needed to rehang it elsewhere, but it was a frame that could be moved and hung like any other door. I'd carry it on my back.

Brand was upon me again. He nodded and stretched. "Really good wind today, isn't it?"

"Yes." I descended back to the main top. Forty years ago I would have stayed and heard his story and smiled. Although I considered that he may have had something important to say, I refused to let my mind be divided. There is value in a quiet mind. Anyone serving with me long enough understood that. Perhaps Allan had asked him to come up for some reconnaissance. I didn't know what Brand wanted, but I didn't feel it was time to grant him audience.

I knew I left more than was fair to my crew and especially the mates and not just during their current month long voyage. There was no reason that Rohad, or Dillon if he ever returned, could not be captain in their own right. Although Rohad was only 26, he had been first mate on a navy sloop before his appointment to second mate on the Transcendent.

In an attempt to regain my mental footing, I ran a finger along the wiry threads of the hemp. I tasted the sea on my lips and listened to the constant wind swirling in my ears. Hesitantly, I tried again to think of where we were all heading. I sighed and descended the shroud.

8

I held the watch glass to my eye. When I was still a child an older retired sailor gave it to me. Seaman Parrish had retired to the gardener's shack at the larger estate beside my family's home in Tremont, where my sister and mother still lived. I wonder now how he had come to own the artifact. At the time I had not yet sailed a day as anything but a passenger. Fond memories of that old man's tales of the sea had a good deal to do with requesting my first appointment.

The beauty of the object still held me as it did then. Although I later learned that only the fabric-like coating on the lenses was from the old stock, the watch glass itself had a very otherworldly appeal. It didn't fog when one breathed upon the glass during cold winter days, and the tube was molded from one solid piece of aluminum, although I could see no casting line. I'd never held anything so fascinating. The actual glass itself was ordinary but flawlessly clear of distortion — I suspected that the lens was German-made, although the craftsman probably had not intended for someone to lay suncloth over the smaller eye-glass.

"Is it there?" Rohad asked.

"The trail?" I put the glass to my eye. The sea went black. The clouds stood out like sheep on a black rock. The tips of the Atlantic waves were bleached like foamed starch. Out at sea, there was no color to be seen through the glass, save a general violet red. "Aye. We are still on the yellow road. It remains due East North East."

"Good. Captain?"

"Go ahead."

"You're concerned about keeping up with the Glorious, but you haven't allowed anyone else but yourself to handle the glass for a week now."

"No. Well, yes. I am. I should say, if you are asking me if am preoccupied with what will happen to the ship when we track it to land, I'm not." A question like that would outrage any captain, but the officership of the Transcendent was far from ordinary — I'd always been as much a passenger as a captain.

"You've been out of your quarters more than usual. I thought you might be having second thoughts."

"If I was too worried about that, you probably wouldn't have sight of me. I could just throw the glass over and be done with it."

He drew a long breath as we descended the galley ladder together. "All is well then?"

"Well enough."

"Mina, we're not following the vessel anymore, are we?"

I looked at Rohad. I couldn't read much in his face, although I did notice that his fists were tensed. I entered the captain's quarters and sat in the chair by the small white table.

"Besides," continued Rohad as he shut the door behind us. "I remember your reaction after The Beam was destroyed near New Haven. I'm just surprised you're doing it again."

"This ship isn't full of passengers."

"There's still a full crew."

"That's not bothering me," I insisted.

"Well, something is off. Mina, if you want help, I'll help you." He stared at me and waited.

"We are no longer following the Glorious."

Rohad exhaled. "Where are we heading?"

"We are heading to Tremont. I know it won't be long until the men realize that. I had hoped their assumptions might largely be that the Glorious had been coincidently making for the capital."

"The day before last, Allan overheard you reporting our bearings and location to the court, coordinates that have nothing to do with our current position."

"I should have been more careful."

"I only know this because I overheard him speaking to Crocodile, who was helmsman at the time."

"So, it is out then. Don't worry, I am not exactly dashing us on the rocks."

"You know I wouldn't think that. None of us would, but I have done some talking of my own, with the crew."

"You could have come to me."

"I am."

"Is this a soft mutiny? You do realize I'm the only one who knows where the brandy is hidden?" I smiled a little. "I am sorry to lie to you."

"I know. But, I really have been sent to tell you of a conspiracy of sorts. I don't think it's what you are expecting." He paused, putting his hands on his knees. "Why don't we break off together?"

I said nothing.

"There are ways to make it work, for mutual benefit."

"You and Bosun," I guessed. "That's how the idea started. And, then Bosun urged you to bring in old Crocodile. You probably agreed to that because he's so direct — if you were wrong about the affair Crocodile wouldn't be afraid to say it. And, then you brought in Emery because he's the great skeptic and a pretty useful pragmatist as well. You could probably use him as the black rock to smash your ideas upon. But then you found that someone, probably Emery, had been sharing your discussions with the others. So, there's been a new rumor going around. Mina is going to steal the ship and set out on her own." I looked up and tried to think of anything I was likely excluding from my guesswork. "How's that?"

"Yes. That's it exactly, actually. That's how it started, but we didn't end there. We are bound to you for the duration of the mission, and we are yours to command until we have fulfilled that oath. I only ask you to let us complete that service."

I felt flush. I'd thought of the men and how I could keep them safe after I turned away from the court. Their ignorance was key. I really didn't want them to follow me so far. So long as they were not involved, my own recklessness seemed several degrees more harmless.

I spoke again after staring at the floor for a time. "I'm obviously not asking this of anyone. If I was to ask for anything, it would be for inaction. I only need the crew to get us back to home port. I'll tend to some business there and then I'll put in for transfers and disband. In fact, I'll tell them all this now." I broke away from the table and moved quickly through the door.

"Wait, Captain." Rohad's voice held urgency and shook a little. "I'm familiar with your contract."

I turned back to him. His hands were outstretched slightly. I was nearly as eager now to speak with him as I had been to run above.

"We've been sailing together for a long time," I began. "I haven't specifically tried to keep that a secret. I mean, look at me. It's obvious. It's no surprise that you're familiar with how contracts work within the court."

"Yes, you are bound by a contract. The length of that contract often, as it must be in your case, exceeds the span of an ordinary life. Death is the only punishment for one who refuses to fulfill that contract."

"Don't forget the copper."

"The copper?"

"It's a liquid, a fuel, but it looks like copper, so I call it that."

"Then the devices really are literal torches?"

"Yes."

"So, you only receive this lamp copper so long as you are fulfilling the terms. Without it, you would age and it would be impossible to fulfill that contract?"

"That is the general idea." I stepped back into the quarters.

"Then, be it by one's honor or fear of death from old age or the hand of another, one is tightly bound." Rohad spoke as if this wasn't the first time he discussed this. "So, I'm watching you break from orders. They'll deny you that copper?"

"I suppose. In any case, I've destroyed my torch."

"You did that before we departed Pomin, didn't you?"

"Yes."

"So, you are already marked then?"

"Not until they realize what has happened. I'm actually a little older now, although I doubt it's noticeable. I suspect that those who have known me long enough will see it eventually." Rohad, for one, had known me nearly all of his adult life. He started as a greenhand when he was sixteen. After that he was transferred, only to return to the Transcendent as second mate years later.

"You could say it was an accident and be given another?"

"I won't." I turned to head back up on to the quarterdeck.

"I know you well enough to not ask twice, but at least know that the core of us would never think of you as a traitor." He reached for my arm, and I didn't pull away. "I won't stand for you to be treated like one, by anyone."

I held still for a moment and then nodded before climbing up the galley ladder. He followed.

On the deck the men had already assembled. They stood where they might stand if I had called them myself. I looked back at Rohad and then to the men. They seemed eager and attentive. Most of them shifted their weight and were not still. As Rohad filed into their line, I noticed that he nodded slightly to Bosun.

"I don't like conspiracies. Rohad, did you call this assembly?"

"Yes."

"Fine. I don't know your purpose, but this will suit mine." I climbed onto the mainsail shroud, although I didn't know exactly why I did so. Consciously I knew they were not assembled to mutiny, although I had seen that once before, when I was relieved of command by a first officer in private. The operation had been amiable enough, as no one wants to have to jail someone, especially their former captain, for the remainder of a voyage. Prisoners can be noisome and tiring.

After scanning the faces of the crew again, I spoke in as authoritative of a tone as I could manage. "I have sailed with many of you for the better part of your lives as men. For you old friends, your mother is probably the only other woman who knows you like I do. I'm not your mother. I'm also not your daughter. By law and in spirit, I have been your captain. This will be my last tour as captain. I know there's been rumors going around. I will answer some of them and leave the rest."

"When we reach the capital I will be resigning. I've had a long career. Isn't it about time I started wasting my days sitting by the shore like the other old women?" A few men laughed at this. I was glad for that. "I suspect some of you know enough of court politics to realize that retirement is not something that is usually chosen, and when it is, it is usually brutally short. However, there are unique circumstances to consider in my case, and I do not feel that I am in any danger."

"I also know that some of you question our current course. By my oath as a long servant of New England, I will not ask any of you to betray your patriotic inclinations. All I ask is that you trust me for a little while longer. You all have duties to fulfill and orders to follow. They are my orders, and there is nothing else for you to be concerned with. If I ask you to beach us on the Bermuda coral so that I may enjoy a thimble of rum, you will do it. Any man who does not will be relieved of duty immediately."

"When we reach the capital, each of you will leave the ship within the hour."

"I will not go," Crocodile interrupted.

"You will, and I will do the same. That is an order."

"You will order me now then. I will follow you until we get there," he said and smiled obscenely wide. "I think then you will be retired and we will not obey you."

"The order is issued now, while I remain in command. It shall stand." I shifted off of the shroud and hung by my hands for a moment before dropping to my feet.

"If we let you just walk off, you'll be killed as a traitor. I know we can do better than that," Bosun said. It was rare for my old friend to speak up in large groups.

"If you are no longer serving the will of the court, how can you hold any authority?" Allan said and turned around. "I don't understand any of you. I think she just retired. It's simple enough, she said she's not serving the court."

"She said no such thing," answered Rohad. He stepped out from the others. "You have no evidence of it. None of us do, and that's not for us to decide. However, Captain Paradis, you have told us of your plans to retire — I have spoken to the men, and, to a person, none of us will sail you to a slaughterhouse. We're much too fond."

"Then, you can do as I say without concern. For your parts, this is business as usual until we reach the capital. There, you are relieved of my duty. You go your way and I go mine." I worked hard not to raise my voice. I was aware that I sounded like a spoiled child when I did. Besides, how could I win a shouting match against any grown man?

"Those are orders we will not follow," Rohad said. For all his talk of unity, he looked uncertainly around at the men.

"This *is* a mutiny then? If you're not to follow orders, that much is plain."

"If you will have it no other way," Rohad said.

"Then you will put my own designs in danger and make criminals of the crew?" I snapped at Rohad. "Is that your plan? Is this what he has explained to all of you? He is a persuasive man. I'll give Rohad some credit here." I began to walk the length of the assembly. "He has called you from your stations. He whispered you into more talk. Then, he talked you into a fervor. Do you see that he has screwed up all your spines straight and pinned you there? In refusing my orders you are complying, not with your lawful captain, but with an overreacting fool. I thought I was mad. You are all proving me sane. Am I actually the only one here in possession of their head? Did you all fall prey to some great reaper that only I avoided, saved by my peculiar relation to the earth? I am short but not stupid. You are children who think they found something worth saying. What say you to all of this? Deliver me by my orders and you are faithful servants to my cause. Drop me off in Montauk so that I may have a good head start or cart me off to Florida or wherever else you may plan to hide me, and you are all forfeit. Take any actions like that and you're all party to my folly. I will be hunted, and you all will be damned as co-conspirators."

"I know none of you want to run for the rest of your life. That is what you will be doing. The free seas will be your prison. You will not be seeing me to safety, as I would wager you have all convinced yourself. Instead, you'll be ruining my chances of a diplomatic termination of duty. You will subject yourselves to a traitor's death for absolutely no chance of gain. There is no merciful mutiny. There will be blood now and blood later. I will draw yours until mine is spilled by your hands or by the bonds you would tie me with and then when you arrive home, your family will watch you hang. Will you even have a chance to kiss your mother's, ladies, or sisters before you are taken away? Will they bravely watch when your entrails dangle over the city green or will they look away?"

I realized that at some point I had lost my calm, but I continued with a raised voice all the same. "They may even watch your faces while it happens. They will see you man up. They will see you look past the pain. They will then see you crumble, and they'll know by the struggle that it is not a shallow capitulation to mere pain. It will be a man's soul spilling out before the body is dashed on the rocks by the next breaker. The court does not care about you. Maybe no one does. I do not. You're not my protectors, and I'm not your charge. You will simply follow my damned orders."

No one opened their mouth.

"The next man who speaks otherwise will be flogged and thrown in the hold."

Brand, inching carefully by Allan and receiving several sharp glances, including one from Bosun, spoke. "I would respect your wishes. I mean to say, I will."

"I will also not disobey the court or my captain," Remmy said. He was a greenhand who had boarded recently with Brand. Both of them were close to Allan.

Rohad did not fall back. He shrugged his shoulders a little. "I have heard what you said. Your men all heard it and know it. We know it well. There are some here who cannot hear you — you always speak so plainly that it can be difficult to understand you at all."

"Come to it or be silent."

Rohad continued. "I have not played out your every action in my mind. Even if I could, I have not bound the men to any course, neither for a mutiny now nor a chance at a good seat during your hanging. If you're after a diplomatic resolution, then we will serve our part. I speak for all of us when I say that we will not break your will, unless you would forbid us this: no crew can survive under a captain that does not value their own skin. I guess I have only really convinced them all of that fact and not of anything else. We will all serve you, our captain; we will carry out your will. *If* you would not steer us to our ruin, then you will ensure your own success in this. If you are destroyed, I know we will be as well, whether we helped you or not. Do you understand?" He looked around over his shoulders. "To save our own skins, if for no other reason, I'll permit you a little room. Shoot me now if you will."

"I can't kill you for pledging obedience. And, that's all I heard." I let my arms fall to my sides. There was some sense in Rohad's last argument, but not enough. I truly did not understand his motivation. "I am not mounting a rebellion. When we reach the shore I will attend to my own business. You said you will not sail me to a slaughterhouse, and I say you will. We are in agreement in this. If you assembled for some other purpose, then go away knowing you failed. If you assembled to remind me that your own fate is at stake and not just mine, then you did that well enough. Back to stations."

"Captain?" boomed Crocodile, unable to say anything softly. "I still have half a bottle. I would ask us to all drink to this last passage. I have served with you for five years, but I am still a green when in the company of such old men."

"Let us drink to our own purposes." Rohad slid through the ranks and took the bottle in hand. "I am a bastard, I say. And I'm going to die as one too, so why should I care if I die as a mutinous bastard. Who is there to mourn me for long? A good piss and a night's sleep should ease the mind of anyone I know on shore. I will drink to this, Captain over country." He took a long pull and returned the bottle to Crocodile.

"Captain over country," boomed Crocodile. The big man drank and opened his mouth in a wide toothy smile. Bosun followed.

Captain over country was repeated and shouted across the line. Without any prompting the men appeared to organize themselves into two groups. Crocodile walked slowly backwards across the deck with the bottle, giving it to each that followed until he drew a majority faction with him. The remaining men moved warily as if they were simply confused by all the fuss. The shouts of captain over country rose in volume and voices.

Allan rushed to Crocodile. He grabbed the bottle from the much larger man and flung it over the side of the ship.

The cheers stopped.

"You're all fools. Look at her. Listen to her. She actually thinks she is the captain. That's your fault. You all let her believe in her mother's fantasy. Captain Paradis this and captain that — we've all played the game, but I will not be strung-up on account of the ship's mascot." Allan threw one hand up in anger and exclamation.

"Stand down," shouted Rohad as he rushed to the third mate.

Allan's shoulder knocked hard into Rohad as Allan pushed past the first mate and advanced towards me. "What will you do? Flog me, bitch!"

I rushed to meet him. Allan threw a wild hay-maker, but I ducked under it easily. I took him by the shirt as I knocked his forward foot to the side with my leg. With practiced precision I brought him to the ground on his back. A wet burst hit me in the face. It was warm on my lips. I realized I was staring at the point of a knife raised up through a red sheet. I scrambled to my feet. He had been brought down upon a knife. Blood spread from the body like water from an overturned bucket.

I looked to the crowd, now a singular mass except for a few stragglers on the periphery. Rohad looked away when I glanced to him. Some hands went to faces. The men were all silent.

I wiped my face on my sleeve. It was a red mess. His heart must have burst. I considered it, pausing a long quiet moment. Still shocked, I willed myself to the dead man's body and pushed him to his side and over, using two hands and the whole weight of my frame. I saw two knives. Allan's dead hand gripped one knife, but he had not fallen upon that blade. Someone had planted another in his back during the rush, and I had likely driven it through when I took him to the ground.

"Someone get buckets of water," I ordered. No one spoke, but Crocodile fetched and filled a bucket. Stake went down the galley ladder. I assumed he was getting the brushes and soaps. "Someone get a sheet."

"I have done you all a discredit. Any man who will stand for it will live or die with me then. I will make cover and arrangements for the others. Take up the bucket and brush and do not speak of this. If you will go your way at the port, drink to that and no one will know you spent the rest of the voyage permitting a traitor to live. You will have done only what was asked and you will have had no part in this."

"But, if your bond to your brothers and me is greater than your will to live in obedience and safety, drink to captain over country or what have you. I will not mock your convictions by discarding them so easily. Your words were never gesture. I knew it already, but how many bodies did I truly want to drag with me? When we get to port you all have orders to leave. Obey them if you will, or, stay and join me in this."

I continued after a moment. "But, for those of you who go ashore, do not get in the way of any who stay behind. I will hunt you down myself if you do." I realized that I said this while smearing Allan's blood off of my face and onto my shirt. "If you choose to leave when we reach the harbor, you will go and live out the rest of your days and service without speaking of any of this. Now, everyone drink to whatever the hell you want. Drink in silence and get back to work. Save for pitching this body, there is nothing else to be done. We go to Tremont together. Beyond that, I leave it up to each man."

9

I sat at my desk and stared at the hole in the wall. I had removed
the torch and its severed head and then locked it all in a small
chest. Even though it was as dull and dark as sea glass, I had treated
the lamp as if it would burst back to life when I touched it, as if the
head would open its tiny mouth and scream and the flame would
relight. It never happened. I wondered if the shrunken head had
always been the thing that screamed with such persistence. The
thought reminded me that I hadn't heard the screaming since
putting the lamp out. I took a moment to appreciate that small
freedom.

Many years ago, on the last day of my childhood and the first
day of whatever followed it, I realized that the window on my
mother's bedroom wall was hinged. It had always seemed like an
odd window, the only one in the house that didn't open. But that
day the window was ajar, not the glass, but the whole frame and the
window — all of it — hung away from the wall. I later learned that
there is a hidden locking mechanism, but the frame was certainly
unlocked that day. When I pulled on the window it swung from the
wall on hinges. Behind it, where there should have simply been a
hole through the wall to the lawn beyond, I saw a dark room that

had somehow been hidden by what I assumed was a transparent window.

Yet even while that window jutted out from the wall at an angle, I could still see directly outside through the glass to the garden, exactly as if the window had not been angled. Swinging it on the hinges didn't even change the view. So, the window was a door, like the ones downtown or the door I would eventually own, but behind it I had found a hole in the wall to another room, which made the window doubly a door. I half wanted to rush around to the side of the house and see what I might see through the window.

Between what must have been two windows that functioned like doors, in the special sense of the word, existed a hidden room. I never did ask my mother where she found the doors. What a waste of a rare thing. Doors could span continents, but Mother's never passed further than ten feet and only that for the sake of appearances.

Within the secret darkness I had found a long brick lined room. It was probably once a closet. Later, my mother did call it her closet. There was nothing in the cramped place but a shelf lined with green bottles and that damned lamp. I recalled my first sight of that torch at the end of the closet and set upon a dais like a fiery icon waiting to consume an approaching pilgrim. I had first felt real fear then. The flame made me feel as if something had died, as if someone you loved had died. I'd lost my paternal grandfather two years before and the emotion was strangely similar. If my sister hadn't rushed in enchanted by the discovery and cupped the flame, I know I would have walked back out and closed the window.

That was a long time ago. I walked to the empty cabinet where my own lamp had been stored. I placed a cup containing nibs and pens within the hollow. It was better than the emptiness. I then selected one of the pens and returned to my desk where I began to write a letter of resignation on my best stationary.

* * * * *

I sat in the captain's quarters with Bosun. There was never any question about whether or not he would stay. I never asked him specifically or insulted him by bringing up the open door. There is point where taking someone for granted is a measure of respect.

"I hear the mooring lines unraveling on the dock," I said.

"Yes. There they are," Bosun said. He tilted his bald head to port. "I don't hear soldiers."

"There shouldn't be any. My last report was made an hour ago. By the court's measure we are a day's journey from Columbia. I'm sure there are several ships there in Fage awaiting both us and the Glorious. I just hope they don't destroy some other unlikely vessel. In any case, we have a little while."

"I don't want to take you for granted," I said. I hadn't meant to say what I was I thinking, although I dearly meant it.

He smiled, which was little more than a deeper squint, but it was a comfort. "I'm not going to go anywhere. I'm too old anyway. What will they do, retire me?"

"There's more than one way to retire an old boatswain."

"Maybe, but they won't catch you," he said.

"I don't know about that. I don't know where we would go. It's very easy to track a ship. Besides, we would be the worst pirates ever."

"We will be pirates?"

I laughed and his smile widened in response. "You like that, don't you?"

"Maybe."

"I suppose I could re-purpose the ship. We could be traders, so long as we avoid any civilized waters." I stood in front of the door with one hand on the prepared chest I'd set upon the table beside me. Slung over my shoulder was my purse which contained the letter. I disliked the disguise, but in a city where so many knew me, there was no costume better than a respectable dress. With my hair down in loose curls, I seemed a stranger even to myself.

"Come, sit," Bosun said. "It won't do to fret."

I sat down beside him. I met Whitman when he was in his early thirties. Over time that crew and I began to only call him Bosun, as it was not only his job title, it was his preference. I didn't like sitting next to most people, at least not so closely, but for some reason I felt like doing so. I hoped he didn't mind. Perhaps he had expected me to sit a bit further off, but Bosun was good company, especially when my thoughts were too choppy.

Someone knocked. I went to my feet. I hadn't heard footsteps. "Crocodile?" Like most Quiripi, he preferred relatively soft-soled moccasin boots.

"Yes, captain." He stuck his head into the chamber. "Pardon me. The men wish to know where we should meet. They told me to wait, but all is very calm on deck."

"Here. If they haven't left yet then I suppose they are in this thing for good. Have them meet in here. I wish to avoid assembling on deck while docked, if it can be helped."

"Captain, I don't think there's enough room in there."

I looked to Bosun and back to Crocodile. I waited for clarification, but the big man said nothing.

"Oh. Well, let's meet in the forecastle then."

In a few minutes Bosun and I joined all but six of the original crew in the forward cavity where most of them berthed. Not a single man with whom I had served for more than five years had left. In contrast, except for the former accountant Crane, all of the greenhands had gone. I discussed what little plans I had and assigned them all rank, leaving the position of 1st mate unmentioned. Rohad would continue as second mate with Emery as third. Able seamen Lasko and Crocodile would retain their ranks and find themselves with more work than they could handle. Although I questioned what authority I genuinely held, I promoted

Crane to able seaman, leaving the ship without a single ordinary seaman. Stake would continue in his role as steward and sailor. Bosun would remain boatswain, which would save them all considerable work since they wouldn't have to come up with a better moniker.

My instructions were for the men to hastily gather some fresh water and a few supplies in preparation for an immediate departure further south to the port of Foundry in Lenape where they could gather more substantial stock without drawing attention.

I left the ship alone on my own errands, carrying the chest and purse. I wasn't sure which weighed more, the chest or the letter I'd written and placed in the purse.

10

An uncomfortable damp heat blanketed Tremont. I felt as if the sun itself were walking beside me, offering to take my hand. I couldn't remember a hotter day falling in mid-April. The dock workers had mostly tied their shirts around their waist or tossed them somewhere else. I had just sailed from the tropics, but there we had enjoyed cool weather and good winds that followed us north along the American coast. Two days ago, before the Transcendent rounded the cape, I had not really accepted yet that winter had fled New England. I had first believed it only when we passed near enough to Montauk for me to see the unfolding green gold of spring. Knowing that spring might be my last spent in the area for some time made it even more sweet.

I entered the yard of a storage area that shared space with the fish docks. I was glad I didn't have to walk far with the small but heavy chest. Dirty snow still hid in the shadows between a pile of wet bricks and the overhang of the large low storage house. Beside the bricks laid other tell-tale signs of winter passing; the melt always exposed trash and often left it heaped in ribbons across the wet and unfolding grass. But as soon as the sun hit that particular pile it must have burst into rot. I wanted to cover my mouth and nose as I wondered what else other than rotting kitchen waste was left thawing underneath. April is not always kind.

Within, I paid the owner of the storage house for six months in advance. That was three times the posted period of required prepayment. I did this after he balked at taking a locked chest from a child. My claim number was 0324. I realized the number was eighteen squared. Most people considered that a lucky number. I didn't, but I decided to use that as a mnemonic for the claim number, not that I ever planned to retrieve the chest myself.

I moved more swiftly through the familiar streets without the burden. By cutting through alleys and yards I saved time, and where I could, I kept to the shadowed side of the streets in order to stay reasonably cool. I avoided streets where I would be most likely to be stopped, even if it were just for some polite conversation. Although difficult, I also tried to shield myself from the dialog running through my head. Still, I was glad to be rid of the chest and the remains of the lamp. To my surprise, I had even enjoyed sweeping up the remains of the torch with a broom and a basket. I was once told by my mother that the lamp itself was just a toy, that the copper was all that mattered. Supposedly a bowl and a wick would suffice. I wondered if my mother would call the little tortured skull a toy, a plaything that a storybook witch doctor might give to his ghastly and appreciative daughter.

On my way through the gardens I passed the south-end entrance to the web. Somewhere in that labyrinth my mother was probably getting drunk with a diplomat. Although I thought it more likely that she might feign a sip or two while urging some fool politician into a malleable and lazy whiskey stupor. Everything my mother did had some purpose. That included crawling on top of co-legislators, petitioners, politicians, priests, and property holders. In any case, I would stay above ground, although it was longer and hotter to cross the city that way. I rejoined the main thoroughfare of York street near the summit of Beacon Hill where the cobblestones completely encircle the memorial courtyard with its raised beds of stone soldiers and lilacs. The flowers were in full bloom; I had smelled them during my march up the hill. Having been greeted by their scent before they passed into view, that anticipation made the flowers appear all the more beautiful when unveiled to the eyes.

A footpath on the far side of the courtyard descended a little ways to a small shop door crowded between a shuttered pub and a goldsmith. A sheet of agate with no writing upon it had been hung above the narrow door where one might expect a sign. I knew of no more appropriate shop sign.

The bells hanging beyond the shop door rang when I entered. The smell of the place usually reminded me of my own door, at least it did when the shop was not so humid and stuffy. Minerals and stones of different cleaves and colors filled little shelves from floor to ceiling, covering all four walls of the small shop. I always suspected that Benjamin Card would someday set some final stone on a shelf and the whole place would collapse inward.

"Hello, little daughter." The shopkeeper greeted me from behind the clutter and debris of the small counter and workspace. He rose and put his hands behind his back. "What can I do for you?"

"I want a huge emerald. It must be grand. It has to be bigger than my fist," I said with a sly smile. I shook my fist. "I must have it!"

The man leaned close to me from over the counter, and his eyes collapsed into little slits. "Well then, you are much too precious to be Mina. Ah, but there you are under all of that finery." The man moved around the counter in a prolonged sequence of short steps, gaining speed slowly like a locomotive leaving a station. He called out my name and hugged me.

"Mr. Card." I returned the hug. "It's good to see you too. Unfortunately, I don't have long and I must ask you a favor."

"Yes, yes." He brought his hands up near his chest as if he was about to begin directing an orchestra.

"I am not expected here for several days, and if anyone finds out then all my plans will be ruined. Still, I need something delivered."

"Oh, what shall it be? Who is this for? We have some tanzanite specimens that must be seen to be believed. They absolutely must be seen to be believed." He began shuffling back behind the counter.

"Actually, I like this granite here." I grabbed a rock within reach.

"No, not that."

"This is dolomite, right?"

"Oh, yes. That is dolomite. You are so clever, but that is not a proper gift, is it?"

"It is perfect, but please, do not deliver it for two days. Is that all right?"

"Of course. If that's what you think they'll prefer. Dolomite it is."

I leaned in close. "And, tell no one. I know you are a strict confidant."

"I am a vault. Actually, just yesterday I told chancellor Wiggins what it means when you entrust something to me. He said the most curious thing about that too. I don't remember, but he said it all just right. A most curious thing, although I do not recall the wording. He said what you were saying, but he said it so well."

"I bet he did."

"Yes. Well, where is this going?"

"Send it to Cotton Edwards."

"The magistrate?"

"Yes. And please deliver this with it." I handed him the sealed envelope. It was a little creased from being carried in my purse. "Since I need you to deliver the gift by hand and not your boy, take these notes as payment."

"Oh, this is far too much. I would take it there for nothing. I haven't spoken to Cotton in ages. He is fine. Painful sharp, but he is soft also. His sister is a cripple you know? That changes a woman. I tell you, it does."

"I imagine it would. In two days. If he is not available, then give the letter to his assistant with instructions that he should open it in place of the magistrate. I am sure Edwards will appreciate the dolomite."

"I will do it happily."

"Thank you. Here are a few more, for your troubles. Remember to keep this meeting to yourself. And, if you need me, I won't be available. I am leaving, immediately, for Salem. Oh, I shouldn't have mentioned that. I can't keep a surprise to save my life." Luckily, I could manage to keep a straight face.

"You're just fine."

"Thank you!"

The purse slung over my neck felt much lighter without the envelope. I doubled back for a way and then began cutting through several alleys until things became even more familiar. By the time I arrived at the back door of my former home my curled bangs were stuck to the sweat beading on my brow.

* * * * *

I stood under the flowering dogwood tree outside of my sister's room. I could see Charlotte through the locked window. She sat alone on a small sofa set close to the lit fireplace. She hadn't responded the first time, so I knocked again. Through the distortion of the old glass I saw leaves of white paper birch bark curling in the flames. Charlotte's eyes remained fixed upon those flames.

"Charlotte," I called with hands cupped to the window. When I knocked again Charlotte finally raised her head and looked to the glass. My sister moved slowly; when she stood she was a nearly dead thing rising up in a sun dress.

"Mina!" Charlotte spoke the name like she were drawing in a breath. After walking carefully to the window, Charlotte fumbled with the lock and opened it wide.

"Shh." I said. "You have to be quiet. I'm not supposed to be here."

"Oh, Mina. Does Mother know you are here?"

"No. Is she here?"

"No. I mean, I was just resting a little, but I don't think so. Come in."

"All right. Go lock your door." I lifted myself to the window frame, using a split in the old dogwood trunk as a foothold.

"Silly, come around to the door."

I looked at my sister and then swung my body inside. As I straightened my dress, I noticed that my sister's fingernails had been bitten to little nubs and the herringbone braid lacing up Charlotte's thick black hair barely held. I wondered how long my sister had been holed up in the house.

"No one is home. Well, the cook might be here, but she's too fat and sleepy to notice anything anymore." Charlotte smiled slowly, but she did look genuinely glad to see me.

"Lock the door." I straightened myself while Charlotte locked the bedroom. "It's so hot in here," I said. "I mean, it's really hot. It's hot outside and it's even hotter here."

"I didn't hear that you had arrived in town. I've heard none of it." Charlotte walked back from the door on the pads of her feet. She hugged me and didn't let go for several breaths.

"I docked at the fish wharf. I don't really want my presence known just yet."

"Mina. I have to tell you what happened. Oh you are drenched. I should get you some cold sumac tea. We have ice, you know." Charlotte sat down on the ottoman opposite me. She held my knees and leaned forward. "Remember Paris? He was that boy that liked to wear a suit while working in the yard?"

"You liked him."

"Yes, but mother did not. Well, just last week he came to the very window where I found you. In fact, when I heard you, I thought, it's him!" Charlotte spoke with exaggerated gestures. "So, he said mother sent him away. I know. I agree. She's terrible. She's getting worse too, really. But, he said that he loves me, and he came in and started packing my things. Can you believe that?"

"Why didn't you go?"

Charlotte looked at me for a bit. "You are always so… something. I couldn't go. He's just a dandy. Besides, mother would absolutely have him killed. She had the guards send him away from work last week because she found out he'd been visiting me almost every night." Charlotte laughed. "And, I do mean, every night."

"Listen. I am going to ask you something, and I don't want you to answer right away. I want you to let it sink in for a minute." I paused to be sure she was listening closely. "Something has happened and I am going to have to leave for a long time, probably a very long time. I'm not even sure when I will get back. In any case, I want you to come with me."

"Is mother angry?"

"No. Well, she will be, but this is not about that. I have quit. I am done. I have written a letter of resignation and delivered it."

Charlotte laughed again, but it was a silent laugh. Her lips could manage it and her body moved, but her breath caught somewhere. "I don't understand. That's not even possible."

"But it is. I am no longer serving the court."

"Oh. You are kidding. You are mad? Your torch will run out."

"I have already shattered it."

Charlotte's breath seemed to return with a start and she nearly choked on it. "But, you'll die."

"Eventually. Abandoning the lamp didn't hurt at all."

"But the contract. You will be killed then." Charlotte's chest rose and fell more quickly.

"They may call me a traitor or an outlaw, but I have still written and delivered my letter of resignation."

"They'll kill us too. You shouldn't even be here. Mother needs you. She says it all the time. *Without Mina we are lost.* She says it. I swear it." Charlotte looked considerably more alert than she had been. Her lids did not raise fully, but her wide dark eyes were sharp and focused.

"That contract can't possibly be valid. We were too young. Besides, we never chose it. I've never even seen any contract. It's ridiculous on its face."

"No one made us touch it." Charlotte looked towards the fireplace.

"What do you mean? How could we have resisted? In any case, it is nonsense. And, I think mother wanted us to find that torch."

"We broke her heart that day. If she didn't talk them out of it, we would have been killed. There's no other way. Really, Mina. What is it you want?"

"Think about it. Mother already had been bound by the contract. She could be three hundred years old for all we know. And, then she has daughters, daughters who will die unless they are bound to a lamp, daughters who wouldn't be supplied with coppered oil unless they had a contract with the court. She *wanted* us to be bound to the torch."

"Not everyone thinks like that."

"We've talked about it before."

"I don't remember"

"But she did try to keep us without copper. For a while we used hers. Remember? You were little. She didn't choose this for us — she wanted to do what was best. Don't you remember?"

"Do you? Wake up, Charlotte. Whatever she tried, it didn't work. She ran out in a month and told us she was sorry. She is always sorry. I was nearly eleven and bound to a state contract of three lifetimes, of at least three lifetimes — I don't even know the terms."

"But, you still did as they said. You've been fulfilling your end."

"Okay."

"Well, I've suffered too! But what you did, that was… implicit acceptance." Charlotte looked back to the fire. "Besides, you're telling me all of this like I don't know it."

"If you know it, ask yourself what you are doing."

"Did you come to say goodbye to me or to take me with you."

"You would come?"

"Oh, you little beast! You know I can't." She stood. "You spend your days sailing with your harem and seeing the world. Well, I sit here taking care of mother. She is not well. She's beside herself."

"I don't care if she's well." I gestured to the air for my sister to be quieter.

"I believe it. She loves you, but you give her nothing. I don't think you even feel anything at all. Even still, I miss you. I miss you so much." She exhaled and her head lolled slightly.

"I miss you too. It's so hot in here. Why do you have a fire burning?"

"I like to watch it."

"She keeps you locked up in here like a doll."

"Well, she sends you out to do errands. You always seem to return. I don't see the difference."

"How are you feeling? You can't even keep your eyes open."

"I am fine. How are you?" Charlotte crossed her arms.

"I don't want to fight. I really, please, do not want to fight. I need you to come with me. You need to get out of here. We both need to be away from Mother."

"I can't. I don't even like boats."

"You can stay inside the door."

Her sister shifted. "You're not even supposed to have that anyway."

"You haven't told anyone, have you?"

"No, but people suspect it."

"Oh. In any case, I have money and we can go nearly anywhere. You can have a house. Boyfriends too if you want them. It will be like it was but better. It will just be us, if you want that. In any case, no mother."

"Mina, I never told you. You were gone."

"Told me what?"

"I lost my baby again. I knew the week you left. I mean, I knew I was pregnant. I didn't know for sure, but I thought so."

I moved close to my sister to take her hands. They were chilly. "I'm sorry."

"I know."

"You have to come with me. I don't think this place is good for you. I know it isn't. If it's not good for you, it can't be good for a child."

"You don't know what you are saying. You don't think I know how to take care of myself when I'm pregnant?"

"I didn't mean that."

"Are you worried about leaving your things behind? I'll help you gather them. We're a lot faster when we're working together."

"Mina, I won't go. Why don't you understand? Look at me. I won't go."

"You don't look well, but, I swear, a month away from this place and you'll feel like a new person. You'll be your old self again. I promise. It will be like a bad dream has ended." I stood and took a few steps towards the window. "Why is it so hot in here?"

"I get cold. It's my stomach."

"I don't understand what your stomach has to do with the heat."

"I've tried everything. I've had more peppermint tea than anyone. I swear it. I should be buried in the mint patch out back."

"What about the powder? Are you still taking that."

"I do, and it's still bad. But, without the stuff it's even worse.

The aches can be so awful that I can't walk."

"How much powder?"

"Just a little. Don't start to tell me what I feel again."

I advanced towards Charlotte. Crouching in front of her, I held my sister's arms. Her eyes weren't right. In Tur I'd seen smoky ghosts with eyes like my sister's. I pulled at her dress. "Don't stay here. You're going to let mother keep you forever? Come with me. You'll get well. I promise."

"Stop pulling at me. You don't know what you are saying. You think you can do anything you want. Some of us have responsibilities that don't come with awards and positions and ships. You want all glory all the time." My sister stood. "You just want another trophy. You'll save your poor sister. I know what you think of me, that I'm mother's tool. I'm wretched. You don't know it. You don't know any of it."

I stood. "I love you. I just want to help."

"Don't we all," Charlotte said. The words ground out of her mouth. She advanced towards me, closing her fists. "What do you know?" She gathered her dress and lifted it past her thighs. They were nearly blackened in places. There were bruises on bruises. "Go ahead and look, captain. You are such a selfish bitch. You are not the only one bound. There are more. I will show you." She struggled with her dress, trying to tear through her corset. She fell crying to the floor. I dropped with my sister and held her.

Charlotte's shoulders bounced. She sobbed into her hands like a little kid. Lifting her head, she began to wail. "Go! Get out of here. Go."

"Come with me," I said softly into her hair. "Please, come with me and you'll never see mother again."

"No. No. No. No. Get out of here." She was screaming. "Go!"

I staggered to my feet, trying to pull my sister with me.

"No! You don't understand. You've never understood anything." She ripped the words from her body. "Go!"

I broke from her and went to the window. I waited there on the ledge. When my sister turned around and screamed again, I dropped to the lawn.

Charlotte appeared in the window, surprisingly quickly. "You will kill us both. I am sure of it." She leaned out the window. Her lower jaw stuck out in anger. "I swear to god. Get out of here or I will call mother."

"It's not too late," I said. "We can make this work."

My sister shook her head and sobbed. Tangles of dark hair fell over her face as she cried. When I made a move as if to advance, Charlotte raised her head and cried out loudly. "Why are you doing this to me? I hate you."

"Tell no one you have seen me, if you have ever loved me." As I walked backwards away from the window I had to restrain myself from rushing to my screaming sister and holding her. When I reached the garden wall I scaled the iron fence, just as I had first learned to do from Charlotte.

"I swear it. I hate you. I hate you." The screams faded as I crossed through the back gardens of some townhouses. With some effort, I pressed through a tight hedge, only to fall forward through the evergreens into the busy street beyond. My face was wet with sweat and tears ran down in streams. I wanted to collapse completely to the street and sob. Instead, I ran. Through my tears I watched the world moved past in darkly contrasted shapes.

I concentrated on the sound of my feet crossing quickly over stone. I ran through another yard and kept running.

* * * * *

I unlatched a back gate and stepped into Pemberton square. A few passing eyes lingered too long on me. I straightened and smoothed my dress. Small sticks and leaves clung to the light teal, but I did my best to pull them off. I was sure my eyes were red and puffy. There was only so much I could do.

From the top of Pemberton hill I could see much of the shining bay. The hilly sweep of road before me curved downhill in a long arc to the wharf below where I could faintly make out the Transcendent as a single dark upward stroke against water line. Upon the same stretch of road where I stood, a group of men jogged. They were moving down the long hill toward the water and the ship. Although my eyes were still blurry, I could see that they were guards. There were four of them. I began tentatively running toward the group.

It was difficult to read the insignia on their arm straps, but the alternating red and blue bands told me that they worked for the court and not the city. Pushed to action by the feeling of uneasy dread filling my stomach, I tried to close the distance between us. I recklessly let the hill propel me forward. It was very rare to see any of the court guards heading that way through the city.

I considered Mr. Card. I had intended for the old stone peddler to gossip, but he couldn't have spread word so quickly. Besides, I had lied and told him that I was heading out from the city over land towards Salem.

The state department — I could see the white and red pillar of the department of state on the arm insignia. The men worked for my mother. They were then surely heading to the ship. I considered my gun. I wouldn't have much time. Perhaps a distraction would work? My shoes alternately appeared from under my dress and vanished while I ran and thought. Left without many options, I decided to really close the distance between me and the men.

Less than twenty minutes could have passed since I left my sister's window, but if Charlotte had spoken to my mother via the house long speaker, it would be entirely possible for the guards to have just emerged from the Brighton street web exit. I tried to consider alternate scenarios that would account for the guards. If some of the crew that chose to leave the Transcendent decided to talk, it was not likely that they would have begun with my mother. But if they did talk, the guards would then be from the armory and there would surely be more of them. In that scenario there might be a crowd of constables and soldiers gathering beside the Transcendent. Ships would close in from all sides. I didn't think that was happening. Perhaps the jogging party was a coincidence? No. I knew what I was seeing. I thought of Charlotte's face and knew that the men were born of that stupid and petty anger, or simple fear.

Instead of drawing so close to the men that I risked running into them, I shot across a side street and joined a parallel road. It wouldn't empty into the wharf, but it would serve my purpose. I began to really run. While I was out of practice, I did know how. Over the years I had learned that there was real skill to the act of running, either in pursuit or flight. My soft boots hit the hill in long forward strokes that rhythmically left me falling towards the hill with both feet off of the ground. I counted my footfalls to let the unfolding sequence itself remind me to place each footfall safely. A bent foot on a stone could pitch me down the hill and spill my skull before the court had their chance to crack it.

At Central Avenue I held to the right, cutting into that corner by as delicate of a diagonal as I could manage without running into a woman weaving forsythia into a wreath beside a fence. As I rejoined the original hill I realized I had lost count of my steps. With some effort I pushed myself to regain the tempo that I had been holding, but my legs were starting to burn. The pain came on slowly, but I knew my feet would become tired and dangerously unsure soon. I focused on the task.

Having rejoined the original path, I examined the still distant ship. Indeed, no contingent had formed. I also didn't see the guards ahead of me, and I couldn't hear their footsteps. Perhaps I had passed them, so wide that I could not even hear them. I urged myself not to look.

The road soon began to flatten there at the deflated end of the hill. That slowed me down, but I pushed harder. Pain in my legs meant nothing compared to losing the race.

I hit the ground. It hadn't felt as if I were falling — the pavement simply rose to my face. When I pulled myself up I was looking towards the ship. Then, I broke a rule and turned back to look at the hill. The men were within 100 yards and they had begun running not jogging. They had to have seen me. Without fumbling, I dug out my pistol. I fired high into the air and began to run. In a continued effort to signal my ship, I fired two more rounds, expending the sad capacity of the little weapon. I threw the gun aside and concentrated on running.

The sails were down, but I looked hopefully for any movement in the sheets. If the ship was still moored, there would be time for the pursuing guards to gather the small contingent of soldiers stationed near the fish docks. Likewise, if I fell again, there would also be time enough for them to grab me. I had the second gun, but they would take me alive eventually. Full-grown men were faster and much stronger. I knew my body — having lived in that unchanging form so long that there was no movement I had not already made a thousand times over. I could move and fight in my skin with a confidence as unique as my long life. Still, while I did not want for skill, that was not always enough. It is wrong to think that experience can always overpower strength. I was a little girl running in a dress that may as well have been a sail.

There was movement high in the Transcendent. The halyards were singing and the sails were dropping. Crocodile stood at the stern. The figure was too big to be anyone else. He had a rifle. Then the ship itself seemed to begin crawling back along the pier. I couldn't restrain a tired smile. The men were ready for me and the Transcendent would soon be set before the wind. Someone else moved into position on the deck beside Crocodile. I kept my eyes on that ship, even as the sound of the men's footsteps drew uncomfortably close. They had such long legs.

The ladder was down and I fixed on that. The ship was already moving too fast, but I certainly couldn't fault Rohad for that, assuming that he was aboard and guiding the vessel. As I drew closer, I hoped all of the remaining crew had returned in time after gathering some basic supplies. Then I thought of my door. While I had not meant to think of it, I couldn't bear to lose the thing. Again, I tried to push the thoughts from my mind and concentrate on moving my limbs.

As my small feet hit the wood of the pier I realized that there were several men further out on the narrow platform, standing to the side. Guards? Fisherman? What kind of idiots would stand there like that? I watched the ladder moving along the pier at nearly half my speed.

Then, I felt my feet pull out from underneath me. Blue sky filled my view as my back slammed into the pier. I struggled to breathe and rise. My breath was caught. Nothing. I could draw nothing. Hands seized me roughly by the shoulder. My chest heaved and I was able to draw a hard gasp of air. Gunshots. I struggled to my feet as the two men beside me let go of my shoulders and fell like limp dolls. More shots.

The starboard length of the ship grazed the side of the dock and the structure trembled. The contact was slight and brief — it was brilliantly done. The ship, at a greater angle now, appeared undamaged but slowed by the maneuver. I threw myself off the end of the dock and hit the ladder. Rungs slipped by and I continued to fall until my hand slipped into a loop and painfully snared my arm. Glad to be hooked, I climbed the ladder and fell over the side of the ship. With my head doubled forward uncomfortably against the bulwark, I focused on my body for a moment before rising. My chest was covered in blood. There was a lot of it. The skeleton crew scrambled around me, and it occurred to me that if I were on my way to a dream, they would be the creatures assembled to construct the stage. The men around me were raising a curtain. They sang out.

Clarity followed a few moments later, on its own terms. I stood. On the shrinking shore men ran about. Some were probably heading to the contingent, which should have been mobilized by the gunfire anyway. Around me the crew gathered to raise the main sail. I added my insignificant weight to the effort while Bosun continued to steer us out of the harbor.

"Do we have everyone?" I asked this of no one in particular and then asked again, louder.

"Yes." The word was sweet to my ears. Sweeter still, none of the men were injured. I was also glad to feel that my nose had not broken, but it was indeed the cause of most of the blood, although some of it may have belonged to the two unfortunates that had been standing on the pier. While I had been scraped up, I was alright. As if to give the garment a finishing blow, I wiped my bloody face, already sticky in the wind, on my sleeve. I then saw Rohad on the quarterdeck and joined him to help with the halyards.

"Just your nose, Captain?"

"Only my nose."

If the Transcendent was pursued, I failed to spot the pursuer. We navigated without escort or challenge through the bay, tacking northward for a bit and then breaking free into the open waters of the cape with a good wind behind us. By the close of the day we would round Herrington and with that we would be in the Atlantic. It was tiring work sailing the ship with half a crew, but it was not impossible.

"This is a stolen ship," I said to Stake. For a steward, he was an excellent hand on deck. Both of us were out of breath from running from station to station.

"Aye." The short cook smiled with his whole face. It wrinkled up like an old purse, but it was a good smile.

Stolen. I considered that. The ship was now stolen and I was not a member of the court. Although I doubted that the word had much meaning, I was free. Despite my anxiety, I appreciated the wind and the color of the sky and the crew. I listened to the snap of the sails and the sound of the men calling out as they trimmed. We were only hours out from Tremont with little between us and ruin, but it was enough. I laughed out loud.

Later I returned to my door to plot a course for Copic instead of Lenape. There, Dillon had been off attending to some task on behalf of Mother. I wouldn't pressure our first mate to rejoin. It probably was not even a good idea for me to make the offer, but we needed supplies anyway and the port at Copic would suffice. Most importantly, it was out of the country, and the Genoans would have no interest in seizing an English ship, at least not for the sake of the English. I wondered if he would choose to come with us in our stolen ship. I was not entirely certain why I had decided to go back for Dillon, but it felt right to include him.

When I returned to help on deck, Emery pointed out that I was still covered in blood. I nodded. I felt good. Everyone should feel that good.

11

I slowly woke the next morning to the orchestration of a ship at full sail. The analogy had occurred to me before, but I had never enjoyed that music while lying idly in bed, certainly not the bed in the captain's quarters. The lines were the strings and they cried out when drawn through their pulleys. Structure came from the tapping of the mainsail hoops and the timpani bursts of the sheets. The crew literally carried the melody as they sang out while pulling a halyard or raising the main. Even with half a crew the whole of the ship's song echoed throughout the belly of the clipper as we cut through the sea.

When I felt ready to pull myself from the bed, I took my breakfast alone at the galley table. Per my instructions, Stake set out the food as I would have normally arranged it myself within my door — a little something of the usual ritual was very grounding. I ate canned sweet peaches over a plate-sized pancake. It was a favorite, although I preferred apples.

I wondered briefly if it were wrong to be pleased that Stake stayed, although not solely for his pancakes. Should I be glad for any of them staying? It pleased me that they did, but I worried that they didn't really know what they were getting into. How could they? The sketchy designs were of my own drafting, and I didn't even know to what end we sailed. The Transcendent was a ship of fugitives.

Root beer candy completed the meal. I often reminded Stake to stock them in the kitchen, although I usually ate more of them than the men did. While I had waited until the others were gone before venturing into the galley, I knew they were near, being within and above the ship. That morning the world felt particularly expansive; I felt a part of the Transcendent and of the men that lived there. We were all of one purpose and that purpose was, ostensibly, freedom. When I rose from the table, Stake met me halfway and took my plates and cup.

I entered the main hold, pausing to breathe deeply and exhale. Through the hatch above I could see terns circling the foremast. A whistle sounded somewhere further within the ship. The intermittent tone grew louder when I opened the green door to the boatswain's workshop. Strapped to a shelf opposite the entrance sat the two long speakers. The one with the wooden base connected to its twin within my door, although the men were told it connected only to the captain's quarter's at the aft end of the ship. The cap on that tube lay still. The other long speaker, the one with the dark metal base that forever paired to its doppelganger within the capital, vibrated with the percussive beat of attention tones. I would not answer it. Instead, I closed the shop door. Although I briefly considered turning around and cracking the neck of that tube, I ignored that opportunity.

The sun was bright, but none of the men above deck were looking for shadows where they might idle. They held full sail for the port of Copic where I hoped to retrieve both supplies and Dillon. The men around me were all activity as they used their combined speed and skill to gather up as much wind as the Transcendent could hold. I noticed that the studding sails had been retracted. Rohad had flown them last evening, but the wind had picked up since then. It was easy enough to dash those stunsails in a good wind. Even in a headwind the Transcendent could make excellent time; without cargo and with the addition of a larger main, the re-purposed trade ship was lighter and faster than most, but I knew that we could still be overtaken by several other ships of the New England line. Some of them probably would have been available for pursuit when we fled. As we left the Tremont harbor I'd even seen the Pinnacle, a newly launched clipper capable of a sustained 14 knots. That ship could certainly catch us if it knew where to look.

I saw that the rifles were at the ready on the deck. That was good. I hoped I had overestimated the court's desire to pursue me, but immediate conflict was possible. In recent years I had become somewhat unattached to court politics, but for the first third of my life I lived almost entirely within the city. I knew too much. Mother would speak endlessly of the people and players. The good ones that I recalled were mostly all dead. A few of the good ones had been bound, but I learned long ago that the very best of the court either gave up their torch or had it pulled from them. New England appeared to hold a good supply of copper, but there had to be a finite supply and scarcity brings out the worst in some people.

Rohad shouted orders into the rigging. I returned a friendly smile when he noticed me staring. He was an excellent sailor, but I thought he would make an even more exceptional captain. I looked at me a moment longer, so I waved at him in a wide arc. He started for a ratline and I realized that I'd unintentionally called him down. I tried to shoo him back up, but he continued.

I explained and he shrugged it off. After an awkward moment, I filled in the empty space by telling him about the long speaker sounding. I loved the way he listened, his face and body moving in time with my words. He listened fully. Not just with me. If anyone had his attention they had it completely.

"You should have pitched the tube over the bulwarks," he said.

"There's nothing good that will come from answering it. Everyone involved knows their business."

"I wonder if they contacted Dillon."

"Why bother?" Rohad rubbed the back of his neck.

"Well, they might expect us to head there."

Rohad shrugged. "I don't expect they'd see us heading there. He's been your mother's man for some time now."

"He's been away on her business, but that doesn't mean he's not valuable."

"Maybe. I don't think I know him as well as you do."

"You think we should sail past Columbia, maybe for Florida?"

"Not so far."

"Well, Copic makes more sense than any other port in Columbia."

"I think your right," he said with a shrug.

"Dillon might not even want to come," I offered.

"Maybe not." Rohad turned away slightly. "Anything else?"

"I didn't mean to pull you down," I said.

He nodded and I watched him head back up the lines. He climbed too roughly, like he'd become disturbed by our conversation. I tried not to let it bother me, but it did.

* * * * *

The calm sheltered waters of Copic glowed warmly as I steered the ship into port. I had expected us to arrive in the city much later, nearer to dawn. Reflected light cast into the water by the tall street lamps illuminated the bottoms of the other ships navigating the circuitous harbor lanes. By that light I began to bring the Transcendent to a gentle stop along the side of the pier. Rohad shouted orders to the crew while I took the wheel. The Transcendent exhausted the last of its speed only as we pulled alongside the fender.

I had visited Copic enough to know it would be active in the middle of the night. Still, it was a little jarring, like walking into a dark house and finding everyone awake in a lighted back-facing room. On shore, woman in bustled dresses, which seemed to be growing in size as of late, walked by like the silhouettes of chickens. Men with canes and tall hats accompanied them. It seemed that the further south along the American coast one traveled, the taller the hats grew. I considered the crown to cap distance as accurate a measurement of latitude as the sextant.

All of the crew were awake and ready too. There had been speculative talk of an armada waiting to seize us after arrival. I hadn't thought that likely. The city of Copic was the northernmost port of Columbia, the Ligurian new world colony that had grown to be the largest of all the Genoan holdings. While the indigenous nation of Lenape just miles to the north was on fair terms with New England, I thought it unlikely that they would dispatch one of their great frigates upon request from Tremont. That held doubly true for the Ligurians, who controlled all of the coast south of Lenape to Florida.

What I had expected was an assault further out at sea. Although it hurt to consider it, once Charlotte betrayed my motives to our mother, everything else should have fallen into position like bricks in a wall. A trip to Copic before heading off to ports unknown would be obvious. Still, even a fugitive ship requires supplies. Actually, what I really needed was crew. Failing a full compliment, Dillon would suffice. Even if I had wanted to overlook his worth to avoid co-mingling him in our sordid affair, the crew knew his value and both Emery and Bosun suggested we fetch him. Rohad's disinterest hadn't made much sense.

While Rohad disembarked to discuss arrangements with the harbor master, I walked off alone into Copic. I dressed as a boy again but not in the clothes from Pomin. Even street kids dressed better than that in Copic. I moved through the lighted main streets and passed further from the central hub of the city. There, things were much quieter. Not everyone in the city burns into the night.

I knew where Dillon was staying since I had seen him to the rented house when we dropped him off in the city. I had only to walk back through the memory palace, although it had been a while and I had not used that particular palace since its creation. Like any other memory, the palace construct fades with inattention and disuse. Although the landmarks looked very different at night, I easily found Hawthorne. I recalled writing out that street name when addressing my last correspondence to Dillon. I'd lavished attention on the calligraphy, something he always seemed to appreciate.

The narrow irregularly stoned street was dark except for one house towards the end of the lane. My assumption that the house belonged to Dillon was confirmed when I drew near enough to read the house number 65 painted on a flowered hanging sign. A man stood with his back to the lighted window. Smoke curled from around the familiar outline of his shoulders. It was surely him.

I continued past the house and then doubled back quickly along my path. Around the side of the house I found an overgrown slate walk. I loved the smell of mint. Without stopping, I plucked a leaf in the dark. I rubbed it between my fingers. It seemed to me that the particular texture of mint breaks down faster under tension than it would if it were smooth and unchanneled. When rubbed the herb turns slick quickly. My fingers smelled cool and pleasant.

Dillon was not the sort to shoot blindly, but I didn't want to walk in without knocking. I tapped on the pane of a back window, one through which I could see light in the main room. Dillon appeared in the lit open hall within and crossed at once to the back door. He opened it without hesitation.

I sunk towards the wall, surprised to see him go for the door so quickly.

"Mina?"

"Dillon?" I asked genuinely. His voice had a surprising urgency to it.

"Come inside." He held the door. His beard was fuller than when I left him and his face a bit rounder. Still, he looked like Dillon and his nearly expressionless smile was comfortingly familiar.

I entered. The kitchen looked as if it had not been touched since I last saw it, which was when Dillon had first seen in too. The man was many things, but he was not neat. The place should have been a mess.

"So good to see you. Please, have a seat. I will put the lights out in front." He lit a gas mantle lantern and left it on the table.

Except for a few hanging pots, the kitchen was empty. They'd probably been hung in place soon after the first walls were framed and there they stayed.

"Captain, it is good to see you. I didn't expect this so soon."

"Are you eating? There's dust on the counters."

"I am a terrible cook, and the restaurants here are excellent. I really didn't expect to see you. Are you here on your mothers request?"

"No. Are you always in the window these days? Maybe that's what she has you here to do, keep watch on Hawthorne street."

"I haven't been able to sleep. There was a rumor though, that you had arrived in Tremont and would be heading inland for a few days."

"Well, if I had I certainly wouldn't have passed by your window." That bit about heading inland was the tale I told the old geologist. I wanted to sigh. If it wasn't for my sister, that story would have bought me some real time, even after the letter of resignation had been found.

"I did see you from the window though."

"Oh. I'll have to be more careful."

Dillon settled into his seat. The two of us stared in the same general direction, into the dark window of the sitting room beyond.

"I left the capital without four of the crew and five less than when we left you here — anyone with any sense decided not to follow me. I quit the court."

Outside of inhaling through his nostrils, Dillon didn't betray much emotion. I looked away from him, back towards the window. After a long pause he spoke. "Who didn't follow you?"

"Seamen Brand and Remmy left. Able seamen Haggard and Anderson also chose to stay behind."

"The fifth?"

"Allan."

"I thought you would have said Allan. I had told you it seemed as if he served grudgingly. There are many men who fought to be appointed to your ship. It is something of an honor, you know."

"Not much honor in it now."

"Well, in any case, I am not sad to see him go."

I looked back to Dillon. "I should have said this immediately; I didn't intend to create suspense. He is dead. Someone put a knife in his back, for my sake, before we entered the capital harbor."

"Were you in danger?" Dillon leaned in. He seemed to notice my arms, running his eyes along the cuts and scrapes. Perhaps he saw the bruises along my left cheek. Out of sight, my legs were bloodied in several places and my chest was one mottled bruise. The gouges on my legs and knees were not too bad, but I'd noticed that they were not healing as fast as they usually did. I'd grown very used to the restorative powers of the torch.

"I don't know. I mean, I don't know what he intended. I don't think so. In any case, I was ready for him. I don't know who did it, but I didn't check sheaths afterwords either. It was a standard issue knife — it could have been Crocodile and probably was."

"Do you mind if I smoke?"

"It's your place, isn't it?"

From the front room Dillon fetched a pipe and satchel. He took a folding pipe tool from his pocket and tamped some shredded tobacco into the barrel. After lighting the pipe he pulled and puffed the smoke from his mouth without breathing it in. With the lighting draw exhausted, he tamped down the embers with the tool and struck another match to resurrect the prepared pipe. I could see he hadn't slept. The match light made that more obvious than the lamp at the center of the table. I wanted to know what he looked like in daylight.

"I am too quiet," he said.

"No. You are quiet though, but I am not sure what I expected. Your business here is unfinished?"

"Yes."

"We're gathering supplies. They should already be loading them into the hold, unless I underestimate the crew. Half the ship set out to fetch what was needed, and they are paying above asking price or at least will if needed. We have more than enough money, just not enough of everything else."

"The harbor company here is soft. Real bums. A little extra money buys a lot here. I don't enjoy this place."

"We are leaving tonight."

"Are you returning to the capital?"

"No. I'll probably never return."

"Tonight then?"

"Yes."

"I trust you will be hunted as a traitor?"

"For putting out my torch? As a contract breaker that's the penalty. Add to that the shooting of some fool men that were taken down for my sake as we escaped. I wish that hadn't happened, but I'm thankful for it all the same. It happened very quickly."

"I suppose you didn't have a chance to look back at the city one final time?" He took a long draw from his pipe. "To reflect."

"I was forearmed to the ground at a full run. I'm surprised I made it aboard."

"Where will you go?"

"I'm not sure. There's no clemency for this crew or for me, but there's freedom to be had out there. I'm sure of it."

"Ten deaths for you if you are caught out there."

"That's a lot of death. I've had it coming."

"There's not much out there," he said. "I mean, it's all the same. If you have a little money it's not so bad, but it is all the same."

"Across the world?"

"Yes. Across the world." He took a long draw from his pipe.

"I don't think that's true. I've seen a lot of it. If it's all the same, I think that's in the eye of the viewer. I have enough money. I have my ship. We would have all we would need to start a small trading company."

"I am a hell of a negotiator."

"Maybe. I don't know that."

"You're not putting yourself on very good footing right now, for negotiations." He leaned in close. Whatever I saw when I first arrived, it was gone. He seemed more like himself.

"I'm not here for council," I responded.

"All right. You are not here for my advice. Why then?" He crossed his arms.

"I don't know. Why are you here anyway?" I waited.

Dillon's eyes locked onto the burning white of the lantern mantle. He shrugged. "I've asked myself that often, but I don't want to talk of it. If I go, I leave it behind."

"Who said I was offering?"

"I shouldn't presume."

"I suppose I could order you."

"By what authority?"

"As your captain."

He gave my leg a slight kick under the table. "You are already here. Out with it."

"We are here for supplies," I said. "The winds may be dying soon."

"Then, I will ask."

"I'd prefer it."

"Why?" he asked.

"I don't know. By what authority am I captain now, anyway?"

"It's your ship," Dillon said. He put the pipe down and leaned back.

"Fine then. Do you wish to resume your position as first officer on the Transcendent?"

"I do."

"Good. Let's go then."

"Where are you docked?"

"Fifth dock. I think it's an open air tavern."

"I know the place. It does feel like that."

Dillon stood up. He paced several times. That was something he often did.

"I can help you gather your things if you like."

"I would prefer, Captain, to meet you there shortly. I must make some arrangements."

"That's fine." I felt tired, but I also felt somewhat relieved. I rested my head on my arms and watched Dillon. He was thinking out loud the way he always did, by pacing.

The first time I had met him I sat under a canvas stretched across the quarterdeck. I had selected the greenhand for extended duty, the only one of the three that had boarded with him on that short trial excursion twenty-two years ago. He paced whenever he was idle. But, that first time, when I was making my selections, he moved so quickly that I had stopped the selection process to watch. Soon the others were watching. It took some time for Dillon to notice that all had stopped while he paced. The other men didn't laugh and neither did I — the young man had looked so damned serious. Dillon had always been so damned serious about something.

"Fifth dock, as soon as possible." I walked to the back door, although I wanted to sit there at the table for a while longer. "We can't stay beyond day break."

* * * * *

The crew received Dillon like a lost friend that had been left adrift. My reinstated first mate did look different in the daylight, much better than he had the night before. I'd glimpsed him several times from across the ship after having finished surveying the supplies in the hold. There was enough there to last until we put in far south, where I also hoped to restore the missing hands. The shelves within my door could be filled then too. In such a state we could set out with confidence to nearly anywhere on Earth.

According to Crocodile, Dillon had been met at the pier by a woman. Through a sly smile Crocodile said that she looked like a bar girl, but I assumed he was just adding some color. Of course, it may have been true. I wasn't sure. Apparently, the woman had made a scene, begging Dillon to stay. I wished I had seen it, not because of any voyeuristic thrill but because I wished to understand him a little better. More specifically, I wanted to understand his peculiarly reserved behavior the night before.

I took the helm to relieve Crane for a bit. He whistled a tune as he walked away; he wasn't very good at it, but he seemed to do it often, enough so that you knew when he was approaching, much like a cat wearing a bell. I pulled the brim of my sailor's cap down to better see the waves without the glare of the western sun at starboard. Looking to the fore, I noticed that Rohad had joined Dillon and the two men were speaking. Neither smiled. They had never been more than professional with one another.

That night the men lit the lanterns in the forecastle and I joined them. At first my presence stiffened up the conversation, but I played cards until everyone began to lounge and speak more loudly. With some excitement, I ran to the door and returned with a bottle. No one seemed very interested in drinking until I offered to lead them in a toast. Stake brought me a glass with honey drizzled across the bottom. I only drank a sip of the sweetened whiskey, but everyone cheered. Crocodile patted me on the back.

The energy ebbed, but the men continued to drink. I didn't have much more, but I could feel it strongly. In time only Lasko and Dillon kept playing, absorbed entirely in a game of Indian Rummy. The rest of us, outside of Crane who remained above, talked about plans for a while. As one conversation gave way to another, Bosun, Crocodile and Stake branched off and talked about women. I hadn't realized that Bosun had been married.

I sat within a berth beside Rohad, who lounged with his hands behind his head. He had no pillow since it was wedged behind Emery who sat on the floor with his back against the mattress and frame. I think that the bunk had belonged to Emery before he was so recently promoted to Allan's old cabin and rank.

It was only when I began to talk about the torch, after Rohad asked several times, that everyone quieted and listened. Lasko kept trying to play, but Dillon put a big hand up. Lasko seemed to pull hard on his cigarette in response.

"The torches couldn't have been from the Moorish cache," I explained, unsure of the argument. At that time I knew very little about the original raid made by the moors through the door that they had found by chance long ago. "New England wouldn't have had them all. Nearly everything else has found its way from hand to hand over time. But only New England has had the torches."

"That's just speculation," said Emery. He took a swig from the bottle.

"True," I said. "But I heard that from Mother too."

"So, why is there fuel still to burn when everything else has gone dead?" asked Rohad.

"Only the tailors went dead," interrupted Emery. "So it's said."

"I don't know. A little bit of the copper lasts a long time. And I think there was a time when less people had the torches." The room had become very quiet, nothing but the creaking of the ship. I took another sip from my glass, if only to fill the expectant silence. "My mother suggested that she was one of the first. She once said something about morons who never realized what the stuff could do. I am assuming she meant the copper."

"How old is she then?" asked Emery.

"Oh, I don't know. I think she was a kid when the doors in Tremont were made."

"That's more than two centuries ago," said Rohad, sitting up.

"The big doors were carved in 1632," said Emery. "Sorry. 1631. It was called the great waste because it used up the English tailors."

"Captain," said Rohad. He was a little drunk but he seemed then to lean on his slur intentionally. "How old are *you*?"

"One hundred and four," I said. I don't think I'd ever said it aloud.

Lasko cursed in Greek, or at least I assumed it was a swear. The others all made some noise.

"You certainly don't act like you're 104 years old," said Rohad.

He smiled as he said it, so I tried to take it the right way. "How exactly would you expect me to act?"

"Like the other old ladies," said Bosun, grinning.

"Yeah, like that," added Rohad while he shook his head.

I wondered then if Rohad hadn't meant more. I could act like a child sometimes, and I knew it. I swallowed the rest of my drink and stood up, smoothing my trousers and shirt. "It's past my bedtime."

Most of the others took the opportunity and stood up too. Dillon and Lasko resumed their game. I went out ahead of everyone and climbed up to the weather deck where I greeted Crane lazily. I leaned by the forecastle hatch and enjoyed the air in silence until Rohad came up and handed Crane a cup. I could still feel my own drink too strongly. I didn't care much for alcohol. Obviously, it didn't suit my body. Even a small amount made me feel hot and dizzy, not drunk so much as mildly poisoned.

The voices of the men below resumed. They must have decided not to turn in. I really didn't know how often they drank together. My evenings were almost always spent in the door.

When Rohad went down the aft ladder, I followed him. I'd wanted to ask if he was upset about Dillon.

"I can hear you," he said.

"I wasn't trying to be quiet. You wouldn't have if I was."

"Old people shouldn't tiptoe. You might break a hip." He laughed and ducked through the arch that led into his cabin. He fell down onto his bed without lighting his lamp.

"Do you think I haven't broken a hip?"

"No, really?" The galley lamp illuminated enough of the sparse room for me to see that he looked interested. I followed him inside. When I sat down on his pillow he sat up cross-legged at the foot of the bed.

"I really did," I said.

"You'd be crippled."

"I got better." I held out a leg and punched it. "It was the torch, I think. I could walk again after a week or so."

"I didn't realize."

"You wouldn't have. I guess I keep it all to myself."

"Have you talked to anyone about it?" he asked.

"My sister," I said. "We're nearly twins. Twins of circumstance, at least." She wouldn't say the same though, I realized that. Yet it was either true or it should have been. Still, that world was gone, fallen in on itself.

"I met her," said Rohad. "You both have the same hair, kind of blondish brown. Same long curls too. I think your eyes are both blue. I'm not much with details."

"She's very attractive," I said.

"Well, you look alike, like sisters do."

"I look more like my father." It wasn't lost on me that Rohad had made a compliment. We both listened for a time to the sounds of the others singing in the forecastle.

"I've never met him," said Rohad. He yawned big.

I yawned too. When I tried to stand up I felt dizzy and fell back again. I rolled with the fall towards Rohad. I knew I shouldn't have, but he didn't throw me out of the bed, so I stayed there in the space between the side of the ship and his crossed leg. The ocean moved and swelled beyond the hull and I could hear it well. That was something I missed within my door. Rohad put his hands behind his head and leaned against the back wall of the cabin.

"I never did meet him either," I said. "But that's what I was told. I have his eyes. My mother and Charlotte have brown eyes."

"Oh. I got it wrong then."

"Doesn't matter. Charlotte's are almost hazel, just like yours. I love her eyes. They're big." I laughed for no reason.

"Yours are too big for your head."

"Really?"

"You'll grow into them," he said. "I wouldn't worry."

"No worries," I said. I sat up beside him, kneeling in the small space. I felt like he should have politely kicked me out of his berth. His eyes remained closed and he feigned another small yawn, but he didn't ask me to go. My skin vibrated with nervous energy, not unlike the way it felt when the green flame of the torch licked at my fingertips.

"None," he said.

"Do you mind me here?" I asked quietly. He should have. I felt very sober and knew better, but he wasn't even hinting that I should leave. Everyone minded when I got too close, always did.

"Should I?" He smiled but kept his eyes closed and his head forward. His breath seemed very even and intentional.

"I guess not." I leaned closer and he didn't move. His nostrils flared and he sighed, but he stayed fixed, pinned. I very slowly touched my cheek and nose to the side of his arm. With some hesitation, I withdrew.

"They're loud tonight." He opened his eyes but looked towards me only for a moment. Rohad's eyes were very watery, catching the shine off of the galley lamp.

I kept my own gaze fixed on his eyes and placed my left hand cautiously on the center of his chest. With more confidence, I leaned in to kiss him.

"Mina." He said it hard and quiet and he knocked me back simply by standing up on the bed like a woman who'd caught sight of a skittering mouse. He stepped down and spoke in a forceful hush. "My god. Don't ever do that. Ever. Why did you do that?"

I didn't say anything or even try to get up. He kept his hands raised slightly in front of him and backed out of the cabin into the bright light of the galley. I sat in the dark of his berth and listened to him ascend the galley ladder.

I wasn't sure if I had kissed him or not, but I knew I had tried. My stomach turned and I knew I would be sick. Guilt pulled at me, as if I should rush to mend the damage. I knew better. Nothing new. Go be sick alone now, I told myself. When I passed through to the other side, I wished like hell that I still had the torch.

12

"Captain?" Bosun was up from the main ladder where he had been working with Emery to thread new anchor bolts for one of the large guns. The ship's keeper took off his hat and squinted into the light of another hot day. His usually roseate cheeks paled.

I realized Bosun was waiting for me to ask. "Everything alright?" I had my hand on the wheel. Seeing Bosun's hesitation, I really didn't want him to answer. I spoke again just as he opened his mouth to begin, before he could say it. "You were down in the tween. The long speaker is there. I thought we were keeping it plugged?"

"We did."

"That's not it?"

"No, that is it. It was fussing, as it does, but we left it. Thing is, we were able to make out what they were saying."

"Without uncapping?"

"Yes. I made a little listening cup from some tin. You know, just something rolled up. I held it to the box so they couldn't tell we were listening, and I could make out the speech well enough. Do you want to know?"

Bosun was joined shortly by Rohad, who was excellent at

spotting a growing storm. I betrayed none of the discomfort I felt at his arrival, besides, I was already uncomfortable.

"Yes, tell me. I doubt you would have come to me if you didn't think I'd want to know."

"It was your mother."

"The message?"

"I mean, it was lady secretary and no one on her behalf. She was screaming like a devil, if you don't mind me saying so. The box had been sounding like that for nearly an hour too. From what I can make out, she will be killed if you do not return."

"What else?"

"Your sister as well." He paused for the phrasing as if avoiding some taboo word of some kind. "Their torches are to be put out. There was more too. Your sister may have been there with her. I think I remember her voice. I met her once at that dinner, if you recall."

I dropped the stops onto the wheel and motioned to Crocodile, who had ceased sanding the ship's boat when Bosun came up from below. I marched across the quarterdeck and slipped down the ladder.

Within Bosun's workshop I found the little box sitting on the table beside a crude listening tube of scrap tin. Emery stood there in the room looking like he'd been caught dipping his finger in a sauce. I immediately plucked the cap from the speaking tube and my mother's voice poured out. Emery walked out hastily.

My mother wailed. It was obvious that she had cried or screamed herself hoarse. There was nothing controlled about her voice. If I hadn't actually heard from Bosun that she had been like this for at least a half hour, I wouldn't have believed that it were possible to make it ten minutes in such a state.

"Mother?"

The tube went silent. A sucking sound pulled from the speaker that reminded me of the retreat of a false tide before a tsunami.

The tide returned in a loud burst of emotion. "Oh, my love. They came for your sister. She didn't deserve it. She shouldn't be the one paying for this. What did you do? Why? You have to come back."

"I can't do that. What happened to Charlotte?"

"What do you think? She was nothing but perfection in this. You nearly shook her to death, but she did the right thing. You know? And what for it? The guard seized her before you even left the wharf. So much has happened. Did you —"

I interrupted, knowing my mother would not stop. "But, Charlotte. Why would they take Charlotte?"

"Your contract. It is bound to ours."

"I'm responsible for my own actions — by what rights would they act? What did she tell you?"

"She told me everything. And, I sent men, just to speak to you — of course — until I could arrive. Now Officer Blarette is dead. You murdered him. What do you think of that?"

"Tell me of the contracts."

"Your sister and you. Both of you. Your contracts are bound. You are my charges. I know you understood this. If you do not return. If you do not relight, we will both be put out. Mina, they will pull her guts from her navel. Think of it. What do I have to tell you to make you realize? You're like a little child." Her voice began to rise again. It reminded me of the hum of a torch. "I put up my life for yours. Do you know how sick your poor sister is? Your treason is more than enough for death, you must understand that, but things can be done. Something must be carved from this. I am hoping. Hoping, my child, that we can all survive this. Together. It has to be together."

"But, why?"

"When I saved you both from yourselves. When I fed you on my own stores, you were both bound, yes. But, they only kept you on because I begged. I signed over myself doubly. Now, I'm paying for it. Your sister as well. She's the one paying for this. Isn't she?"

"What does that even mean?" I paced with my hands behind my back fidgeting.

"I have been trying to free you from your contract. You know that. If you had just told me, I would have tried another approach."

"Why are we bound together? I left. You are speaking to me of a contract I've never seen, of a deal I have never made. It's an obligation I never agreed to and one Charlotte never agreed to. Where is she being held?" I sat down at the table on the small wooden stool. The little room felt too big for me. I crossed my arms.

"We are all bound together. That is all. Why do you speak to me like this? What are you? You're a hateful monster. Blood. Mina! See, I bit my lip I am so beside myself. So long as I serve, you will serve as my charges. There is only one contract. And, in breaking it, you have screwed us too."

My ears rang. It was not as if the court was above execution for treason, but I had not expected to hear Charlotte's name dragged into this.

"Please, Mina. I beg you. End this madness and return. Will you return?"

"I want clemency for my crew. All of them. Complete."

"That is fine. Who cares about them. They are nothing in this."

"We will all be unharmed?"

"I will try. There are powerful people at work here. Will you come?"

"I need time to consider." I replaced the cap and walked into the main hold. Bosun and Rohad were waiting. Dillon stood further back, towards the forecastle. I wasn't sure if he had heard, but the others must have.

I broke to the right and walked through the galley, counting my breaths. I opened the door to the captain's quarters.

"Wait." Rohad jogged to me.

I continued into the room as he followed. I felt my lip twitching.

The awful flood of emotion building within me could not be held back much longer.

"You're not going back, are you?"

"I don't know."

"You can't go back. Forgive me, but that woman is not to be trusted."

"I don't trust her." I stood just in front of the cabinet that hid my door. With the white-slatted false panel pulled over it, the door looked like any other section of the under-bed storage area. I wanted very badly to see the Nantucket red of my door. I wanted to rip the covering panel off, open my door, and fall backwards inside. "I do expect that I will be killed if I return."

"No, I don't only mean that." Rohad motioned into the air in front of me as if he was softening a pillow.

"I am sorry. I am. I don't know what is happening right now."

"Just go slowly into this. You don't have to decide now. I can see you deciding. What I meant to say was that you can't even trust that she or your sister are in any sort of real danger." He shut the door most of the way behind him without latching it.

"And how could I know that? I don't have much to go on."

"Then you cannot act. You should not. You've come so far."

"I'm nowhere. If I am, I don't see it."

"But you are. Look, I see it. I saw it. I've seen you excited about life for the first time in so long. That's worth hanging onto."

"At what cost? Am I so important that I should be throwing these lives around? How many lives have I ever claimed, directly or indirectly? How many deaths should my sister die? At least I've lived." That last thought caught me and it took all of my concentration to fight back tears. I paid attention, hard attention, to the room. I focused on the listing of the ship and the angle of the light from the mess hall. Even noticing the shadow Rohad cast upon me helped steady my sense of place and time. I felt light-headed.

"We all pay our own way." He paused. "I mean to say, that we all must. Are we all such children that we can't decide for ourselves?"

"You *are* children to me." I caught his glance and we both smiled a little at the humor of it.

"Just think about this first. You have a lot of living to do yet. You're aging for the first time in who knows how long — that has to be worth something. Do you not realize? I mean, you always have in mind, but in body too. That's something."

"I can hardly stand it," I said, wary of the change of topic. "I swear I feel it."

"I don't doubt that."

I turned to the door.

"Just let what she said go."

"How can I? It is my carelessness that brought this on them, on my sister." I turned around. "You don't know. You didn't see her. She was not well."

"I'm sorry for her, I am, but do you honestly doubt your mother's ability to fix that situation? That's if it's even true. Please, forgive me if I over-speak."

"At ease." I smiled again. "I don't know what she is capable of, but that extends in all directions and to everyone else in the court. Actually, I know more about what she is capable of than I can stand knowing. I put it out of my mind with great effort. It makes me want to tear myself in two. I feel it. I can feel it in my stomach." My lower abdomen ached and I felt a little nauseous. My own muscles felt tight around me, like I would double over and die from the force of it all.

"I'll leave you, but I think you are wrong to even consider this. How's this? Your mother is a murderer. If she cannot keep you, she will kill you."

"She's still a piece in their game."

"I just don't believe it."

"I'm sorry." I opened the door.

"You, I believe and believe in, for what that's worth."

"Thank you. I would like some quiet."

"As you wish."

I shut and locked the door to the captain's quarters. I had nearly considered entering my door before he even left the room. It was not as if they didn't all suspect or know it. They must. I did, however, need to keep the means of entry to myself. Or, was it more than that, of keeping it secret out of security? Opening the door felt like something more. Shame? That was the least of my concerns.

Upon entering the door, the cool of the tunnel brought breath to my lungs. I remembered Charlotte's breath at our last meeting. I remembered the child Charlotte had once been. I had only brought her within the door once. My sister was so overjoyed by the place. I had thought we would live there together and travel. Yet the next time I returned to fetch Charlotte, she had lost all enthusiasm. She claimed then that she had no interest in the door at all. How did mother do it?

I screamed, in anger, and then screamed again. What kind of parent was my mother, what kind of person? What a monster. I wailed again into the dark and advanced the last few feet of the short passage. My body ached in earnest. My stomach hurt. My chest ached. It was a pain I could feel in my soul as well as my body.

I crawled through the inner door and stepped into the foyer. My face was on fire. I didn't even wait before undressing, and I didn't bother to count breaths. I threw the clothes on the floor and marched into my apartments. I smashed everything I saw without touching a thing. It was an idle tantrum executed in my mind only. Nothing moved yet everything was destroyed all around me. While I didn't throw anything, I felt my arms twitch like they had actually hurled a book. Towels flew. Mantles, in my mind, were smashed with bronze sticks. I brought the walls down with my fists, using arms that never actually left my side. Were someone able to watch me within, they would have seen me standing still — red faced and naked too. Unless I was out of my clothes I was never really in my door, was I? I would still have been half out there, in their petty and flat world.

When the thought of Charlotte's tired, sad eyes returned to me, I began to cry hard. I dropped to my knees under the dome of the library, under the constellations of my own design. I cried like a child. When I couldn't cry anymore, I crawled to the bath and let the water run down the drain while I sat in the tub. The water was nice. It was endless. The sound of the rushing bath was endless and intricate. I let the sound of that flow replace my own thoughts.

* * * * *

When I emerged from the door I went to the weather deck and faced the wind until I heard Dillon's heavy boots approaching from behind. I looked up at him. His face looked slack and inexpressive in the descending vesper light.

"Captain?" Dillon spoke as if I had summoned him.

"Full sail, for the capital."

"As you wish." He turned.

"Do you wish to be returned to Copic first?"

"No. I don't think I'm in any danger. I wasn't part of your revolt." He turned back and added, "It's like I told you, it doesn't much matter where you are. It all measures about the same."

"Well, full sail then."

"Aye." Dillon walked towards the quarterdeck.

"There's not much wind, is there?" I said, but Dillon did not hear, or at least he did not respond. I returned down the forecastle ladder into the relative darkness of the below. The door to the workshop and ship's supply room was ajar and lit from within.

There I found the boatswain surrounded by small wooden bits and fasteners he had fanned out onto the table before him.

"Bosun?"

"Aye, captain." He stayed seated and smiled amiably from behind a silversmith's anvil set by a peg into the table.

"I have three old guns I was hoping you could look at. One is the navy revolver. I would like very much if you could check the sighting. The other is the modified howdah pistol. I would like shot prepared for that. Any additional noise and smoke from that thing would be appreciated. The third is that small pistol you tooled for me about 15 years ago. Do you remember it? I want that smaller — I need it thinner. I don't want to blow up my hand, but anything you could shave would be appreciated. The firearm is built to be compact, not necessarily thin. I am willing to sacrifice a good hand feel for that, so don't be concerned if there's nothing much to hang onto but a little stick. I'll make do when it's time to shoot it."

"I'll see to it. You think there will be opportunity to fire it?"

"Yes." I had no idea.

"Well, I'll see to it."

"Thanks," I said. I realized I had a headache again, although I hadn't cried in hours.

"Also, Crane's glasses are broken. There's a curious story to it too. I didn't know this, but the man is almost completely blind without them — they are bottle bottoms."

"Aye, Captain. Are you sick?"

"I don't think so." I relaxed my stomach and put my hands behind my back. Crying usually made me feel sick. "Also, did you see that woman with Dillon?"

"No? When?"

"It's not important. Have you seen Rohad?"

"He's helping to thread the port stunsail."

"I thought I saw it flying?"

"It is, but I think he's out on the studding boom anyway."

"Thanks." I ran back above. There was Rohad, a silhouette against the early evening sky. I wasn't sure how I had missed him when I was speaking to Dillon. Perhaps, to erase the memory of the other night, I had pushed Rohad out of my head so successfully that I hadn't noticed the man at all.

I took the Jacob's ladder in hand and rose to him. Emery and the half-blinded Crane were there with him far out on the yard. Emery held a line fastened around Rohad, who leaned out over the sail, relying on the rope to prevent him from pitching over. The end of the rope behind Emery's white knuckled grip had been secured to the fore topmast as a safety. Emery nodded to me as I approached. While I returned the gesture, I said nothing, not wanting to break Rohad's concentration.

It was unlikely that he would fall. I didn't expect that, but I also didn't want him missing a needle push on my account. Up there where the earth is a loose thing and clouds move and sails shift too, there is the natural sway of the lines and sound of the ship on the sea that guides your fingers and hands. I didn't want to be in the way of all that, to be the reason for the slip of a needle. I imagined that Rohad's universe had been reduced to his fingertips. He was actually a master with a needle, if there was such a thing on a ship. He was an excellent swordsman too.

I watched him sew. The act was a uniquely curious thing to watch. We were moving at around six knots in a weak, but unpredictable, wind. It was nearly full dark then as well, and he was repairing the sail at the furthest end of the boom without letting it drop. The staysails go out to catch all the wind they can. The kite-like extensions jut out far over the edge of the bulwarks. I remembered when I first saw studding sails on another clipper, and I had shouted to Dillon that we needed them. As a matter of form, they were exactly right — a ship should become something else, something winged when one wanted such flight. I wanted that then. I wanted the ship to be as a butterfly seeking warmth and finding something else entirely, finding itself, but not itself.

I watched the needle. It was a curious thing. It went in one place and came out the other.

I thought of my door. Doors such as mine had been made using a tailor. The device could punch a hole in one place and connect it to another. While Rohad sewed I thought about the energy it must have taken to create the door. No wonder the tailors did not last. I wondered what my world would be without my connection to that stitched place I called my door. Over the years I'd stopped distinguishing the rock carved fortress from my own self. Retreating within was not unlike escaping into a dream.

I watched Rohad at the needle again, working in the last light of day. The sun existed only as a warm smudge mostly hidden behind some clouds near the horizon. No one tried to speak above the winds and now and then light would glint off of the needle. Knowing that there would be no moon that evening, I expected to soon see many stars. When Rohad finished, I thanked him and then asked him to later gather the men for a briefing. He told me that he wanted to talk, but I shook my head and told him that Bosun waited for me below.

That night, under the stars, which were as bright as I hoped they would be, I told the crew of my plans. No one commented after I spoke, and I was thankful for that mercy. After the men dispersed, I threaded myself through the entrance to my door.

13

After I finished tying up Crocodile's braid, I pulled out one of his wiry gray hairs. "See, it's real."

He held it up to the light and bent it between two long fingers. "This is Bosun's."

"Bosun is pretty bald," I said.

"That's only because it all fell out. He's been shedding."

The rest of Crocodile's hair was lustrous black. Around the time of each new moon he washed it in fresh water and then ran a comb through with some oil he kept in a corked brown jar. For the past year or so I'd sometimes braided it for him. He'd offered to do the same for me, but I always declined.

To his usual braid I added a white ribbon. He didn't mind. I appreciated how the fabric looped through the pattern like crocodile teeth, although Crocodile had no real association with the creatures. His given name was actually Querouac, but someone had once given up on the pronunciation and called him Crocodile, which stuck.

On my way out of the forecastle, Rohad again asked if I would talk. He must have been waiting for me to finish. I thought I had heard someone lurking in the hall. "Okay," I said. "Go ahead."

"I just wanted to apologize."

I squinted at him and raised my eyebrows. "You? I expected an admonishment, not an apology." I walked away from the fore but stopped by the door to the galley storeroom. I was going to take him to the captain's cabin so we could speak in private, but my stomach hurt and I thought I might have to cut the conversation short.

"It's my fault," he said. "It is."

Even as he apologized I felt newly awkward, too aware of how close he stood. I started to respond, but I stopped. "You'll have to excuse me."

Please wait. I want to explain."

"I know, but I have to excuse myself." What I wanted to say was that I was out of line, and if he could pretend it didn't happen, I could too.

"Just to give you some context, I've been out of sorts since Dillon came back. I know it, and I'm sorry. Call it envy if you want, but he's the first mate and I've no business questioning that. You made the right choice in going back, and I don't want you thinking I really opposed his joining."

"This is what you wanted to talk about?"

"Yes. I'm not sure what Dillon told you, but I wanted to explain my actions."

"Well, Dillon hasn't told me anything. Okay. I have to go." I had no idea what Rohad was talking about, and I kept fighting the urge to bring my hand to my stomach. It hurt. Rohad put his head down in what looked like frustration, nodded, and walked off. I turned around and made it past the galley table when Crocodile stepped out of the dark corner by Bosun's berth. The sailor must have gone above, run across the deck, and dropped down the galley ladder while I spoke to Rohad.

"Captain." He pursed his thin lips.

"What?"

"Forgive me. Has Rohad been bothering you?" Crocodile faced the hall out of the galley, as if he were standing guard.

"What?" I asked again, with a slightly different intonation.

"Has he been harassing you?"

"I have to go. It's fine, really." Just then I realized that I very much needed to head to the washroom. "Even if he was, I can take care of myself."

"The other night," he started. "It made me think of something Dillon told me about Rohad."

"I'll listen. I will, but I have to go." I escaped into the captain's chambers and through my door. As I crawled through the tunnel to the inner door, I reached back between my legs and then jerked my fingers away.

Once through, I stood up into the foyer and stared at my hand. It was red. I felt faint. It felt like my blood had run out of me completely. I would die in the door, in that tomb. No. That was not it. I pulled my breeches down and looked.

I thought I would cry, but no tears came. In fact, I wanted to cry as if I had been cut across the eyes, as if I could bleed out tears, but I wasn't capable of it. Instead, I sank to the cold floor and stared at a smeared line of dark blood on my leg. I could feel new blood pooling beneath me as my chest heaved. As I sat there, the blood on my fingers eventually dried, and the humor of the moment finally came. I managed something near to a laugh. A century old and I found myself inconsolable over a little blood, over something so inevitable and common. Torch or not, there was something to this. I felt wary of myself without knowing why.

14

I left the door early that morning, after having woken on the foyer floor and accepting that it had not been a dream. I had cleaned the floor and spent an hour bathing and dressing. Twice, when I thought I was ready to leave the door and return to the ship, I became unsure of myself again and returned to check in the washroom.

And then, back in the ship, things still did not feel right. I told myself that the nervousness should be expected. After all, what more proof did I need that I had pushed myself down a path I could never retrace. But it wasn't only that: I had never really felt alone on the ship or anywhere outside of my door. Of course, I didn't mean physically alone but alone in the sense that I was by myself. Standing there on deck just after sunrise with the wind off of the sheets surrounding me, I missed my sister in a way that I had heard others speak of but perhaps I'd never actually experienced. I missed her in a way one couldn't express out loud to someone else because it would sound overdone and saccharin. I needed, at least, to talk to someone. I was alone though, out there on the water, learning then what everyone else must always have meant when they said they felt lonely.

I looked back to the line I'd been securing. Working dulled the emotions for a time, but they returned. It was as if my mouth was bound by cloth and that feeling seemed to be growing more intense. When I had a big idea and wanted to share it, it was my choice. But what I felt presently was an unasked-for urge to connect that would not pass. I expected change, but it was too much and too fast.

"Lasko?" I called to him and approached the sailor as he climbed down the rigging and hung by one lanky arm before dropping to the deck. "Did you make contact using the long tube?" I had asked him inform the court of my arrival. I'd chosen Lasko because he was a particularly poor communicator in anything, one assumed, other than Greek. I suspected though that the deficiency had less to do with his heritage than it did a general lack of interest in what most people had to say. In any case, I suppose I wanted to annoy my mother's men.

"I did," he said. It was another hot day and the man perspired heavily, darkening his shirt. It can be very cool up on the rigging, and lowering oneself to the deck can bring on a quick sweat. "They asked when we would arrive."

"What did you tell them?"

"I told them about the wind. How can I know the wind? You know what I said, I said I am not a god."

"Thank you." I smiled and looked for Rohad. Before I reached the stern I stopped and thought about my gait. Was I taking longer steps? It was not impossible.

The timing of what happened to me made very little sense — I'd only been off the torch for such a short time. I wanted to talk about that and a thousand other things. Instead, I waved to Rohad when his head bobbed up from the boat secured to the deck. He'd been right in front of me while I searched for him. Did I feel all right? Was fog a symptom? I already knew all the specifics of what to expect. A very long time ago I witnessed my sisters struggles, and I had known many girls and women and heard too many stories to recount them all. I knew everything I needed to know, but none of that applied, somehow. Wasn't I different? So long connected to the torch, wasn't I an unknown?

"Rohad?"

"Aye."

"I changed my mind about the lit lamps when I go ashore. I want real fire instead. There should be dipped cloth torches. Lamps are seen, but torches are talked about." He was looking at me for too long, as if he somehow knew everything. He knew somehow. Maybe he did. I knew I had to focus. We would be in the capital within a day and there I would descend into the web. Whatever I lacked in intelligence and body, I usually made up for with planning, but my head was in a cloud. There would be no clarity while my mind was wrapped in a thick layer of haze like a dried-over coat of paint.

"That's all," I continued. "I may not be available for a little while. Don't hesitate to use the speaker to call. I'm sorry I'm not of more use."

Rohad stopped whatever he had been doing in the craft and looked at me, putting an arm on the side of the boat. "I don't understand."

"Well, for one thing, why it would matter how you lit the boat on the way in. It's really not a funeral barge."

I shrugged and stepped onto the first step of the galley ladder.

"I guess it makes as much sense as any of your plans," said Rohad as he bent down to resume his work. I noticed that Crocodile was watching us speak from the forecastle deck. It reminded me that I hadn't asked Rohad about what happened with him and Dillon.

When Rohad's words finally seeped into my bones I grew annoyed. "What would you have me do?"

"With your mother?"

"All of it. I want to be done with the whole business, but I won't leave Charlotte dangling."

It was Rohad's turn to shrug.

"So, we just continue on and I tell my mother to... what?"

"Tell her what she wants to hear and then do as you please," said Rohad. He flicked his gaze upwards and then bent back down.

"Carry on," I said.

"It's good advice," he said from the boat while I turned my back and returned below.

I felt like someone who had just stuck their head up into a beehive and watched the inhabitants buzz around for a while. A few steps away Bosun was busy at the galley table. Stake and Emery assisted him with some task, but I couldn't see it from the door. One man shy of half my crew was nowhere near the weather deck. The mental equivalent of a shrug passed through me.

The ship could almost fly itself if the wind held, but I knew I shouldn't be melting back away into the door. However, I wanted another bath, mostly because my stomach hurt, and I knew a hot bath was supposed to help. I had heard that, although I had heard it in the way you might hear about some remedy for some condition that someone else might have.

I counted my steps to the door, but then I stopped. There were not enough men on deck. I would focus, and I would stay. Grudgingly, I returned to the above. Crane had taken the helm again. He wore the new twisted-wire frames Bosun had fashioned. I took the wheel from him, hoping the activity would push it all from my mind. I had known others who had been bound and then were cut from their Copper. They didn't die or suffer from sudden aging or anything of the sort, but I'd been bound young. Maybe I wasn't supposed to feel like this. Perhaps I would be dead in a year.

The Transcendent rounded the cape in the late morning. The windows of Provincetown were white with reflected sun. The last time I was there in that cape city, surrounded on three sides by water, I had sat with Dillon and Rohad and enjoyed cold sumac tea. The two men made comments about the passing woman on the boardwalk. Sometimes those women would stop to chat. They often asked which one was the father. I had thought it funny. Everything is humorous in the right slant of sun.

I returned to my door to prepare what things I would bring. Bosun had done incredible work in making the little pistol as thin as he might dare. I took delight in packing away the easily concealed gun into a bag with the ammunition, clothing, and other supplies. I also found that I was no longer bleeding, and that too was pleasant.

The bag still had room for some more clothes and some canvas, which I would use to wrap the other two guns. Reaching low for the long barreled revolver, I chanced to look up into the floor-length mirror on the other side of the closet wall. How long had it been since I stood in front of that mirror? I didn't know. While slight, what had just been the vaguest rise in my chest, nothing really, had become something else, soft and useless. It was undeniable. My chest had grown. Not overnight either, I thought. Don't be silly. I moved closer to the stranger in the mirror. Still gripping the gun, I brought both hands to my chest. It felt sore to the touch. The icy cold of the pistol barrel brought me back to the moment. If living for a century didn't convince one that breasts were meaningless, what would? I decided to pay them no mind.

On another, more practical level, I felt sure the puffy mounds would kill me. They wouldn't murder me in my sleep, but a shift in the balance of my body might throw me off at the wrong time. Someone would move to shoot me and I would dodge, but I would move as if I still had *my* body and not the new strange one. I considered that a practical concern. Having lived in an unchanging form for so long, I felt that even a centimeter more of height could prevent me from walking straight. For the first time, I felt a little uncomfortable standing around naked within my door.

* * * * *

"This is Mina." I spoke into the long speaker. "I need to speak to my mother. I will only speak to her."

"Acknowledged." There was a pause. "Lady secretary is not available at the moment."

I covered the tube and leaned towards Bosun. "That's my mother's closest guard. He hasn't left her side in years. I don't think he removes himself while she's in the privy. And, I mean that." I uncovered the tube again. "Tell her that we are approaching the cape, but we require safe passage. We will be in the harbor in less than eight hours. We need a guarantee of safe passage."

"Mina," said my mother.

Why does she even play these games, I asked myself. How far from the tube had my mother moved in the past few days?

"I do not control the court. You overestimate me in some ways and think so little of me in others. What can I do when you think of me like this?"

I hardened at the words and looked over at Bosun. He was laughing quietly.

"She's ridiculous," he said.

"I will come to shore, just me. The others will take the ship out of the harbor. I will do nothing, consent to nothing, until they have passed beyond the cape."

"More demands. That's what they are. When will you understand that you are the only one thinking in these terms. If there is trouble, and I suppose there is, it is of your own making. I can say nothing for authorities beyond my control, you know, but I will not hold your poor crew members at fault here. But yes, I promise you safe passage home, if it can be had. Although, you will be escorted."

I shrugged to Bosun and replaced the tube. "I don't know what good all of that did, but she doesn't appear to be too concerned about the crew. In any case, Rohad was probably right about her not being in any personal danger."

"Then you'll just forget this madness?"

"That's enough of that." I left the boatswain's workshop.

15

The crew stood on the deck beside me. At my request, they had assembled before the evening lights of the city. The night was warm and humid. The pressure had dropped and it felt like rain, but no drops had yet hit me. Preparations had been made on the boat, with torches arranged across the bow of the small craft. I wanted to be sure that my arrival was noticed by everyone in the harbor. I had no particular plan in desiring such, except for the knowledge that my mother faired poorest when the lights were the brightest.

The prepared bundle containing my clothes and the guns had been trusted to Dillon. I also gave him detailed instructions for the hiding of that satchel within the hollow of a beech tree at the edge of Mount Auburn. I assumed it would be better to offer up myself empty-handed, to prevent any escalation and as a show of good faith. There would be no shootout, but I wanted the things accessible.

"I will see you all again. It should be soon. If you hear reliable reports of my death, I have entrusted Crane with my last will and testament. He was a clerk for a while, so he's the closest thing to a lawyer we have or need." I smiled. "If I do not arrive in

Portsmouth, or upon the isle of shoals itself, within one month, Crane has a second sealed envelope. That one contains instructions for your removal to another port, where I ask that you remain for another three months. If I do not return there, or word does not reach you of my expected arrival, that self-same letter contains further instructions for the sale of the vessel and transportation of my personal goods. I don't think it will come to that, but I don't have the luxury of time. I act to save my family, and I think I can do that without putting your lives in danger."

"What will you do on shore, when you are bound and prepared to be hung?" Crocodile asked.

I sighed. "I don't know. I'm going there for my family."

Rohad shook his head. The others followed in expression and gesture.

"Lower the boat," I ordered.

When the rowboat sat in water, I climbed over the bulwarks. I looked at no one.

Dillon followed. After settling into the craft he produced a box of matches and lit each of the nine torches. He untied the boat and took up the oars while I pushed us away from the ship.

"Mina," called Rohad from the Transcendent. "Don't forget all I have said. You are fighting for your life. Please don't forget it."

I nodded.

After a time looked to Dillon. He was again a stranger bathed in yellow light. He had said nothing since we left the ship. "You don't approve of this?" I asked.

"No."

"And you're rowing me there."

"Tell me to turn back."

"I can't."

"Then I'll row."

The fuzzy circles of light on the docks grew larger, shifting into little pointed lamp heads only when I focused on them. At that time I preferred to look at the approaching shore through the starry fog of unfocused eyes.

I checked for my guns but remembered that I carried none — I had nothing edged or explosive on my body. On the boat launch, about 150 yards ahead, a small crowd had assembled. I didn't focus on them either. I wanted no memories of that night, desiring to put it out of my head even as I lived it. Instead, I thought of my sister.

Dillon leapt from the boat and pulled us onto the hard packed mud of the north pier launch. I stepped into the cold water, watching the legs of my breeches float on trapped air and then descend. As the water seeped upwards, the fabric of my trousers grew heavier. I walked from the lapping bay onto the launch until men surrounded me. Then, I watched their feet and we all began to walk together. I looked back. Dillon was walking away in the opposite direction, with no particular haste. I felt I was no longer in any particular hurry either.

The soldiers were not court police. They were almost certainly from my mother's private guard. If I had looked up, it was not unlikely that I would recognize a few of them, but just as I didn't bother counting my steps or looking forward or backward, I didn't bother to look up. The guards carried no lights, and I preferred that. I wanted them all out. The cobble stones, dirt, or gravel of each street came to my eyes in intermittent slices from outdoor lamps or still-lit homes. I passed wordlessly over the path to my family's estate. While I had not expected to travel there that night, I was not really surprised by the destination either.

The lamps were not lit in the house, but the smells were familiar. The creaks of the floor were there. Only when all were inside did the men stop to light a lantern. I saw no lights in the house save that lamp. A hand guided my shoulder and I walked down the hall to my room. I hadn't slept there in decades, but the room was as I had left it, although it smelled like an old steamer trunk. It struck me as a curious thing that I had not even looked in on the room during my previous visits.

The men said nothing, they simply shut the door and left me there in my old room. I listened to the noises they made in the hall while shuffling about. When the flickers under the door steadied, I surveyed the room. Some light came in from outside through the curtained window, but the moon was still too new and the streetlights too far. I walked slowly around the perimeter of my room, running a finger across my old desk and feeling around for other furniture. The shape of the painting hung over my mantle could just barely be seen. Although not visible, the painting was of a cutter named the Pattern. I loved that painting. As I rubbed my fingers together, I noticed that little dust had accumulated in the room. Outside of my old clutter, the place felt immaculate to the touch.

Two guards stayed at my door. Their boots had reflective buckles. There were also at least a few other men making noise outside in the vegetable garden, which lay fallow that year. I sat and waited, sat until I was hungry. I did feel better, bodily, and that was something. However, it was my sister, and my mother, that occupied my mind. What was my mother doing right then? I didn't know. Whatever her activity, my mother had a certain style of action, as if she were operating several marionettes while half concentrating on animating her own undying body. Something like that.

After at least an hour and a half of nothing, I knocked on the door. No one responded, so I opened it. A guard faced me, standing in the margin. I knew how easily I could strike him in the groin. I could take his throat when he doubled forward. His pike would be near and I would have it. A minute to the street. What then? I may as well shove that pike into my sister.

"I must speak with the secretary."

"She's unavailable. You are to wait here for her."

"Under what authority?"

"The authority of the court." This he was ready for, and he said it like he were reciting a script.

"You are my mother's personal guard, but you answer to the court?"

He shut the door with his foot.

I persisted for a while and then sat back down. Morning did not come quickly.

* * * * *

The next day passed imperceptibly slowly. I asked for food, but no one answered. I asked for water too, although I had found a little in the pitcher by the wash basin. When my patience ran out, I called for my sister, which did nothing but exhaust my breath and make my throat sore.

The second night passed as the first. The room was hot, but the guards outside objected when I tried to raise the window. It was a siege. My mother would exhaust my resources. I would neither send for word nor receive it — the supply routes were cut off — the blockade would win out. By the time the sun lighting the lawn sank below my window pane I was feeling constantly lightheaded. Only uneasy nausea broke up the monotony of my fast.

In the early morning of that next day, when I woke with my back still against the door, I heard a response to the question I had been asking repeatedly, a single sweet low response. At first, I didn't even understand the softly whispered words. It was necessary to roll the syllables around in my mind until they made sense, but when I had it, I knew that it was exactly what the guard had said. "Charlotte is safe." Soon afterward, another guard rejoined the man who spoke behind the door and then the day moved only as fast as a shadow can crawl along a wall.

Something there is that doesn't love a wall. I didn't know why the words fell in my ear, but there they were. I think a poet had read that line when I was young. I most clearly remembered that the audience had worn their finest, mostly suits and layered dresses, but it was too hot that day to reasonably be expected to wear anything at all. Even the lemonade was warm. Worse, the pulp floating on the top formed a waxy layer, like the afternoon had melted a candle across the top of your drink. At the sight of it I had refused the cup. There were small sandwiches there that I did eat, tepid cucumber and cheese. They were delicious. Still, nothing and no one was comfortable in that room except for the sound of that poet.

His voice was coarse and he spoke the sort of verse that didn't settle with most, although I wasn't sure why. I hadn't heard of him since that reading, but I had been impressed at the time. For me, the sound of it was comfortable enough. It fit the room, if not the politics of the day, which is probably what the man intended. The words tumbled out of my mouth as I lay in my old bed. I had forgotten most of the poem, but the echo of the words remained. I played with them while I considered a vision of a cool stream flowing over a stone dam.

I drank the last of my water directly from the washing pitcher. There was a stubborn villainy to the room. I saw it plainly as I waited. In my head I had lived out so many scenarios, each of escape or useless persistence. The designs piled out around me. Each new idea was a burden, as I had to revisit it countless times to remind myself of why it could never work. I thought too of my last conversation with Rohad. I thought of the night before then and felt foolish.

When I pounded on the door, no one scolded me. There were no sounds elsewhere in the house. My sisters room would be next to my own, but nothing stirred there either. I listened for any movement with my hands cupped to the wall. Nothing.

* * * * *

A short, thick-necked guard woke me in the middle of the night by shaking my leg. I launched to my feet immediately, but then I tottered to the side and had to steady myself against my old dresser. He left the room and I followed. The man was Mother's private guard, probably back from the shitter where he kept vigil. While I saw no other men, I could hear them bantering in the kitchen. He led me through the house, but I could probably have followed him with my eyes closed -- we were walking to my mother's room. At the end of the steep, carpeted stair lay the door to my mother's chambers — an inevitable place. The landing at the top held space for little else aside from a window stool and myself.

My feet dragged. I could smell myself, although I felt I didn't even know how to smell like myself anymore. My armpits were foul. My clothes were soured with sweat. I had spent the days in a hot room with no open windows, and while the air out of that prison felt cool, it was not necessarily refreshing.

The guard had left me alone there at the top of the stairs. I wanted to open the closet and look for something, perhaps a misplaced butcher knife. I looked at the window treatment. Maybe the rod could be cracked into a crude spear. That would work. I remembered doing that once before, although I didn't recall when, and it couldn't have been that window. Perhaps I had not.

After a few minutes of nothing, I shook my light and loosely attached head. I opened my mother's door.

* * * * *

My mother existed by the head of her bed. She neither sat nor stood nor lay there. I supposed she was reclining. Outside of a single taper burning on the nightstand, all lights were out. The room smelled like it always had, vaguely sour. Here and there I would encounter a whiff of something sweet like overripe oranges, but as a rule, the room smelled like fermenting grapes and Mother's strong perfume. I wasn't sure if it was the cosmetics. Vinegar. The room smelled like vinegar most of the time.

I shut the door behind me and locked it as quietly as I could. I wasn't sure why I had locked it, but it seemed like a good idea. The humid attic-hot room felt impossibly long as I moved through the dark tunnel towards her, towards the light at the end of that darkness that was my mother. I reminded myself that what I saw was only the reflected glow from the candle.

She was visible only where the yellow light of that dying taper fell on her. The single source of illumination left her full of holes where the shadows lay, like a patchwork sculpture of herself. There was a nose there and a cheek near it and a hollow where her eye should be fitted. Her hair appeared only as wisps and a candle-shimmer. The nightgown she wore was sheer and luminous where the light hit but dark and unending where it did not. It was a very thin gown. I thought my mother may have been soaked with sweat, but it was a trick of the cloth — she was impossibly dry in the awful heat.

"Come here."

I continued walking towards her.

"Take off your shoes. You are rude." My mother whispered, but in that quiet room, it was loud enough.

I did and came closer.

"Come and sit beside me."

"Where is Charlotte?" I asked. My voice was dry. It could have been the heat or the screaming, but I suspected it was disuse. I wanted to clear my throat.

Closer still, the nightgown was so sheer that she would be naked if not for shadow. I could see a thick downward pointing nipple. My mother's stomach bunched up and was etched with deep furrows. I stared at the spidery veins in her legs until I thought to raise my head. My mother's hair was down. It was not long, but it was unkempt and greasy and looked endlessly wired. I could see knots embedded like burrs.

"Sit."

I sat on the unmade bed, lacking even a top sheet. Up close my mother smelled like urine, not vinegar. It was not strong, but it was stale.

"How I have missed you. Is it so awful to be here? Look at me. You never looked at me, even as a child."

I stared at the candle, watching my mother only from the corner of my eye.

"When you were a tiny thing — probably too small to remember this — we were laughing about it, the way you wouldn't look right at me. All of us, father too." My mother smiled before she continued. "And, it was a joke to them. It was a joke to you too. But then, I stopped laughing. I felt so wicked. I made Charlotte fetch you. Do you remember this?"

"She caught me and wouldn't let go."

"Yes, and you were laughing so hard."

"I was going to pee. I stopped laughing though, and she held me down. I hated her for that."

"But you did laugh. And, I told Charlotte." She paused. "I think I told her to hold you still, and you fought. Oh, you screamed. Remember that?"

"Yes." I could see it in her face now. She had that same expression that I had remembered from my childhood. It was a certain tight-lipped intent, like a threat.

"And, you bit, and you kicked, and all I wanted was for you to look at me. Your nurse didn't like it."

"You told her you would kill her. I think you said you would slit her throat."

"I did not."

"You did. I was afraid of it for weeks."

"You never remember. At least, you never remember right. I

could make you face me. I could make your eye socket line up with my own — you weren't strong. But, I couldn't make you really look at me. I moved back and forth to catch your gaze. I did everything I dared, but you never looked at me."

"You hit me too. You slapped me while Charlotte held me there."

"You were such a beast. I held your lids too. I stopped just short of binding you, I think. I doubt it would have worked. You never looked at me. Why? Do you have so much contempt for me? Am I so loathsome that even as a babe you should shrink from me? I am asking you now, why won't you just look at me?"

"I am here for Charlotte."

"Yes. That little bitch that betrayed you? Didn't she? You'd throw yourself into hell to save her, right? How many times must she hurt you? I don't know. I just don't know anymore. You hate us so much that you can't lift your arms to receive me, either out of fealty or mercy. It would mean so much to me and it's such a little thing to you."

"Am I free to leave?"

"Stay."

"Lay your head. I am not well, and I ask so little."

Her hand wrapped around my shoulder and guided me down to her lap. My head rested on my mother's stomach. It was warm. I could hear the sounds of digestion.

"There. Lay your head. You make such a show of all this, but you are just a baby aren't you?"

I said nothing, but I thought of Charlotte, not the one that did as Mother said and not the sad-eyed addict she had become. I thought of the bright twin, older but not unlike, that had always laughed with me. I felt safe with my older sister, although Charlotte never could protect me from our mother. Although, she did once beat a boys tooth out after he'd pushed me to the floor — I missed her. My mother began to pet my braided hair.

Neither of us said anything. I could see the candle dance in the patterns cast on the furniture. Against the wall I made out the edges of the curtained false window where I had found the damned torch.

A hand reached under my shoulder as Mother pulled me against her chest. She rocked back and over again. She gathered my body tight against her with arms, bony and cool. She continued petting my head.

I let myself drop out inside, my mind falling to the floor. I thought of nothing but an empty space. It was a large open space where nothing could survive. It was that empty. I existed there but cast no shadow. In that place without any shadows there was nowhere to hide, but I needed nothing in that place, and so there was nothing within to either cover or cast. There would be nothing new, but I didn't want for anything. In some distant place my mother stroked my cheek with her fingers. My mother would be there outside my mind like that forever. I didn't know how old she was, but I accepted that she had persisted for centuries, probably for at least three. Why not assume her immortal? I could smell her sweat, a dry sweat. It was so humid in the room.

"Look at me," said my mother.

"Please," I said. "This isn't a game to me. I don't want anything to happen to either of you. That's why I am here. Don't you see that?"

"Look at me."

"Mother, stop it."

"Look at me!"

I turned my head aside, crossing my mother's chest and trying to move away from her embrace.

"Stop it, Mina."

"Do you want me to pull away?" I grew louder. "What is it you want? Just tell me what it is you want."

My mother relaxed her grip. I moved slowly, tentatively, like a caged thing about to try a barbed wall one more time.

"Mina?" She sounded surprised by something then grabbed my hair. She tugged it hard and I reflexively sat up and pulled away from the snag, which hurt me again. She yanked my head back so hard I crumpled backwards, flailing.

"What? I don't. I don't understand."

My mother's hand was at my chest, scraping across me, patting and feeling. Before I understood what she had discovered, I questioned if I had perhaps hidden a weapon there in my hungered confusion. My mother screamed.

I was flung from the bed by my hair as Mother shot to the floor like a terror. I tried to steady myself, struggling dizzily to raise my head and keep the world level. She pushed me from the side and I stumbled to the paneled wall. Shadows moved. I saw the door and rushed towards it. The door seemed to grow higher, unreachable. Then I saw the floor rising to meet me. I hit and the room flashed white. I had tripped over something. No.

I was looking at my hand. It moved. The wrist was still, but my hand twitched, like a horse might when throwing off a fly. I hadn't tripped. While my cheek hurt where my face had hit the floor, pain like fire was spreading across my crown. It was white too. It was an empty white pain. I realized I must have been hit with something. It struck me as funny that I had not merely tripped. "There," I thought. "I wasn't so clumsy after all."

16

I woke to the feeling of pain before sight of light. The illumination came from the window that was not a window. I woke in parts, moving each limb slightly. My lips stirred, and I attempted to wet the inside of my dry mouth with my tongue. I swallowed. When I moved my neck, nausea woke and moved inside of me.

I sat up faster than I had intended. I only rose to keep from vomiting, but the movement triggered pain in my head that carried with it an even stronger need to throw up.

Cautiously, I looked around at the room. The end table was over and my mother had gone. There was blood on the floor where my head had been. Had it all been spilled out? Had I emptied my head there? I brought my hand to my head. I felt blood, mostly dried. Some of it was still damp and spongy. The angle of the shadows around the room was not too steep. It was easily late in the day.

My shirt was open, so I tried to close the buttons. Several were missing, and others were torn off as if I had been attacked by some animal in the night. It hurt to hold my head down for so long.

I tested my legs. They wobbled but held as I pitched forward and back, needing to reach for the bed post until the room stopped listing. I doubled over and vomited on my mother's bed. I did not have much in me to vomit, but the heaving made my head cry out. I wasn't certain if the gnawing in my stomach was hunger or more nausea — the first waves had come from my head and traveled down to my stomach until I threw up. I might again. Still, I knew I needed water. Carefully, I walked to bath adjoining bath and opened the faucet spigot. The dim light within the washroom was much appreciated.

The water was cold. It tasted like life. I vomited into the sink before I had drunk three mouthfuls, but I drank again. In the mirror, I saw that the entire left side of my head was smeared with dried blood. My hair was crisp with it and very damp in places. I bathed my scalp in the sink, despite the awful feeling of blood swelling my bent head. There was a wound there, a wound on top of a large crescent-shaped mound. The cut stung terribly and my head pounded.

Blood came off in chunks and streamed red down my cheek and over my ear. I didn't stop washing until the water ran clear. I tried to look at the wound, but it was hard to see under the hair. Perhaps it didn't look as bad as I had expected. I shook my head gently and looked into my eyes in the standing mirror. They were hollow. Perhaps they were also a duskier blue. I wondered if they would change as well. Would I know myself at all? I heard a scratch in the other room and spun around, ready to defend myself. I saw shadows by the window in the other room. It was probably a bird.

When I finished bathing my wound, I searched my mother's room for a weapon. I walked the perimeter, throwing things to the floor and pulling out drawers. I found two hat pins and a letter opener that may as well have been a Spanish steel stiletto. From a sheet stored in a lower dresser drawer, I cut a long strip of fabric and a single large swatch. I wrapped the letter opener in the fabric and secured it to the inside of my calf by wrapping the long strip in the alternating pattern I had seen on the shoes of gladiators in paintings.

My hair was disgusting, but I didn't want to take it down, not there. I left her room and stood in the upper vestibule. There were no guards visible and I could see the sun's position from that window. It was late, maybe three o'clock. The view from the stair made me nauseous again, but I held it back. What I truly needed to do was keep down the water.

Quietly, I descended the wooden stairs. I could hear guards outside, but I seemed to be alone in the house. Charlotte's room was empty of my sister. It was stuffy there too, but not as it had been before. At least a week's worth of dust lay on her things. I also found far too many empty packets of my sister's powder. The crumpled empty envelopes were beside things and behind things. They filled the trash. My sister would prepare them with water like tea.

In the kitchen, I ate some dried meat and half an apple. Although I had a legendarily strong stomach, it took considerable effort not to vomit. Usually I couldn't even force it with a finger down the throat. The nausea did not feel right at all. I prayed I didn't have pressure building up against my brain. I knew that could happen, although I did feel slightly better than I had when I woke, which was somewhat hopeful

There were knives in the kitchen. I knew of some hiding places too. Perhaps I would find a gun. The horror of the next question hit me again, as it had for days. Then what?

I had not come to Tremont to drag my sister away, although I didn't doubt my ability to do so. I was there for them, for both of them. I remembered my mother's touch. Was there not something there? There was something hateful but also loving. It was in that sigh. I had heard a mother's repressed desire simply to comfort her daughter.

And the image of the screaming head inside the lamp came to me again. I moved to the kitchen window and looked into the sun. I considered a new offer. I would agree to serve my mother, agree to stay close, if that is what she demanded, but I would only do so for the duration of my natural life.

Outside of the house there were two guards standing at ease. When I walked by them onto the front garden path, they stood at attention but said nothing.

"I suppose the secretary is on an errand?" I asked after I had cleared the entrance by a dozen feet.

"Parliament is in session. I trust she is in the House," said the man on the right. I thanked him. His name was Gar, and while I did not know him well, I remembered when he had first been appointed, perhaps ten years ago. I wondered if mother ever beat his brains out at night. How long would it take to heal? This time I didn't have the regenerative powers of the lamp — I still even had bruises and scabs from the fall on the deck a few days ago.

And, with that thought in mind, I passed without incident out of the garden and through the picket gate. It was likely that my mother was in the web. I considered finding Dillon, although we had made no particular arrangements for me to do so. I considered simply leaving the city, accepting that the ridiculousness of my situation bordered on madness. Instead, I followed familiar streets toward the nearest entrance into the hill and the web within.

I entered a small courtyard with a stone arch set into a steep hill which rose behind it. Several sentries were stationed by the large entrance. Others stood above on the hillside. The guards at the base held older, mostly ceremonial rifles. Of course, so long as they still fired there was more substance than ceremony in the old guns.

The well lit cavern beyond the arch, with its smooth walls, not unlike those within my door, rose to twice a man's height. The corridor was long. I didn't know where the actual carved cave beyond that door resided, since the arch was no different in mechanism than my own door and the transition was always seamless — air passed as freely as people, so one couldn't detect any sudden difference in temperature or pressure. The city had nine known arches, and they all led to the same interconnected labyrinth, which most citizens called the web. This was not a common thing for a city to offer publicly.

Well before my time, the builders of the arches, the doors, and the caverns, they all expected their tools to last. They wasted so much fuel. What idiot punched a hole through one side and sealed it to my mother's window frames? While the window frame had probably not been created for use in that house, how did my mother come to own something so valuable? I had spent nearly half my life in pursuit of my door, and even that was found somewhat by chance. In any case, the English founders had wasted all the fuel left within the tailor tools while carving out the tunnel system. I thought it was not unlike my own wasted life, regarded as finite and valuable only at the end of things.

In times of siege, the place became a sewer of unwashed men and women. In all times, it was a place of storage, of commerce, of the government, of travel, and of colonial secrets. The long gas-lit passage where I walked opened into an enormous round chamber. There were people, so many people. They entered from various side tunnels that all bent away in one direction or another. Some hurried while others looked like they were without purpose, merely being pulled along by the rest. Perhaps they only wanted some time in the cool tunnels. A man with a wheelbarrow of gravel walked behind a couple with a uselessly open parasol and a top hat. That man with the gravel could emerge with his burden on the other side of the city without having to physically wheel the load more than a comfortable eighth of a mile.

I had no real idea why I was stalling in that chamber. The way to my mother was well known to me. If parliament was in session then I was near enough to her already. I wondered if I would see the same ghost-like woman in a gown I had encountered the night before. I knew I would not, as surely as my mother knew I would not flee the city. My mother had strange motives, but I too knew a good bit about my mother's personality.

Just then I realized how ridiculous that claim was, that I had learned anything at all about the woman. While I could type most people, with fair accuracy too, after only a short conversation and some observation, someone like my mother was an open book in a foreign language. For all the time I had spent observing her, I had been watched more closely in return and always kept close, by hand or speaking tube. In the reverse, I had known only a portion of my mother's days. She knew all of me while I saw only a portion of her. Of course, even that bit I wanted to cut out of my mind. None of it actually helped. In the end, my mother always had what she wanted. I always gave her whatever she wanted, even when I went a world out of my way to avoid falling into that old trap.

I descended a stair so that I would cross near to the sixth gate, which would have brought me a quarter of a mile from the fish docks. Even without leaving through that exit, the smell of the sea was delicious. It brought strength to my aching head and even steadied my legs. I paused near the exit. Hunger had gripped me tightly again, noticeable in earnest even through my nausea. I had made for the gate to stop by a push cart that sold knots of cold clam fritters. I asked the vendor to charge it to the secretary. While I didn't know the walrus mustached man, he seemed delighted to see me.

"Of course," he said. When he looked closer, his smile faded a bit.

I hoped I wasn't bleeding again. Although I had a degree of celebrity within some circles of the city, it was not something I appreciated. Dressed in stinking dirty breeches and a shirt bound by only a couple of buttons and a few pins, I was a little disappointed that I was recognizable. The fritter was good. It was a little greasy, but it was familiar and I had a craving. The nausea remained, but it was more in my head than my stomach.

* * * * *

I entered the halls of parliament after waiting for the guards to discuss the matter amongst themselves and make several checks. I had no identification and was certainly not dressed for the part. So far as I could tell, someone must have recognized me.

Municipal and federal halls, offices, and auditoriums filled the section of the web that ran underneath Beacon Hill. While I was briefly nervous when the first guard had left to consult with an officer, I had been permitted entry without incident. Most of my life I had enjoyed free access throughout restricted areas within the system, although it was a privilege I rarely exercised. The operation of the government itself was of little interest to me, although sometimes I fantasized about what it would have been like to have been a part of the revolution, before the tides turned and all sides began to make concessions. I considered it again but was soon distracted by my pounding head. Whenever my foot hit the stone floor, it felt like someone was tapping my skull with a ball hammer.

I drew curious stares from people that guessed who I might be and some who I assumed did not. My bloodied outfit was typical of a sailor of higher rank — I never wore the bands of a captain, seeing no reason to do so when it only made me more conspicuous, and no one had ever insisted otherwise. Besides, I felt I relied more on my mates more than most. In any case, I knew it looked ridiculous to see a child wearing the real white and gray. Was I still a child physically? I didn't know. How blurry does someone's vision have to get before they can be called blind? I doubted that it mattered.

Gaslights were set to burn progressively hotter the further one descended past the checkpoint to the inner levels. The halls narrowed within and took on a true labyrinthian quality. Clerks shot from side halls carrying papers. A navy ensign saluted me as I walked past. I returned that salute, noticing the usual hint of a suppressed smile from the man. The upturn was small and certainly not deliberate. I may have known him, although familiarity with me was no inoculation against the comedy of it all.

I turned left and left and right. My mother's office remained in the senator's wing. She had not wished to move offices even after her promotion from junior senator to secretary, which predated my binding. It was not a grand office, but it was private and I loved the space itself. When younger, I had often spent time there, particularly when the city was too hot. And, at that moment, the cool of the web did make my headache just a bit more bearable.

While I hoped my mother was not behind the studded Ligurian bronzewood door, I could already smell the perfume. There was no crack too small in a doorway to keep out the smell of my mother's flowery perfume. I wanted to turn around, but I knew I would enter the chamber and I would sit. I did enter, without a comment or a knock. She sat behind her large ebony desk. I didn't look up, and I was unsure if my mother even raised her head. Neither of us said anything for a time.

A life-size portrait of Charlotte hung on the wall to the right of my mother. Charlotte was not more than ten in the painting. She held me, awkwardly, on her lap. We only had four and a half years between us, and I was certainly too big to be sitting there on my sister's lap. Observing it now, I decided that perhaps the painting was slightly larger than life size. The office held no books and few papers. There were three couches, too many for the confined space. All light in the windowless room came from the large gas chandelier, the body of which had been formed in the pattern of a full enneagram. My mother had it commissioned, and I had picked it up for her from Amsterdam nearly thirty years ago. I looked down from the fixture. My mother sat staring at me with her hands folded under her narrow dimpled chin.

The older woman smiled as I sat on the couch directly across from her. The cushions were thick and the couch too deep. Despite myself, I found the well-conditioned leather comfortable and the smell familiar, reminiscent of my childhood. Mother looked so much different in the diffused and scattered light, without the nightgown and the sunken eyes. Her hair was up in the old imperial fashion. She wore dark lips. They were moist as if she had just licked them. The mineral powder on her cheeks gave the old woman's face a bit of life. My mother unfolded her long and slender fingers. In that light they were much smoother. A copper plaque at the front of the desk read Secretary Genevieve Paradis.

"I am glad you came."

"Oh?"

"Let's not keep that up. Please, I have made a breakthrough today. I wanted to share it with you." My mother rose and crossed to me.

She sat down on the leather couch and carefully flattened her dress. It was too revealing and silky for either the halls of government or good taste in general. However, it was fairly typical. The woman had changed little, but her fashions did creep along with the times. Whatever the style though, she managed to always walk the farthest edge of accepted modesty. The men didn't seem to mind. Perhaps they appreciated her power. I wondered exactly what power did she hold?

My mother sat far too close. I pushed myself to recall the pain of waking, to remember that this was the same woman who struck me with something. Was it a candlestick? She stank. It was as if her nose began dying a century ago and each day she put on a bit more perfume until she could smell it herself.

"I am sorry for last night." She reached her hand out to my head.

I leaned slightly forward and lowered my head a little, maintaining eye contact the entire time. I thought of a cougar I once saw standing above on a rocky promontory in Leith. I hoped she saw that same expression now in her own daughter's eyes.

My mother's face didn't move, but tears swelled above the waterline. After the first drop fell she began to cry without expression. Her shoulders shook a little.

I don't think my expression changed. I said nothing.

"Look at you." My mother took her hand away and held it to the center of my chest. Tears continued to fill the same wet path down her mother's face, having carved some trail through the mask of makeup and powder. "I will take you to your sister tonight. She asked about you and I told her I was angry. I get so angry. Why do I get so angry?" She then broke down and cried outright.

I looked to the floor. She brought her arms around me and sobbed harder. I moved my head to my side, away from her. After a few moments I exhaled and moved towards my mother, opening my arms slightly. She fell forward at once and put her weight upon me. We hugged while she sobbed. The woman was an actress, but not like that. I felt uncomfortable. It was awful to see and hear and feel the weight of it all.

"What was the breakthrough? You mentioned a breakthrough."

She continued to sob until I found myself growing physically uncomfortable under the weight. At some level though, my mother was a warm comforter in a cool hall. I hated myself for it, but I loved my mother.

She answered in a whisper. "They want you to keep your position. You are to be reinstated."

"I don't understand." When my mother sat up I felt the cool air fill the space between us.

"You will be bound again to a torch without penalty. And I," she paused. "I cannot keep you here. You may return to service out there." She made a gesture towards the world, the sea. "You can be free as you like."

"What of Charlotte?"

"Charlotte is fine." My mother looked away, with a bit too much melodrama in the particular craning of her neck. "I don't think she even realizes what has been happening."

"And the crew?"

"They will continue their posts, if they will have them."

"But what if I am not bound?" I asked.

My mother stopped moving and said nothing.

"What if there's another way? Certainly I can serve without being bound."

"You do realize what I have just offered you?" She looked at me in apparent disbelief. "This is a pardon for a condemned man. This is mercy. This is more than anyone deserves. It is certainly more than I've ever been shown. You didn't even ask what I had to do to pull these kinds of strings. You'll be free as a shrike to sail about and do what you do. And that door also. That precious thing is still yours I imagine?"

"No, I don't think I can accept the terms. How could I? And, in any case, I don't think you would let any harm come to Charlotte. I just don't. I can't see it."

"I see we're lowering ourselves to this kind of discussion. Well, it is not up to me."

"Why not? I mean, you managed to force out some kind of clemency for an entire crew. What was next, a promotion and medals all around? Of course it's up to you. Besides, I could smash that next lamp as well, before I even left the Tremont bay."

I stood and counted three steps from the couch to the desk. "I want to make a counter offer. A serious one."

"Please, why do you always fight like this? Just when I think there is something in you, something decent and human."

"I will serve you in whatever capacity you desire. I will sit at home and let you comb my hair sometimes. I will travel about, and short of some things, do as you require. I will be a partner again — I know you want that. But, in return, I will remain without contract, without a torch. Charlotte as well. You will have the rest of my days and probably hers, but that's it." I wondered if I had thoroughly considered what all of that might mean.

My mother stood and calmed the wrinkles of her skirt with her palms. She spoke to the floor. "So, you would have me watch you die, and you would do the same for your sister?"

"I just won't be bound again, that's all." I stood and walked slowly across the room, putting the large desk between us.

"And your men, they will be dashed on the rocks? Left for the gulls to eat their eyes from their living sockets? Yes?"

"I'm not asking that," I said. "Why the threat? Let them serve with me as I serve out my natural days. I don't fear old age."

"No," said my mother.

"Then what? If I don't agree you're going to kill them off and take a knife to Charlotte? You would permit the court to pronounce her a traitor openly? I don't think you could stand it. I don't think you want any of that."

"What about you? You're going to do what? Wander off and die? How ridiculously poetic."

"Or I'll die before I ever leave the web. I don't care anymore. I call your bluff. Charlotte is fine. You're certainly more than alright. Kill me if you wish." I rounded the desk and moved towards the door.

"Portsmouth, right? Well, not Portsmouth proper."

"What?"

"You little bitch. You're an incurable thief. You know that? I know where they are. I've already dispatched a regiment northward, to Portsmouth. Hmm? More specifically, past the far side of the isle of shoals. Yes. That's where they are, aren't they?" She sat down into the couch. "There. Now, just tell me at what hour you will be bound."

"I don't understand."

"Your little boyfriend told me."

"Told you what?"

"Shh. You don't even know him. I do though. I know him well, much better than you might think."

"I don't understand."

"You do. Why can't you just be happy? Anyway, Magistrate Edwards is preparing your binding. You resume your contract, and they will not be killed. You refuse, and there's nothing I can do to prevent the court from bringing you up on charges. Even if they spare you, there's no alternative for them."

"What do you want?"

"I want what's best for you."

"You're taking everything."

"You're the one committing suicide. To me, you are just a brat who won't take her medicine." She leaned forward to the edge of the seat. "Sit in the fucking capital and relax. Take your goddamn binding and live forever." She threw her arms up and laughed. "Oh, how I twist your arm! Men kill to get a position worthy of a torch. Kill. Wars have been fought over control of the copper. There are three in our little family. Think of it. What do you think I have done to secure that?"

"Awful things. I know because I've been your damned hand. I've done what you've asked for so many years. Yes, then. I suppose it's a suicide of sorts. I would rather die than be bound to you."

"At the risk of only your own punishment, I guess. What if I did have your sisters guts spilled? Maybe you want to watch little kids poke them with a stick? Maybe you want *me* in the guillotine. Would it be any different if I ended up an old lady waiting for time to kill me off? You must want that. That's what you're asking. Think about these things."

"I never asked for harm to come to you."

"But it will come. I just want you to live. Is that so bad?"

"You can end this. I know you can. You've spent your lifetime weaving yourself into the court. There's probably not a man in the web that doesn't fear you in some way. Hell, you're even sleeping with the magistrate."

"I am not. I haven't in years."

"It doesn't matter."

"If they will slit my belly, let them. I don't think you will let them drag you down or kill Charlotte. I call your bluff. I call it."

"If I do not send an order of restraint, the Transcendent will be seized."

"You don't even know where it is."

"I just told you. Dillon told me they're hiding at the damned isle."

"But that's not where they went at all."

"Come. Look here. "

I looked. My set of revolvers lay in the top draw, laid out like pinned insects in a tray.

"Did you harm him? Where is he."

"Harm him? I paid him and then some. He had some debts to settle, but I told you, men will kill for a torch." She laughed. She laughed as if she even loved the laughter itself. "He hasn't been yours for a long time. Why can't you just accept it? I am old. I am too old for this. Are you just willfully blind? I think so."

"What do you want?"

"You will reseal." My mother's chest heaved. "Yes, I will take you to Charlotte. She is fine. She is no prisoner. I only worried for her safety, with you out there breaking contracts. So, I hid her. Think of that. I hope she forgives you. You should hear her curse you. You will renew the contract out of love, and I will respect my original offer. You and the crew will leave." She crossed her arms. "And, clean yourself up. You're a terrible mess."

I turned to the door.

"Wait." She opened her arms. I saw that she had the eyes of that cougar. "Come to me."

I did. As I allowed my mother to embrace me, I considered the letter opener strapped to my calf. And Dillon. How could he? I found my arms rising against my will. Instead of reaching down for the hint of pommel sticking out of the cloth by my right foot, my arms encircled my mother. I began to cry, which made the pain in my head sing out. She wiped the tears from my face with her fingers.

"Look at you. So different but the same. I love you, little one. Don't you know that without you this family has no chance of survival? We're in this together."

I nodded. I walked slowly out of the office and into the web. The tunnels through which I passed grew increasingly dim until I staggered into the street, like a man pulling himself onto a boat before drawing breath. My lungs burned with a rage that grew hotter in the open air.

Bowdoin street smelled of pitch, but I breathed deeply anyway. I held my resolve like a balled fist. I moved away from the web in a straight line. I tried to think of the path in front of me as something linear. I tried to, but there is nothing in life that is truly straight. Even if you walk in a line upon the earth, you move in an arc. Ships arc across the sea and birds bend across the sky. If one could travel long enough in a straight line they would even return to the same point on the earth. The truth of it was that life moves in a spiral, a great counter-screw bringing you to the same vista on each pass up or down upon that unbeatable machine. Of course, that was still something. You could complete an entire journey like that without ever truly doubling back over your own path. And, if you never looked up, you would never know you had been going in circles the whole time.

I found a shadowed place behind some apple trees and between two shops. A rain barrel further into the alley hid me from view when I crouched down. I adjusted the make-shift dagger on my leg until it moved freely enough to allow a reasonable draw.

With renewed energy and the weapon ready to be drawn, I returned to the street and reentered the web. I passed by the guards without challenge. Within the span of three minutes I traveled unchallenged to the gates of parliament. I looked around and then sat on a stone bench. There were others there too, probably professional petitioners. Everyone waited in the large room outside of the even larger parliament hall with its magnificent buttressed ceiling. I supposed I was there to petition as well. It seemed fitting to wait with the rest.

After a count of 648 seconds the imposing double doors opened. Preceded by the noise of their own glad-handing and riotous laughter, officials and senators and the other notable people of parliament streamed out of the round hall. The crowd broke past me and filled the room like a tsunami. Men stood in places conversing, establishing and violating little imaginary circles of territory etched on the floor. Suited men moved around like dancers changing partners. Some laughed loudly like hunters returning home with some meat. Others hid behind cautious submissive smiles. I moved through them, knowing that the men and women of the innermost court usually exited last.

I saw him, the magistrate Cotton Edwards. He was a chubby little man with a big smile. He wore it as if had been pinned to his ears. He was speaking to two other men, both much taller than he. One of the men picked up the tassel hanging from Edwards' long sleeve and dropped it, as was the local custom of respect. Another followed.

The magistrate looked at me and then immediately past me. Another man walked between the two of us. I stepped to the side, but Edwards had gone. He reappeared through the crowd nearly twenty feet away. I navigated through the swells until I edged past his pear shaped bottom and stepped in front of the man. He stopped like a moving ship that had dropped anchor.

"Magistrate."

"Ah, Mina." He said it as my mother did. It was an old pronunciation of an old name. It sounded odd coming from anyone other than my mother.

"Your honor. I must speak with you. Would you permit me that?"''

"I don't see why not. Oh, your hair. Did you get hurt?"

"May we go somewhere more private?"

"He looked to either side and smiled wider. There's no one lurking about." He motioned around him. "You underestimate how interested everyone else is in themselves."

"I think you'll change your mind about that."

"Oh?" He leaned down to see me more closely and at my own level.

"I wish to make my own counter offer." I considered how I would get this man back to his chambers.

"Counter offer?" He shrugged. "Did you know that there are over six-hundred masons in this city?"

"What?"

"That just sounds like a lot. That's all. I am sorry to interrupt, but I thought that was truly something. I just learned that."

"Magistrate, a counter offer. I've just spoken to the secretary."

"Oh. Good. How is your mother today?"

"You don't know what I am talking about?" I saw he did not. "What of a rebinding?"

"Ahh, yes," Edwards said. "You are lucky there. Limited resources and all, but we know what's of value, don't we?"

"So there is to be a binding?"

"Tomorrow night, if I recall. I am sorry to hear about the accident during your last voyage. That is unfortunate. Is that all?"

"I think so." I felt as if I had woken up from a dream only to fall into another, foggier, stupor. He had no idea what I was talking about.

I wished him a good day and left the court. He wished me the same. I traveled down a long hall that took me out of the secured section of the web. For a while I ran, although it hurt my head to do so. I entered the tunnel known as Faneuil Hall. The area smelled of every sort of food. There were clams and beans and roasting sausages. I remembered that those things had smelled wonderful, but now it seemed to me only to be a crowded place that brought nausea back to my lips. I wanted to be back out of the web and into the sunlight.

Although I noticed no difference between the places, I knew that at some point, I had passed through an underground arch that took me to another section of the web, far across the city. I stood there in the large underground hub of Central Square. From there I could ascend several levels or go deeper. I circled upwards around the outer ramp while others descended using the inner ramp. Through the center of those opposing helices rose a great pipe that carried water out of the web tunnels. Small windows were set into the pipe while evenly spaced blisters concealed lighting. The effect was such that the inside of the tunnel was very bright, and one could see a constant stream of rising bubbles there. It was a sort of a contained fountain. I tried to keep pace with those rising bubbles as I wound around the perimeter. I couldn't ascend quickly enough without breaking from a walk, even as I pushed past the other the pedestrians. It hurt my head to even try, but I wanted it to hurt.

I wasn't sure where I was heading. I considered how to get word to the Transcendent. If what my mother said was true, then there wasn't much time. My thoughts returned to what the magistrate had said. Moments later I found myself leaving by the exit towards Cambridge and Dillon. My first mate was either the cruelest traitor I had known or a man who succumbed to torture. I considered another possibility — perhaps he was floating face down in the Charles on his way to the bay?

If he had been true, and he lived, I could use him to get word out to the crew. I stopped by the tunnel exit. People passed me in both directions, while I stood still in the center of the arch. For a moment I again thought of that passage down the Charles. Not for the first time, I seriously considered shoving the letter opener into my heart. I knew where it was, where exactly it beat. I could drive the blade in confidently to puncture my aorta without striking a rib. It would be violent and bloody. I would drown in the blood. If it was to be done, it should be done in my mother's office, not near any river.

I turned around and went back towards the central hub. I descended. It is cured by walking. I knew this, but I said it again to myself anyway. It was not the first time I repeated that mantra to steady my own hand. And, just when I began to doubt the words, I found myself facing the south hill. I jogged off, a little stronger than before, although the effort caused my head to pound again and I constrained myself to a fast, less painful, stride.

* * * * *

The geologist's shop was open. There were customers inside, which was rare. Mr. Card waved at me from between a pair of older women. I paced the shop, dimly aware that it was rude to do so, but I had been within the place too many times to occupy myself with the displays. If only to verify the number, I counted the minerals in the front window. The women were asking to have a mother of pearl inlay repaired. That was something Card used to do, but he had been sending out a lot of the finer work to a younger man. I was sure he was nearly giving away his work at cost. Perhaps he ran the business out of hand.

I rushed to the counter when the woman left. "The letter. Who did you deliver the letter to?"

"Mina. How good to see you too. I think you're a little too familiar with me. What kind of a greeting is that?"

"Please, who did you give the letter to? The box. Did you deliver it?"

"Yes, of course." He pulled back, shaking his head as if he were very concerned about me. "I delivered it to the magistrate myself.

He was most displeased. At first I thought it was the rock. I did think that, but it was an exceptional specimen. No, it was the letter. He read it to himself several times. I didn't get a glimpse. Between you and me, I tried. I certainly did."

"He read that letter and he was displeased?"

"He was. You know I don't like to speak, but he was actually furious. You made that man terribly unhappy."

"Cotton Edwards?"

"Yes, Magistrate Edwards."

I backed away to the window display. I sat down on the plush bench without looking behind me. "I don't understand. I really don't understand these people. I can't understand them."

"Oh, Mina." He moved cautiously and sat beside me. I wanted to move but did not. "You are fine."

"I saw him. He knew nothing. It was as if there was no letter."

"I've known you for a long time, but I have never known you to cry. Don't cry. You look as if you might cry." He took out a handkerchief. "I have never known you to express much at all. So, don't start now."

I tried to gather myself. Perhaps it was my head or the days in that room without food or enough water. Maybe it was Dillon. It was probably all of it, but I found myself reaching some dark final conclusion where I simply wanted to put it all out of my head. I rose like a ghost.

"Child, child. Look at you. You are always so damned ageless that I have to tell myself, remember now, she is no kid. She is one of the bound. She is a withered old woman in there. She is fit to sit and crochet by a sunny window. But, you know? I don't think you actually are. There is something to holding the mind within a body that cannot grow. Do you know how much I have learned from being stuck, in my own common way, within this old body? I tell you, it is not the most fun, but it certainly has been instructive."

"I'm sorry to come here and blather like this."

"I say all of this because I want to forgive myself for treating you like a child. If I have avoided that before, I won't now."

"It's not your fault."

"So, I am apologizing. I am apologizing for more than you think. I did actually read your letter. I took lemon juice to it and I heated it under a kettle. I did everything I could so no one would be the wiser and then I resealed it with a little glue. I am sorry for that too." The old man looked forward down the shop and away from me. "I will tell you this then, and perhaps it will explain some confusion. There is word that your mother and the magistrate have been having an affair, for years even. The magistrates wife, the Grand Madame of the senate knows nothing. I think your mother used that to hush the whole thing up. To make it go away."

"They haven't been together in years. I know of all that. I thank you though, but I doubt the affair is part of all this. Do you?"

"It is possible."

"And yet the magistrate wishes for me to be rebound?"

"Apparently so."

"And if I do not? What of my sister?"

"Why would you not?"

"It doesn't matter."

"Your sister. What of her?"

I considered him for a moment. "You are a terrible keeper of secrets, you know that?"

"And, I still wish to have another anyway. Please, go on."

"Well, if I do not submit to this, if I am not signed back into service, the contract will be truly broken. But, we are bound to my mother's contract. Are we not?"

"Yes."

"Of course you know that already." It would be easier to catalog any gossip the older man had *not* already heard.

"I was one hell of a petitioner in my day, you know. I didn't care for the game much myself, but I loved to hear people tell stories."

"Well, if I invalidated my own damn contract, I could run. I could hide. Maybe I could even make a good life of that, elsewhere. But, the problem is that doing so breaks the terms of my mother's contract and my sister's. I suppose I don't doubt her ability to avoid sentencing. Maybe I do. In any case, it would be a risk, too big of a risk with my sister's life at stake."

"What does your mother's contract have to do with this?"

"Our contracts are all bound."

"Yours are bound to hers. I mean, only to hers," explained Card.

"I don't understand."

"When they discovered your mother had been sharing her copper ration with you and your sister, she was to be put off entirely. One can't share like that, and it was a strange and uncomfortable business for her to be binding children in the first place. But, she fought like hell. She was newly appointed as a secretary, but she had a lot of pull and in the right places. Somehow she cornered the city's governor at that time. I think it was Michaud, that Frenchman they hung. I don't know how, but I don't think it was pretty. He conceded to let her be given more rations. In exchange, you would both serve the kingdom, but you would do so for her. They washed their hands of the business of locking up a child like that. How that last part, about being bound to your mother, became a concession, I'll never understand. In any case, it is *entirely* up to her to set the terms of the service. I thought you knew."

I met his eyes. They were watery, but not from any of this — they were just old and glassy. "You didn't really think I knew, did you?"

"No, I suppose. Not really."

"There is no crime in my leaving is there?"

"Oh, I suppose there is. You are in service to the court, in some manner. So is your sister though." He shrugged. "Well, perhaps there is no crime if your mother does not call it such. You might be a deserter, I suppose. Or, they could make the case for treason. I don't know."

"So there really isn't anything to all of this, is there? It's all up to my mother. You don't have to answer that. And, what of my sister's service. She doesn't honestly do much. And, much of my mother's recent power comes from me. I'm the one who carries her will out to sea."

"Well, regarding Charlotte. I don't think she is so strong in the way you are. At least, in your particular way. Still, that is how your mother chooses to have her serve. I suppose she could have done the same with you. It is a most brutal arrangement, but what I wouldn't do to have had a torch myself. Oh, back when I was young. I was strong too. And, pretty. I was a handsome man, wasn't I?"

"Yes, I remember." I gave him a strong hug, as strong as I could manage. I rose.

"Where are you going?"

"I'm not sure."

17

I lowered myself from the window, moving intuitively and feeling more shadow than form. My motions were nothing more than a pattern of a wind-caught tree bough cast upon a wall by a streetlight. I certainly did not feel as if I were in my own skin, but I hadn't forgotten how to move. The dark denim trousers of my uniform and the shirt I had pulled off of a line before setting out served me well in the darkness. Once within the room, I sat down below the window sill. I held my head low and stared at the side of the bed, waiting for my eyes to adjust to the dark room. I counted their breaths, focusing on a hand that hung off of the couple's bed. It was his hand. I was looking at his side of the bed. I drew my knife and stood. After noticing my own shadow raise suspiciously on the far wall, I moved away from the window.

There were two of them in the bed together. She wore a blanket. One of her legs was out of it and wrapped over his as he snored open-mouthed on his back. The man had a sheet draped across his midsection as if to intentionally preserve modesty. Perhaps he expected company. I hovered over his face, close enough to smell his sour breath. Sailors without half that man's amenities didn't let themselves go like that. I blew softly. His eyes twitched. I blew again. He inhaled as if suddenly short of breath. When I breathed once again, his eyes fluttered and then opened.

He met my eyes. I watched his pupils focus on me and retreat and return. I held a finger to my lips and mouthed a hush. Where the fat man's throat should be I pressed a knife, enough so he could know what it's like to have the metal against his skin. I leaned even closer to him, passing my face over his like a spirit. When I brought my mouth near his ear I could make out wax and hair. Had he ever cared about himself?

"My mother's contract is terminated," I whispered. "It is done. She has served. It is complete. Her contract and her children's contracts are through." His breath was more rapid now. I thought he might wake his wife after all, if only for that. "If you do not enforce this, if this is not the end of that terrible deal, then I will paint this town with your secrets. I will start with my mother and you. I have letters, but it won't end there. I will end it by cutting off your dick."

"I..."

"Quiet. Or I'll not end, but begin, with your parts, and you'll spend your precious torch-bound eternity dickless. Bind her again afterward if you will, but her contract is terminated and her children are free."

I backed unceremoniously to the window. The man did not turn his head. The sheets were wet with urine. I leaped from the window sill to the great magnolia. I hadn't thought of threatening to cut off his pecker before the visit. Although, it occurred to me just then that I did mean it. The drama of that made my giggle. I climbed back over the tall fence and dropped to the street. My soft boots flapped on the wet stone.

* * * * *

The first of the globes hit the floor, and I smelled that bitter and metallic fragrance which I couldn't help but enjoy. The room had already reeked of the stuff, but it was sharper when lost upon the floor like that. The copper had a way of burning the nose a bit.

The humor of my actions was not lost on me. Like a child in a tantrum, I threw the next globe to the floor. The liquid spread across the floor in an explosion of droplets. They were perfect little copper marbles with a smoky greenish skin. Each bottle I pulled became a new omni-directional burst that scattered and danced across the floor until joining the growing metallic puddle. Little beads of the syrup rolled across the floor. The drops collected into bands and pools. I smashed the fifth bottle. The tenth. I walked through the swamp of glass and mercurial liquid to reach the thirteenth. The bottles were issued one or two at a time, with a single sphere generally lasting months — my mother had managed to build a sizable hoard.

I regretted that she was not home. I was disappointed that the lamp was gone too. After I emerged from the closet and shut the window that was not a window, I walked on down the hall and left by the kitchen door. At the edge of the property I moved the loose slats in the back fence and came out in my neighbors garden. I crossed the slick grass that wet my boots. When my feet hit the pavement, I ran on.

* * * * *

I crouched in a closet beside a dried and shrunken head. It was not the sort of thing one usually left around to be found, but he was full of surprises. I had put down my doubts one by one, strangling each of them as they surfaced. Still, I could not shake the feeling that I was wrong or that I was overreacting. However, there it was. After I had put his lamp out, I had stepped on the little head and the spear of seemingly metallic vertebrae upon which it had been set. The thing did not snap like my lamps ornament had. The head was leathery. It had give. How old was the head? It seemed fresh. The thing was comically small as if someone had decapitated a doll and pulled the things head and spine out of the body like beads on a wire. Shrunken heads were not so small as that, but I didn't know what else to call it. I picked up the ornament when I heard the apartment door unlock. It was in my hand, the little crushed head facing my palm.

He entered and was busily engaged in some task within the other room of the apartment. I heard water. He was making tea. He put his gun on the table. His shoes came off in a thud. I tucked the horrid head into my belt, spine first, behind my back. I waited there and considered how best to reach the Transcendent when my business was complete within the city.

After a while he finished his tea, his released sugar spoon banging against the side of the cup. He didn't, from the sound of it, do much in particular after that. Then, light danced through the louvered doors, and I prepared myself. The doors opened and I pushed off of the floor like I was leaping a chasm.

"Dillon!" I cried. I rushed to hug him as he stumbled.

"You scared me."

I wrapped my arms around him. He walked backwards as I hung from him.

"What are you doing here?"

"I was looking for my things." I did not let go.

"There's blood in your hair. What happened to you?"

"Just let me rest a moment," she said. He smelled like cherry tobacco. "I know what my mother did, to you. I understand now."

"I don't." He tried to pull back.

"Don't go. The location of the Transcendent. We can't let this ruin our friendship."

"I didn't say anything."

"It's alright."

He moved in earnest to pull me off. "What is wrong with you?"

"Mother told me about the lamp."

"What lamp?"

I moved as if to withdraw and then I brought my hand back and swung it forward, twisting my whole body to give it momentum. The lamp-head assembly hit bone. I could feel the little head itself squishing against my finger pads.

Dillon screamed and flailed as I stepped away. He was on the pads of his feet and reaching around to his back as if he was on fire. I had put the lamp spike in his shoulder. It wouldn't come to much, but I had hit bone — the pain would be awful. I once had shot scrape against my scapula, and it was indeed awful.

I walked towards the small open closet and put my boot through the thin panel at the back where the rest of his broken torch was concealed. The panel fell to the floor.

"Wait," he called. "Mina. I am sorry. You don't understand. I had no choice." The light from the kitchen illuminated the blood on the spike in his hand.

I considered his words before responding. "You always had a choice." I had said that before, but I thought it meant more now, like an idea circling around you until you have the right to say it.

"I can take you to Charlotte."

Enraged, I rushed forward and took him down to the floor without any struggle on his part. I brought my makeshift knife to his throat. He didn't struggle. "Where is she?"

18

Tired, hungry, and thirsty, I stood in the street beside Dillon's apartment. What energy I still had within was unsteady and hard to restrict. I wanted to lose control. After refusing to let Dillon come with me to Charlotte, I wondered why I didn't kill him and leave him there with the shards of that damned lamp.

The first glow of morning had begun to crown over the north city. I thought I would have an hour perhaps before the first light hit the tops of west city and the day began in earnest. If I waited out that hour, the trip would be short, since I could use the web after curfew lifted. Instead, I ran. I ran like I hadn't been nearly killed the night before. My exhausted limbs carried me over the morning damp stones. I ran like a close friend had not sold me out for a chance at something no one deserves. I ran like my sister wanted me to show up at all.

Unless Mother had already attacked the ship, I did have some time on my side. I would get my sister, dragging her from whatever hell she had fallen into. I recollected the slightly perfumed but mostly vegetative and unpleasant smell of opium smoke. That's what I suspected her hair would smell like for weeks. According to Dillon, my sister was with friends, and he had brought her there himself.

Before that, Charlotte had been locked in my mother's root cellar. When I had been imprisoned in the house, she had been less than a hundred feet away. According to Dillon, my sister was terribly sick when he moved her, at the request of my mother. He had left her in the care of a woman named Ellis. Even when I pressed him for answers, Dillon claimed he had asked no questions. I knew what it was like to do what my mother said and ask no questions.

I passed working men with their carts and brooms and picks. They were all walking across town after their early morning resurrections. I could not see their shackles, but they were there. I imagined great lengths of chain falling off behind each man. They tied them to one another. Alone, they could struggle to escape. Together, they were bound.

The third house on the left side of Brighton after the intersection with Galley street looked like a boarding house. I wished I had my things with me. I wanted my clothes, wanted to be prepared for whatever or whomever I might find inside. What I had instead was a pair shaky legs, a headache, and a tired nervous energy that made it difficult to think. Through all of that, I was sure of one thing, I wanted my sister.

There were lights on in the house, towards the back. I circled the place completely. Most of the windows had drawn curtains. I looked at the intervals of the windows in order to locate a larger room, hoping to find a good candidate for Ellis' apartment. The place was much larger and cleaner than I had expected. I reminded myself not to trust Dillon.

I wished I had my climbing spikes. No trees grew close enough to the two storied structure, so I returned to the front and used the porch to get as high as possible. Standing upon the porch railing, I walked myself carefully up the wooden column that ran to the roof. From there I could get my fingertips onto the overhang by extending myself out with only my legs wrapped around the highest point of the porch pole. I then let my legs swing out, and I pulled myself onto the roof.

There were four front facing windows. None of them were lighted, but one was open. I accepted the darkness within as an open invitation and lowered myself inside. The room was large and connected to the adjoining space by an archway. Across the floor, mats and a few mattresses were laid out evenly, much like a military encampment. I counted nine heads as I moved to the only door, which was slightly ajar. The floor creaked as I crossed. A head turned and eyelids moved. No response. The face went slack again. I lowered myself against the wall nearest the door and stared into the darkness. I tried to use the periphery of my vision, as one can most easily make out shapes in the dark that way. My sister wasn't there. She wasn't one of the sleeping young men and women. Most were in their later teens but none of them much beyond.

I moved into a hall where I stood before a row of doors on either side of the hall. There have been too many times in my life where I was not sure what do next, where I was certain only that my actions had put me in an unworkable place. I had hoped to find a large room where Ellis could be found, hoping that I could persuade the woman to take me to my sister. But I had seen no pipes anywhere. The halls were clean and empty. I had no idea what the place was and that made me feel like a genuine intruder.

The nearest door was locked. I tried another, but it was also locked. The locks were so simple, but I had no tools with me. I felt unarmed in so many ways. I wondered if my mother had been hiding along with Charlotte in the root cellar, huddled and sweaty.

I prepared myself to kick in the next door. It would attract attention. Then, I would be a scared kid looking for my sister. It was obvious and hopeless. I didn't feel it was too far from the truth either. And, the oatmeal. I smelled oats. Someone was cooking oats. I moved quietly down the hall with a rolling stride. I felt like I had lost a little weight; that made me feel very unsure of my body. The key to walking quietly is a confident balance, but I was only vaguely familiar with my changing form. I could almost feel my limbs lengthening as I walked. I imagined my toes breaking through my favorite boots. With some humor that could probably be attributed to sleep deprivation, the thought came to me that every item in my closet was of the same size, give or take. I would lose the entire wardrobe.

I descended the stairs, which were hopelessly creaky. Letting my hands pass over my face in preparation, I prepared my best tired smile. I moved my facial muscles and sub-vocalized the sound of my first squeaky words. The smell of oatmeal pulled me to a little kitchen adjoining a long table set with at least twenty chairs. I stood in that doorway and smiled at the tall plump woman in a dirty apron stirring a pot.

"Hello," I said. "I am supposed to get my sister."

* * * * *

Charlotte looked better than when I had last seen her. The woman, named Harriet, not Ellis like I expected, had told me that my sister was doing much better and that she had been moved to a common room. When I asked what the purpose of the house was, Harriet had told me that it was someplace safe. My sister did look safe, so I didn't question further. I stood beside Charlotte's bed. There were two other women sleeping in the room. They were both older. Charlotte looked more shrunken than when I had last seen her, but her eyes sockets were not nearly so hollow.

I knelt to my sister and woke her gently. When Charlotte opened her eyes I saw it.

She was... better. Charlotte was rising from a natural, healthy, sleep. Her eyes opened wide. She always had such large eyes. My sister greeted me, seeming to say my name without speaking. We embraced. I noticed that both of her arms were bandaged.

"What are you doing here?" I asked.

"It's complicated," she said. One of the other women in the room rolled and drew the covers over herself. Charlotte lifted her head to get a better look at me then glanced towards the window. Her long hair was matted. "The sun's not up yet. Why don't you ever sleep?"

"Are you all right?" I hugged my sister again. "Why are you here?"

"I'm alright. Mother was worried, so she sent me here."

"I suspect there's more to it than that. She was trying to keep you from me."

"Mina, there's more to it than that too."

"Let's get you out of here."

"No, I can't go.

"Why?"

"I need this."

"This is a safe place to go clean, isn't it? I'm not an idiot."

"Yes."

"But you can leave if you wish, right?"

"I don't know if they will let me, but I won't try. I need this."

"I'm back here because Mother pulled me back. She said a lot of awful things. She said you would be killed for my breach of contract. All the kinds of things you would expect her to say and more. But, it doesn't matter now. We are genuinely free. It's done."

"What's done? Please no. What did you do?"

I recoiled. It was strange hearing something like that from my sister now that she was more fully conscious. I felt something awful stirring within. How many children had run back from the yard with a bouquet cut from their mother's best rose bush. I looked away from my sister as I spoke. "I want to give you another chance to return with me. You are clean now. You and I, we can leave this place, together."

"That. That again. Mina, I do not want what you want. I…"

"That's not true is it?"

"No. It is. I just don't know how to say it so that you understand. How did you find me anyway?"

"It was Dillon who brought you here, from the cellar."

"Yes."

"Feel my head. Feel that? It's a good lump and dried blood. She tried to kill me herself, she nearly did."

"I don't think she meant it. She loves you."

I looked at the sky through the window. The sun would gain on me soon.

"Is everything all right?" asked Harriet from the doorway in a hush. The woman lingered a moment and only moved on after Charlotte nodded.

"Charlotte," I said. "I know mother has her hooks in everything. She makes it all feel so complicated and connected that you're probably tied with a knot through each arm. Why would you ever stay with a woman who would hold you for three lifetimes? Does she threaten my death? Is there a condition of some kind?"

"No, Mina. When will you believe me? I hear you are to go back into service?" Charlotte sat up. "I know what a burden all of this is. There is something in being relied upon though. There really is."

"Shut up," said one of the woman sharing the room.

Charlotte giggled. "Mina, you don't have to throw everything away just to make some changes. You're so dramatic, and solutions aren't always so simple."

"She lied about the contract. We have never been bound to the state. We've been bound only to her. You are her pet and I am her servant. She's a villain."

"She is our mother."

"Listen." I stared at Charlotte's eyes. They were surrounded by dark crescents, but they were clear. I felt like my vocabulary had been reduced to a grunt and it would do nothing to serve me, but I kept speaking. "Our contract was to mother. We served at *her* pleasure. She received enough copper for all three of us, to do with as she wished. If there is a legally binding contract, it is with her. You are free to go."

"Go where?"

"Anywhere you want." I smiled. "The magistrate should void our contract in the morning. It is over."

"No," she said. "You have to stop him. What have you done?"

I stood and backed away. My sister looked completely horrified.

"No! What did you do?" Charlotte's cries dissolved into something less audible and more terrified.

"What's wrong with her?" asked one of the women.

"Charlotte, no. It can all be so much better."

"Harriet!" Charlotte cried. "Harriet!" My sister screamed. "Make her go. Please, make her go."

"You heard her," said the tall woman in the apron, already by the door. "Go on. She needs her rest. Go on."

I ran to the front door beyond the eating area. I fumbled with the lock and ran into the street, nearly colliding with a carriage. I stepped back from the road and put my hand on the fence. The sun was visible through the trees at the horizon. After closing my eyes for a moment to stare at the sun through closed lids, I knelt to tighten my laces.

Someone called my name. I turned back to the house, expecting to see my sister. The door was closed. I heard it again and realized it came from the street. Dillon was running towards me.

"Mina," he said. He was out of breath and carrying a parcel. "Here."

I took the package from him. It was mine. "The guns are here?"

"Yes."

"Mother had them."

"She gave them to me yesterday." He paused. "At the

ceremony."

"They weren't hers to give."

"I know. I'm returning them."

I tightened the bindings on the satchel. "Before I go, what happened with you and Rohad on the ship?" I realized I might not have another chance to ask.

"Oh, a nothing, really. We had a short fight."

"Over?"

"A rumor," said Dillon. He looked upwards to the left. "I told a couple of the guys about how Rohad ended up transferring to us."

"Okay." I felt I shouldn't have asked.

"He was made first mate of the Elan, but he was caught sleeping with the captain's daughter."

"Jern's daughter? I've met her."

"Yeah. Laura and her mother would often sail on shorter jaunts."

I didn't have the time for gossip. "Why did you even share that?"

"I shouldn't have," shrugged Dillon. "Rohad's a good man."

"So that's why you fought?"

"He threw the punch."

"I have to go."

"I want to come with you. I never wanted any of this."

"No. Absolutely no."

"Wait. I know it all looked bad," he started.

"Thank you for returning my things though," I said.

"Mina, I fell in love. I never expected it."

"Oh?"

"I met her in Copic. That's why all this happened. It's the only reason, I swear it."

"For her sake or to keep her safe from mother?"

"Both, I suppose."

"It doesn't matter. Goodbye."

"Listen, I never betrayed you, or them. I did my best with what I had, with how I was forced. Look, you're safe and untouched. I've just received word that Laika is safe now too. I don't even care about the torch. Really, I never did."

"Laika?"

"Yes."

"I have to go." I spoke as I walked backwards. It was all suddenly so perversely funny. "Did she have red hair and almond eyes? Very short too. Not much taller than me?"

"Yes."

I was twenty paces from my former first mate when I looked back. "And, she has a Petrovis accent? She says hello like *hizzo*?"

"Yes," he called. His arms hung limp, and his head was raised slightly as if preparing to be gathered like a stalk of wheat at harvest.

I had to call out for Dillon to hear me. "She was my mother's handmaiden." I turned to run. "Bye."

19

The first time I tried to ride a horse it had thrown me to the ground and stomped on my hair. I was nine at the time, so in order to mount the horse, I'd led the poor creature to the side of a shed, climbed on the roof and leaped. While I later considered myself lucky that the tossing and near-trampling had come to nothing, I remained terrified of horses. The introductions that followed, all to gentle and experienced mares, did nothing to save me from the impression that I had been set down on a lit stick of dynamite. Knowing that even if I tried I would not be able to ride one at any useful speed, I left the city in a small two wheeled cab that vaguely resembled a handbag.

The driver sat high above and to the back, connected to a pair of horses by some lines, although the team seemed to be connected in spirit by the whip. The driver didn't seem the sort to actually use it on the animal, but there it hung and moved, sometimes idly brushing up against the backside of the horse.

Still, it is an interesting thing to ride, even in a cab. It's not unlike sailing. The fields of wheat pass by slowly. Orchards too. But, if you let yourself sink back into the cushioned rest far enough, one can let it all roll by like a stage play. It is good sometimes to let people and the places they inhabit pass you by as if they were just waves at sea. The ride wasn't pleasant enough to keep my mind from thoughts of what I might find at the end of the trip, but it helped distract me.

Something similar to sea legs must be acquired when riding in a buggy. Occasionally, when both wheels would hit a bump, I'd find my injured brain nearly scraping the cabin roof. I certainly would have hit if I was even a head taller. Soon enough I would actually be taller. In time I probably wouldn't be able to pass myself off as a boy any longer. I doubted it would matter much since I would no longer be in the same line of work, but the costume had always been socially useful. It was a shame to lose. I thought I had nothing to gain in inheriting all the trouble that comes along with being a woman. I'd learned to tolerate being set aside and dismissed as a child, mostly because the advantage was mine -- people are surprised when they encounter a child with the intellect of an adult. When you are a grown woman, men already expect some intelligence; they just try their best to dismiss or ignore it. That is an entirely different thing.

After I had first entered the cab, the driver lowered the privacy cloth which blocked me from his view. If the cabbie was aware that the girl in the seat would make a complete change of clothes and arm herself with a good knife and three guns while still finding time to hastily re-braid her bloodied hair, I suspected he might never have dropped the screen. Even I considered myself to be curiously entertaining at that moment.

It took nearly an hour to reach the north gate. From there I paid the toll and we rode through the leaning and buttressed Portsmouth gate, which took us almost sixty miles north along the coastal corridor in the time it took to roll across the span of five feet through the old gate. Large gates were generally unstable and almost impossible to move. I was surprised that the Portsmouth door still stood after the sabotage fire some unknown group had set two years back. I suspected the arson was motivated by the potential for rail development in the area. I had wanted to investigate the attack, but my mother had refused.

The team continued with haste northward as the road wound through tidal areas dotted with egrets. The path of the road there mimicked the scores of thin estuaries that snaked through the tall green marsh grasses towards the ocean. Encouraged by my instructions and a few extra coins, we reached the banke before nine. I paid the driver the rest of his fee after stepping out beside the well-named Puddle Dock. He left without acknowledging or commenting on me having changed into the boy's outfit and cap, perhaps because the tide was low and he wanted away from the biting flies and the smell. The Strawberry Banke was a favorite departure point for lobster and crab fisherman, and I picked the area because I knew how rarely any police concerned themselves with a place like that.

Old and young men carried traps to and from small boats while I surveyed the area. I noticed a wrinkled mouthed woman in a sack dress glaring at me senselessly from a crooked doorway. The streets were old and narrow there, leading away from a muddy tidal pool towards a larger dock to the east. I passed through the Widow's Association Rose Garden. The memorial to the dead fisherman and sailors, according to the plaque, had not been there last time I was in the city. The tribute seemed well-placed since I soon passed several men who could be nothing but sailors and a lone woman, who may or may not have been a widow. As I walked towards the pier I realized that I had never asked half of my crew about their loves or family. Outside of an overheard remark or two, I generally assumed the men had sprung to life when they set foot on deck. I felt eager to ask and a little ashamed.

Most of the foot traffic moved by me in the other direction as fisherman unloaded. Lobsters were cheap and plentiful. There was not a lot of money in trapping the scavengers, and that meant that I was not going to find the prettiest ship at a lobster dock. My hope was that it also meant I could buy something outright with no questions asked. Perhaps I would get a few traps in the deal. I actually enjoyed the underrated foodstuff. When steamed with fresh butter, they were delicious. When had I last eaten a real meal or slept?

There we no guards that I could see posted by the busy pier. The lack of a presence at the port strengthened the possibility that all that had occurred was indeed orchestrated by my mother — posting someone at any and all piers would probably be beyond her. If that was true, I had a distinct advantage — *I* was my mother's strongest arm. At that moment the secretary's good arm was not tied behind her back, it was actively struggling.

I walked onto the dock. The old boards sounded hollow. The planks were gone over in white where feet hadn't trod, layered in the soil of pelican and gull droppings. As much as I liked the smell of the sea, I didn't think so highly of any place where the land and water met.

I had a particular distaste for fisheries. Year by year they were becoming more like machines chewing on the teat of the sea. I'd heard that expression from Lasko. Overfishing had moved beyond an issue of respect to one of sustainability. Even the Puddle Dock had been new and fine once. Forty years ago fisherman set out from the area for bigger fish. Then they brought in the big vessels but they only stayed until the shelf was exhausted. The next time I visited, the men only went out from there for bait-fish, not that I didn't love eating mackerel. In short course the old salts who remained by the banke only bothered to scrape up big insects for folks who couldn't afford any better.

"Hello there," I said. I greeted a fisherman on a short skiff with what looked like new rigging and a large mast. The boat itself was old, and I'd have hated to see the underside, but it did look like a vessel on the near edge of what I could handle alone. Any larger and I wouldn't match the boat. The white-haired, dark-tanned fisherman looked up after a time and then went back to his knot. "Sir, I just need a few moments of your time."

"Bugger off."

"Here, let me help you. You've got the bight there caught under the standing end." He corrected the knot only after shooting me a look.

"I said get out of here."

"I think you misunderstand." I moved in closer to the edge of the pier where he moored, standing on the bumper and nearly positioned to fall into the craft. "There's a good bit of coin on me, and I know you'll see a healthy share of it if you permit me a little audience."

"Whatever you got, I don't want."

I reached into my pocket and shook my purse. I produced a coin and the man responded to the flash of money like it had been a muzzle flare."

His hand shot out and had my arm. He squeezed tightly, like a sprung trap. "Where did you get that?"

I struggled to free myself. "Let go. It's mine by rights. What do you think you're doing?"

The man pulled me into the boat. I was already on bad footing, but it wasn't like me to be caught like that. I recovered only after hitting the deck in a roll. I crouched, ready to spring.

"Whoa. What's wrong with you?" He bent down and picked up the coin. "And, what exactly are you buying, boy?"

"This craft." I wiped off my pants and stood. "I'll give you 200 pounds for this and another hundred for your troubles."

"Oh, you will?" He reached for me again. I dodged his grasping hand.

"You're missing out on a hell of a chance here." The ship moored in the berth next to the old man's boat was empty and near. I thought I could probably make the jump if I needed. "But, more importantly." I evaded him again. "You're wasting my time with this."

He danced with me around the mast. "Trust me, I have the money."

"I bet you do."

"I realize how I look right now, but it's mine." I knew how impossible that must have sounded. It didn't help that I probably appeared as gaunt and desperate as my outfit.

The man made another determined leap and caught my pant leg. I tripped, and he was on me. He elbowed my lower back hard. I felt his hands digging for my pocket. "Where is it you little thief?"

"I'm not a thief." I tried to roll to my back so I could kick the wiry fisherman off me.

"Where is it?" He was loud, too loud.

I caught him with two feet square in the chest, and he tumbled backwards. I rolled back and then forward hard, bringing myself to a prepared crouch. I ripped my threadbare breeches halfway up the leg and withdrew the little pistol, not raising it much higher than my knee. I switched the safety.

The man shut up and went blank in the face. He didn't speak or move. I seemed to have the whole of his attention.

"I'm going to pay you two hundred pounds for this piece of shit. That's twice what this is worth. I am adding one hundred on top of that for you to spend on whatever it is that rotted out your teeth. You want to shut up about the whole affair and find yourself a new boat. Am I right?"

"You're right."

I fished in my pocket for the prepared purse and threw it at his chest. It hit him and then fell to the deck of the skiff.

"Pick that up and get on the pier." He complied wordlessly but watched me the entire time. I wasn't sure he even blinked. "Don't say a damned word to anyone. If they ask you, tell them to fuck off. Understood?" He nodded and picked up the purse, his eyes never leaving me.

I prepared the boat for sail while the man stood on the pier like a fool. The money was more than enough, but I was sorry for the rough treatment. As I worked, images of my crew burned through my mind. I'd already wasted too much time getting to water. At least no one seemed to pay me or the near-catatonic fisherman much attention, but I wasn't shocked by that. I'd come to the right pier. If the wind stayed with me and the water didn't have much chop, I should make the Transcendent long before any ship from Tremont.

Unfortunately, I made terrible time. It is an awful thing to look at cerulean waves from nearly the surface of the water, to face the milky green beauty, and then to feel something other than awe. I hated the choppy sea just then. Each swell, however modest, stood between me and the crew. It took nearly three hours to cross to the small cluster of islands. I navigated past Haley Cove with its painters swatch of sky blue shallow waters and then tacked beyond the lingering fishing boats, careful to avoid not only the rocks but also their nets. I headed north from there, guided by the ships bent compass arm and wishing I'd not overestimated the time savings of a northern passage over land.

There would only be time enough for one good shot at finding the ship that day. I knew the coordinates, and that was something, but I didn't have the tools for that on the fisherman's skiff. What I had was a compass, but I could only use that to shoot straight out from the isle. It was a terrible way to navigate. If I was on my mark then I would pass within the lucky mile or so of sight and spot the ship. If not, I would be forced to turn around and book something more substantial to carry me to the designated coordinates. That would surely be too late.

When a spare moment came, I caught myself thinking again of what had happened in the last trip to Tremont. To derail those thoughts I closed my eyes and stared into the lowering sun. I felt I would find the Transcendent. In any case, I was glad to be heading in a straight line, even if it were not the right one. Any movement away from Tremont was progress towards a goal. Without me, my mother would likely, eventually lose her seat of power. My sister would probably be married off like cattle too. That said, I guessed that the reality probably fell somewhere between my assumptions and the best case scenario. Perhaps my mother and sister were somewhere together at that moment.

In all of the scenarios I pressed into shape within my mind, the crew survived. I would reach them and we would sail. It occurred to me then that I was already sailing. A little guilt crept into my mind for taking some pleasure in the voyage while the men were marked targets. However, the nature of the work did tend though to bring one back into the moment. I was an excellent helmsmen when moving against the wind, but to make any progress the little vessel required an intensely physical approach. I ran from side to side, grabbing at lines and tying extensions. When I had the chance I planned to revisit the hastily tied knots and secure them fully. Occasionally, even the weight of my entire body could not pull a line to tension, forcing me to compromise speed. Everything took longer than it should have. There was a level at which I hated my body, but as I had no choice, I battled against the alliance of waves and time.

* * * * *

I sighted the Transcendent far to the starboard at the furthest reach of my vision. The masts were mere scratches against the sky, but that was enough. The sails were half raised, giving the ship the appearance of a lost mountain range at the horizon.

At a quarter mile from the ship I noticed that perhaps a hundred yards beyond the Transcendent another ship anchored. I made preparations to drop my own anchor. As soon as I was reasonably close I let the sheets fall, doing my best all the while to keep the Transcendent between me and the uninvited sloop beyond it. As soon as possible, I lowered the anchor and also dropped the little worm-eaten dinghy stored at the back of the fisherman's skiff. With that little boat I rowed steadily to the side of the Transcendent. Climbing only high enough to look through the bulwark opening, I neither saw nor heard anyone on the deck. There were voices, but they were farther away, probably carried on the wind from the sloop I had seen.

With the fisherman's rowboat attached to the side of the ship, and certainly visible to anyone up in a mast, I pulled myself and my pack onto the Transcendent. The landscape was familiar. It was like returning home, but to an empty house. With no one on deck the ship felt like a dream place, a memory palace. There was blood. When I came around to the fore, I found long heel-scraped streaks through the blood drawn upon the deck, like a man had been shot and dragged by the shoulders.

I kept low and looked through the railing supports to the sloop off of port. There were court guards, but the vessel looked like a civilian sailing sloop, which was curious enough in its own right. I could think of no link between that ship and my mother at all. On the far deck between the legs of the bulwarks, I saw heads. It was my crew or at least most of them. I counted them like a mother might count her children after an outing. They were not all there. Neither Crane nor Bosun were visible. The men appeared to be sitting and bound together by rope lengths that formed an interconnected lace. Some men walking idly about the ship looked like they were neither of the court guard nor of my mother's men. They were soldiers. I wondered if they could even row, let alone sail.

Staying low, I crawled to the hatch and slipped down the stairs. Once out of sight, I ran through the ship. It was empty, but I found more blood in the workshop and a wrench on the floor. I hoped it was from old Bosun braining someone. On the galley table I found blood that was still damp and sticky to the touch. It was not enough for a man to have bled out, but there was splatter. Someone had probably been stabbed, but I saw no trail and remained hopeful.

I went to my door where I wanted the long rifle with the telescope and as much ammunition as I could fire before they picked me off. I brought my hand underneath the door frame. The locking slide was shifted to the far right, leaving the door unlocked. I drew my revolver and entered. After throwing my pack through to test for a reaction, I exited the end of the tunnel feet first, gun pointed and cocked. The foyer was trashed. The tumult stretched off in all directions. The soldiers must have passed through the door.

I sprinted down the hall of keeping. I raced back and down the artificer's hall. In nearly every corner I found something smashed or knocked about. I ran into the hall of being. Shot had torn away most of the stars from my ceiling mosaic in the library.

Save my own footfalls, I saw no one and heard even less. The place was too large to search thoroughly. I ran to my bedroom. It smelled like piss. The mirrors in the closet were smashed, and the armory had been raided. There were some pieces still there, but the long gun I needed was missing.

I felt very unarmed and exposed. I had never had anyone back there, not since Charlotte's visit. And now, to see it torn up — I tried to let it remind me of the crew. It was nothing. It was not me. It was not even a part of me. The whole of the crew were tied up or injured on that sloop. I tried to focus, if only to stoke anger. I wanted to channel the emotion. The other ship should burn with it, like the sun concentrated in a magnifying glass.

I ran back to the foyer and out the entrance, crawling out of the tunnel into the ship.

Explosive pain in my neck. I hit the cabin floor in front of the door. I was being kicked and there were hands closing around my head. The skin was rough and they were strong.

I tried to pull myself backwards through the tunnel with my feet. The gun was no longer in my hands, and I couldn't grab onto anything to prevent me from being pulled out by my head like a tick. A bag, maybe burlap, went over my face. More boots kicking my back and chest. There were at least three of them beating me to death. I tried to protect my head.

20

"Mina?" Mother asked. "Wake up my love. I am sorry. I'm sorry they did this. I am really sorry." And then water. Had it already been flowing? I didn't know. The world was a massless gray sheet. I was waking to cold water against the side of my face and the voice of my mother. A dream perhaps. It was difficult to move.

I began to struggle to sit up. My hands were tied and my feet slipped and skidded against the porcelain-smooth basin floor. I was naked, and there was blood, water, and hair swirling into the drain. Feet and legs slipped uselessly against the wet stone, like I was spinning in a giant cooking pot.

"Oh, relax. I'm not going to kill you. You deserve it though."

"Untie me!" I cried.

"You have to relax. I am cleaning you up." My mother held her hand over her own mouth.

I finally saw that I was looking up from the wash basin within my door.

"My poor thing," said Mother with lullaby softness.

"Release the crew. Release me!"

"Once again, my love. I am not in charge of all this." She spooned soap and water, now warmer, over my shoulders and head. "You have one hell of a reputation. I think they were scared of you."

I breathed so hard I swore my lungs would explode.

"Mina," my mother said with that drawn out first syllable. "Whatever you said to the magistrate frightened the hell out of him. I don't pretend to understand you anymore. But, it also made him very, very angry. He actually declared that all of the defectors involved in the tow-line incident shall be hunted dead. Do you have any idea how long it's been since I heard him order something like that?"

"Then let me go. You can't want to see me die? You just can't"

"Be calm, please. You are being spared because I begged for you. Begged. I had nothing, nothing to offer. I begged on my knees."

"I don't believe you."

"Oh, you are so rotten."

"I am surprised you didn't just kill me the other night."

"You know I didn't realize you'd been without the torch for so long. I wasn't thinking. Besides, I thought you were going to attack me. Calm."

My chest heaved. "What of the men?"

"The court soldiers are all on board the Transcendent now. They left your crew on the magistrate's sloop and scuttled it."

"No!" I struggled again to stand. I stepped on my hair, awakening the fire in my neck. My left side hurt so damned badly.

"Relax. It is done."

"You murderer!"

"You don't know what you are saying."

I cried out and struggled. The water ran into my mouth and I spat.

"My god, shush! You did everything you could — more than you should have. We all protect those we love. I do it. You do it. You've never loved me. I know that, but I do love you."

I tried to wiggle through the binding, hopeful that the soap would assist.

"I really do. So does your sister. She is doing well, you know."

I tried again, attempting to break the rope using a snap technique that works with lighter lines. More pain.

"Shh."

I let my body go limp. I began to count. When I reached one hundred and eight, I asked, "is it really done? Is it sunk?"

"Yes."

I set a goal of fifty-four seconds and waited in as relaxed a posture as I could manage. I tried not to clench my teeth. "I did love them, you know." I was taking Rohad's advice. There was nothing else to do. *Tell her what she wants to hear and then do as you please.*

"I know. Here, sit up."

My mother helped me to sit up. She looked awful. Her eye makeup had run amongst older, darker dried streams of mascara.

"When was it sunk?"

"At least three hours ago."

"Did they shoot the swimmers?"

"They were tied together. There were no swimmers. Look at you."

"Why sink it?"

"That's not your business."

"I want to feel my head. Please untie me."

"I will, but not yet. I'm a little afraid of you, you know." She smiled. "Once we return I will take you to doctor Prit. He replaced Dr. Burroway. He's very good."

I nodded and my mother smiled.

I shifted in the tub, grimacing as if I simply could not get comfortable while she cleared blood from my forehead. Before I sprung at her there was a shared moment when I saw the woman look at her daughter's legs and feet, which had been carefully moved into a well-planted crouch. What I saw there in my mother's eyes was horror. I watched myself spring from the tub and nearly through my mother. The rope between my bound wrists caught her head and she fell back against the sink basin at the opposite wall of the small room.

I landed atop her and scurried to my feet. I slipped twice before reaching the carpet of the hall and wheeling around in a defensive posture. My mother was splayed out on the stone. I wanted to rush to her, but I did not. There was no blood. I realized it was my own turn to cruelly trust in the restorative powers of the torches.

After cutting the cord binding my wrists using a pantry knife gripped between my wet knees, I tore through the satchel in the foyer and pulled out the custom double-barreled howdah gun. I fumbled for shells, at first loading the wrong ammunition for each of the differently choked barrels. I ejected them from the gun and reversed the order. Worried all the time that my mother would emerge from the curtain behind me, I then loaded the caplock navy revolver. My hands moved swiftly, but I could feel them shaking.

I ran to the outer hatch door and slid the big howdah gun through first. I entered the little pass-through tunnel, keeping my pistol at the ready. When I busted through the outer door, I emerged bare feet first. I waited for the pain of ambush, but there was none, or at least there was nothing new. I grabbed the howdah and shut my door. Thunder. A blast of thunder shook the ship. My ship was firing. I looked around in the small room for materials.

I threw my guns on the captain's bed and picked up a nearby chair by the legs and smashed it on the ground. Again. Against the door. Again on the ground. The back was off it, and I set the broken furniture so that the four legs and seat were wedged between the near wall and my door. There was still enough space for the thing to shift. Books. I shoved in one volume and another. Using my dictionary, I hammered in a book of verse until I felt sure the door could not be opened from within. Another cannon boom snapped me back to the present danger. I grabbed the guns and ran.

I burst onto the deck wet, naked, and armed. There were just four guns on the Transcendent. I faced the aft gun. It was set to fire. The man standing there with the firing rod stared dumbly at me. There was no fear in his eyes, just an acknowledgment that the universe was a funny place. At least, that's what I thought I saw in his face. He screamed before I leaped off of the step. I struck him squarely in the chest with both knees, and the last chord of the man's yell was pushed out of him in an explosive gust.

I turned from him, keeping my pistol trained on the soldier. The sloop still stood on the water. The mainmast was down, and it was badly damaged, but it was not yet sunk as my mother had claimed. It looked like the soldiers had the guns shooting balls instead of grapeshot. In either case, my ship was outfitted for extremely close combat, not for the distance from which they were firing. All around me the deck of the Transcendent was a growing panic. I saw two men preparing rifles.

"Pull!" Another cannon sounded.

I looked around me. I laid out some fire from the revolver simply to buy time. In the shape of the smoke drifting across the deck I saw my own death as well as that of my men. I decided I would go down as poetry. Men approached along the starboard while the Transcendent continued to fire its cannons. I dropped to the deck, flat upon it. To my left I saw the downed guard scrambling towards me, red faced and clenched. I fired the revolver and took his throat.

Briefly, I looked up from the deck over the raised galley hatch and then dropped low again. The ship I had seen stretching out before me was impossibly armed and too large to be overcome. I pulled to my knees and looked at the sloop through the bulwark supports. I then narrowed my attention to the tie lines beside me. Setting down the navy revolver, I braced the body of the howdah with both hands as best I was able. I pulled one of the two triggers back and fired upon the thick rope that bound the loaded cannon beside me. The shot ripped through the rope and left it smoking. I pulled the remaining threads apart and loosed the line. Shots struck the deck near my feet. I remained partially hidden by the galley hatch, but the cover wouldn't keep me for long.

I dropped the heavy pistol to free up both hands. Keeping low, I threw my small frame backwards and rolled the powerful gun off its mount. I felt a hot streak form against my hip and near to my arm. Involuntarily, I snapped back. My side had been hit with the slightest possible graze, like a burn along my hip. Stepping again into the line of fire, I wrapped my arms around the neck of the big gun and pulled backwards with everything I had. I pulled until the beast began to move. My back felt as if it would snap, but I swiveled the cannon so that it faced up-ship towards the fore.

Another explosion. At least one gun team continued to fire on the sloop, on my crew.

Low peripheral movement by my right flank caught my eye. Dropping again, I picked up my navy pistol. The crouching soldier hesitated for a moment, granting me just enough time to put a bullet in his chest from ten feet.

Again, I rose and struggled with the ship's gun. That time I didn't angle the cannon, I pushed it forward. I pushed until my legs flailed out behind me and the machine rolled. The almost useless front caster wheels dropped the single step off of the quarterdeck so that the cannon faced the belly of the ship — it was a gun turned upon one's own body. Quickly, I seized the box of matches that the first dead soldier had abandoned.

I did not really remember lighting the prepared wick, but I looked into the unsteady flame. It was not at all like the candle on my mother's table, but to me, the sky seemed to darken, and that is what I saw. I saw the image of a flame that pulled in all available light. All became pitch then, and only that flicker and crackle remained. I hugged the deck again as more gun fire came down from up high. I considered the possibility that they might not be trying to kill me.

The cannon beside me, angled down at about twenty degrees into the ship, boomed. I was too fascinated by the light to cover my ears. All sound narrowed into one screaming, ringing pitch, like the singing of a steady finger pulled across the wet rim of a glass.

The shot did not hit the main mast — a round, inward splintered entrance wound appeared mid deck exactly where I wanted to see it open. It was a mortal wound. I stood and watched the men. I saw a scene of smoke and hell. They all moved towards me then, in form or gesture. They left the big guns. I looked to the sloop. Although I heard nothing, I felt splinters hitting my legs and a shot pass close to my head. I did want to live, even if I had not expected to survive. They are just poor shots, I thought. All of them. I threw myself over the side of the ship.

Salt water filled my throat and sinuses during the hasty and awkward crash into the sea, but I paddled to the surface and cleared my passages. I began to swim. If they fired I didn't know it or hear it.

When the world is silent, the sea is a painting that moves. It is really just like a good painting where one can see movement in the strokes and know the intention of the artist. For what seemed like the tenth time that day, I appreciated the blue of the sky. The weather could not have been better. The sea had some good chop, but you can't have it all. I was constantly amazed at where my mind went in times of crisis.

I swam towards my friends. Knowing that my aching arms would not hold out in a straight shot, I switched to my back and took the distance in long slow sweeps. The soldiers and guards aboard the Transcendent were all activity. I saw that they were loading their boat. That was not good, but they were also running about in obvious panic, and that was of some use to me. The ship had already begun to list, and even if they knew how to use them, I knew the pumps would not be enough.

What I did not see was my mother. When would she awake? If she was smart she would lock the inner door. I had shut it, but that was not the same as sealing. It was a barrier hatch door, but unless one spun the wheel, it was as useless as the true outer door in keeping away the sea. Of course, if my mother opened the inner door and let in the full force of the sea, I doubted my mother would have the strength to shut it again.

I was sending the door back to where I found it, at the bottom of the sea in the Gulf of Maine. After turning to swim face-forward again, I wondered if the circumstances that sunk the original ship that held my door were very similar. I doubted it.

Years ago when I found my door in the wreckage of some ship that I could not name, found in a field of other hulks that had already been picked over, I did not open it. I knew enough to leave it shut until I could bring the door, and a section of the hull itself, out of the water. When I had first opened the portal, the door was flat against the deck. A stream of water, perhaps two inches high, poured upwards as if raised by some force and prepared to fall into the sky. But the stream ran out along the deck of my old ship as if it had always been running horizontally. There was not much accumulated water within, perhaps six inches deep across the interior. It had taken me a long time to clear out the sea creatures and muck that covered the floor. The place was disgusting then but also already so beautiful. It was actually my father's notebook, the only thing I had of him, that led me to that field of wrecks.

I reached the sloop, reached it ahead of the boat. Behind me, on the Transcendent, the panicked men had decided to gather everyone aboard the dinghy rather than attempt to save the ship. I suspected though that the Transcendent had at least an hour in her. Of course, the men were mostly private soldiers, not sailors. The best sailor among them, my mother, was likely sealed inside her sepulcher, headed to the sea floor.

I took the tie-line in hand and pulled myself up. Halfway up the side of the sloop my arms began to shake. I didn't have it in me. For the remainder of the climb I inched forward using my legs wrapped around the wiry rope to propel me upwards while my hands did little more than secure my body to the line. Pieces of shattered wood and metal dug into my back when I dropped myself sidelong onto the deck. Debris covered the ship, but I did not see any of the men. They had likely gone over the side to escape the fire, drowning as the weakest swimmers sank first and pulled the others with them. I continued crawling low across the sloop. When I opened the hatch, relief moved through me in a wave.

My crew-mates were piled in a sad but moving heap below deck. The hatch was small, mostly for ropes and access to the ballast, but it was filled with my men like so many netted fish thrown into a hold. I leaned over, my sopping hair raining down on their backs and faces. I spoke but could barely hear myself over the ringing. "Are you hurt?" Crocodile's face became visible in the heap. His lips moved, although I couldn't tell what he was saying. Breaking away from the hatch, I scoured the deck for a blade and found a cracked fishing spear by the fore. All that time I expected my pursuers to board the craft and place another sack over my head. I crawled into the hole with the men and began to saw at the ropes. It was difficult to know what I was cutting or where. I hoped it was rope and not flesh, although I doubted I would hear it if someone screamed.

The first to emerge from the heap was Crane and then Emery, whose long face had been bloodied. I gestured to the sailors to find weapons. I mimed a knife until I remembered that I could speak, even if I could not hear myself. "The boat. Don't let them board."

After Crocodile's hands were free, he took the blade from me and began to saw. I crawled up the ladder to the deck, too tired to stand, while the men began to fill out the craft. I heard a faint gunshot behind me. To my surprise, Emery had found a rifle.

Lasko was beside him loading another. Lasko was an excellent shot. By the time the two men had positioned themselves properly against the bulwarks to fire on the approaching boat, it had already turned. They were rowing to a side.

Someone, Rohad perhaps, put a shirt over my shoulders. I stared at the Transcendent. It was already swamped. The ship was sinking faster than I had expected. If my mother was awake, or alive, perhaps she could free herself. I did hope so. Rohad buttoned my shirt up the front.

"Shouldn't we try to pursue them?" Emery asked.

"No," I said.

"Where is the secretary?" Bosun asked. The words were not said quietly, but I heard them as an absolute whisper.

"I don't know," Crane said. "Rohad?"

I looked at Rohad. He said nothing.

With that the men seemed to unnaturally cease that line of questioning. To a person, they were all preparing the sloop to sail as best it still could. Under continued fire, I saw that boat full of the court guards retreating as fast as the men aboard could pull.

I spoke to no one in particular, although I knew Rohad was at least near enough to hear. "I think she is on the Transcendent. I mean, she is on the ship, unless you see her floating."

The ship had not sunk yet. I had seen several ships sink. My second command, The Alkyd, was scuttled in battle after capture. Then too I had stood on the deck of another craft, watching my ship slip into the ocean. It had floated there for almost an hour and a half before we lost sight of it in the water. Even then, my captors had wasted six shots before the main mast of the sturdy frigate sank into the dark. Ships want to float, but without the displaced water, they will eventually go down.

I stood. "Find me an iron. Get a hammer. We are saving my door." I looked around. "The mizzen mast here still stands. Let's use it. Raise anchor and approach the Transcendent. Rohad, get to the wheel."

We had to move a wide circle to come across the side of the sinking ship. It was dangerous. The masts and shrouds towered like trees, like trees that threatened to fall in a gale. It would not be unexpected for the ship to list more to port than it already had, but it also would be possible for the wind to switch and send the masts smashing down on our small craft.

I didn't doubt that the rowing boat of fleeing, confused soldiers would make it back to the isle of shoals, but I strongly doubted our own ability to do the same if all we had to cling to was the wreckage of two ships. What hell that would be.

I decided my next ship would be the Transcendent II. I had money put away in more places than the capital. It would be another Baltimore Clipper too. It was difficult to change something you are used to. It is not impossible though, just difficult.

"Where would she be?" Crane asked.

"Fetch me that length of rope. Yes. Cut it at the end." I began to tie the rope to myself.

"It's too long for her in there," Stake said.

"Could there be a pocket of air?" Crane asked.

"We are not going back for my mother. If I don't have to lose the door, I won't."

"It is real then?" Lasko asked. "The door?"

"Very."

The ship remained swamped. It listed more strongly than it had been, but it was leaning to port and away from the hobbled sloop. The stern was riding dangerously low in the water. If the ship was not rolling over, exposing one side, or if the sea were any choppier, there would be nothing to stand on aside from the rigging and masts.

"Crocodile?" I asked. "Will you jump with me?"

"Aye, Captain."

I climbed the side of the small sloop and lowered myself down. I went into the water, careful not to let the safety line catch me. The water was cold and the Transcendent looked much more dangerous from the perspective afforded by the water. It could not be long until it dropped. I swam to the side and pulled myself into the swamped ship with renewed energy. I walked up the deck at a twenty percent grade and mounted the railing at an angle. From there the ship felt sturdy enough.

Crocodile climbed to me, pulling a ballooned cloth sack with tools. The two of us moved cautiously, swaying with each swell until we stood by the wheel, firmly above the captain's quarters. I considered the hatch again. However we entered, there would be enough time for me to reach the door, although I doubted we could actually break it free before the opportunity was lost to the water.

I reeled in the tool line and handed Crocodile the hatchet. I pointed to a spot beside the wheel. A hole there would drop me above the captain's bed. I should have called it my bed, although I rarely slept in it. The little tool wasn't much, but the strong man went to work. If the ship went down, I had no doubt he could reach the sloop safely. Chips of wood on the deck lifted in the water when the swells came, like designs on a beach washed away by a rising tide.

As soon as Crocodile had broken through the board, I switched him to the iron. With a great heave the plank snapped and he went to work on the next. Two boards would be enough for me. I hadn't grown that much in those few weeks. I could feel the air rushing through the rough gap as the ship moved, half expecting my mother's hand to snatch upwards through the wound or float passively into view. Had I killed her at the tub? I may have murdered my mother. It was possible. If I felt anything about that, I was not aware of it at the time.

When the second board snapped I took up the hammer. Spray snapped up from inside the cabin as the ship moved in the water or the water moved in the ship. Soon the two would be inseparable. I saw my pillow. It was that or a body.

"Wait. I will go," Crocodile said.

I ignored him and lowered myself into the ship.

Water filled most of the stateroom. It was my pillow I had seen. The banging of cargo and possessions within the belly of the ship was constant. I moved from the bed and dove down to the door. It all felt right, where it should be. I moved my hand around the edges. The door was still secured by the chair. Although the outer old, wooden door was the far flimsier of the two, it was the real door. It was the door connected to the halls that lived somewhere else, carved into a mountain. Wherever they were buried, that space began at the edge of that little wooden door I had once pulled from a sunken ship. The stronger inner door beyond was built into the stone, but it was a part of the far off structure. All I needed to do was remove the old wooden door without severing the frame.

I felt around the edge of my door to the actual cabinet-mounted frame until I had to come back to the surface to breathe.

In the dark I bobbed while above me Crocodile freed another plank. I dove again into the water, hammer in hand. I opened the cabinets on either side of the door, but then I was back at the surface and out of breath sooner than expected. While I didn't have a lot of strength remaining, my muscles had yet to entirely fail me, although they burned fiercely. Above, Crocodile continued to lever the boards away from the wreck. I noticed that I was floating closer to him now — there seemed to be less space in the cabin.

I went under again, trying to wedge the pry bar of the claw hammer between the cabinet wall and the frame of the door. Failing that, I made a second attempt only to fall short yet again. That time I was gasping for air when I returned. Hammer in hand, again I went down and pulled the corner of the frame only a half inch from its mount. Bosun had done his work too well. The quarters were more cramped than they had been, and the captain's bed was fully submerged. I felt the ship was listing more as well. It is sinking, I reminded myself.

I dove again. That time I had it. The claw of the hammer was in a crack wide enough for me to walk it in substantially further. I began to pry and work along the edge. My lungs burned and my head swam. Shoving myself upwards with my feet to draw another breath, I hit my head. Above me I could feel kneed cabin wall and ceiling instead of air. I began to feel around. The ship had gone under. This is how it is? I opened my eyes. There was still some light by the hole torn in the ship. Even as I swam towards that light it blinked out and became a glow. That glow dimmed and went black.

Was it the bed I was kicking? It was. I felt for the cabinet and my door. With panicked fingers I released the latch and swung open the door. I pulled myself inside, unaware if I was swimming up or down. My body began to spasm for air, forcing the last of my breath out entirely. Desperately I pawed for the inner door and I had it. It was open. I jettisoned myself out through the hatch and into the dull dim light beyond with all I had left. Letting my body go slack, I put my trust in buoyancy to determine which way was up.

Air filled my lungs. I gasped and coughed. I went down again but recovered. More air. The air was sweet. I was swimming within the nearly submerged foyer of my door. The chamber was dark except for a single gas lamp still burning above. It seemed impossible to consider, but I took the largest breath I could handle and dove back under. It was difficult to find the door through which I had come. When I did find it, I feared irrationally that I might slip back through it, perhaps finding myself at the bottom of the sea. I shut the bulkhead door, spinning the wheel until it sealed.

Again I found the surface. There was a lot of stuff, my stuff, floating all around me, but none of it would keep me afloat. I grabbed wildly at a cushion and some clothing. My limbs all wanted to collapse. It was all so much more than I could handle. I felt sure I would drop from the gap of free air too near the foyer ceiling. And, I did. My arms fell and water covered my crown.

21

It was my mother who saved me. I knew this when I realized the warm chest to which I was cradled had breasts. I couldn't hear at all and there was not much to see. A lamp filled my field of vision and then passed, either moved by a hand or swinging freely. My legs were in water. Focusing tightly only for a brief moment, I saw that the pock-marked ceiling above was my own, painted with my own constellations. I coughed. I felt so tired.

When I came to again I was staring at the same lamp. It was still moving. I wondered what damage I had done to my brain. It occurred to me that it was only the lamp that was moving and the lower ceiling beyond it was steady. It was also not the same lamp, and my mother was no longer holding me.

I turned my head to the side. I was looking through a wood planked crawlspace toward a shaft of sunlight. Although not the Transcendent, I was on a ship. There were crates around me, but I was alone. It was the hold of the magistrate' sloop where the men had been tied. Shadows moved in the column of light coming from the hatch above. There was some movement. It occurred to me that I was glad it was not the Transcendent. Not only because it was probably at the bottom of the gulf but because then it all would surely be a dream, probably my last before final darkness.

When I tried to roll to my side, I found my arms were simply too heavy to move. I coughed and lost what strength I had recovered. Wherever I was, it was dry. I went back to sleep. When I awoke again all was dark beyond the lamplight. Rohad sat beside me. He was smoking, something that he rarely did. I smiled. He dropped the pipe and swept me up into a hug. I tried to embrace him back, but I was still painfully weak. I began to cough and it hurt.

"Oh," Rohad said, pulling away. "Forgive me, captain. But, all of that *and* a smile."

He sounded very far away.

"Did Crocodile escape?"

"Yes."

"Did the sea dry up?"

"No."

"You recovered the door and with it you found me and my mother?"

"We did. When the ship rolled Croc went into the water after you. He wasn't the only one either. You were gone. It was Bosun who figured out where you went, but Crocodile and Stake pried the frame off of the cabinet. They had to go in through the hull."

"The ship is gone then?"

"It sank completely, but not before we took some of the spare sail to rig up onto this old boat."

"The door?"

"It is on the deck. When I last saw it, it was still draining."

"I'm glad it wasn't lost."

"We're glad you weren't lost. That was close."

"Thank you." I closed my eyes. It felt good to rest them.

"You didn't ask about your mother."

"No." I opened one eye inquisitively.

"She is alive and bound."

"I'm glad she's bound."

"We hadn't tied her at first, but she tried to throw herself overboard."

"Sounds right."

"Your orders?"

"Gag her if you need. We should make land in Rye. If it hasn't washed away, I should have more than enough funds stashed within the door for us to charter a ship immediately."

"And what will we do with your mother?"

"Well, we're certainly not going to take her with us."

* * * * *

The Cormorant was a good, strong commercial frigate. We boarded her after booking a short passage from Rye to Provincetown on the cape. It would not take long for the capital to determine how we had left and for where, but by switching ships, I hoped to complicate the matter. For a while I felt a loss like none I had ever borne. I didn't know when I would see my sister again. The same went for my mother, although not in exactly the same way. I mourned the ship too, in the way I suspected one mourns an old house. Perhaps it was more than that. It was not just the time one had put in there, it was the potential for more time spent. The ship was freedom. I had never really experienced the loss of a home, only of a ship. When I thought of Tremont, I thought of Charlotte, but I didn't miss the place itself. I certainly didn't miss the swearing, gesticulating woman we abandoned in Rye harbor.

The wind was good. In the evenings the crew and I worked over plans for the Transcendent II. Until we thought of something better, that would be the name. We also worked on something else together, plans for the space within the door. I had no answers, at least none for which I could form words, to explain why I had never taken the crew inside. There had been a security concern, of course, but there was more to it.

I had long suspected that the choice had more to do with how fleeting our time together had seemed to me. They had been strong friends, but even the strongest ties would eventually be broken by old age or death. I still suspected I would end up at their funerals, but I would also be old in body by the time that happened, I hoped. Knowledge of your own death is the lens that brings life into focus. In any case, we planned the layout within the door together. I would maintain firm ownership, but the men would pass freely within. Interior doors would likely be hung within for privacy. I still knew there was sense in certain walls and barriers.

During days, the crew worked with me to salvage the interior of the door, so far as we could without raising suspicions on the Cormorant. Two weeks after the sinking, my limbs still ached. The cook on the Cormorant said it was growing pains. He was probably partially right. The second floor of the library was entirely untouched and the rest of the door had mostly drained. The place still felt like an extension of myself, but it had changed. I tried my best to love its changing face, along with my own.

Bosun wanted to begin drilling upwards, to find out where the tunnel system had been laid. Rohad sided with me, preferring to leave such alone. It is valuable to have a passage from one place to the next or a way out, should they need it, but it's a particularly risky thing to open the tunnels up to local detection. At that point there would be a pass-through. Nations would fight over such things. I thought of the doors in Tremont that could once deliver colonists to England inside of a short march. Those same doors had been used by the Dutch and the Iroquois confederacy to raid London.

Whatever the crew chose to do, we had the door. In time we would have a ship. I saw that the stars were out in force that evening. It would be three more weeks before the Cormorant would arrive in Italy. I lay on the deck that evening and looked at the stars. I had no desire to put them out. I watched them flicker while I made plans. I had less time than ever, and yet I had never felt I had so much of it.

GLOSSARY

able seaman: A more experienced seaman.

aft: Near or towards the rear of a vessel.

apparent wind: Combination of the true blowing winds and the wind caused by the movement of the vessel.

below: Beneath a deck.

berth: Either a location where one moors a vessel or a place where one sleeps on a ship.

bight: A loop or curve in a knot.

boatswain (bosun): Crew member responsible for the maintenance of the ship.

boom: Horizontal pole extending from the bottom of a sail.

bow: The forward part of a ship.

bowsprit: Pole extending from the front of a ship.

bulwarks: Fence-like structure extending above the weather deck.

chronometer: Extremely accurate timepiece that can be used to determine a ships longitudinal location.

clipper: a tall ship often used in trade when speed takes priority over carrying capacity.

crosstrees: Horizontal beams crossing a mast, to which the shrouds are attached.

deck: Structural portion of a ship covering an area or forming a floor, not necessarily the uppermost exposed deck.

dinghy: A small boat often carried by a larger vessel.

dock: Area between piers where vessels may be secured.

fender: Cushioning between a vessel and the pier.

first mate: Second in command after the captain.

fore: Near or towards the front of a vessel.

forecastle: Area below deck at the front of a ship, often where the crew quarters.

frigate: Moderately sized warship.

galley: Ship's kitchen.

grapeshot: Smaller cannon shot, particularly useful for tearing apart rigging or personnel.

green hand: A novice sailor.

halyard: Lines used to raise, lower, or shape a sail.

helm: Entire mechanism (rudder, wheel, area securing the wheel) used to steer a vessel.

helmsman: The one steering a vessel, often a shared task.

hold: Compartment(s) on a vessel where cargo is stored.

hull: Structural shell of a vessel.

knee: Angled support connecting a deck beam to the hull.

knot: Speed of one nautical mile (1.1508 miles) per hour.

ladder: Steep stairs on a ship.

line: A rope.

list: Lean of a ship to one side, often due to flooding.

mast: Vertical pole supporting booms, rigging, and sails.

mess: Dining area and kitchen on a ship.

mizzenmast: The mast to the rear of the main mast.

moor: To secure a boat to a pier or a buoy.

ordinary seaman: Less experienced seaman.

port: Left side of the ship. The word has the same number of letters as the word left, which is a useful mnemonic.

quarterdeck: Rear area on the upper deck.

ratlines: Lengths of horizontal thin line tied to the shrouds to make rungs that one may climb to rise into the rigging.

rigging: General term for the system of lines, shrouds, sheets, masts, etc. on a vessel

schooner: Sailing ship of at least two masts where the foremast is no taller than the rear masts.

scuttle: To deliberately sink a ship.

seaman: Sailor.

second mate: Commanding officer after the first mate, often in charge of navigation.

sheet: A line used to control the angle of a sail in relation to the wind.

shrouds: Rigging running from the sides of the ship to the mast to support it laterally.

skiff: A small flat bottomed boat, usually operable by a single person or a small crew.

sloop: A small to mid-sized single masted vessel.

square sail(rig): Sails and rigging set perpendicular to the keel of the vessel.

staysail: A triangular sail attached to a stay (line), not a mast or yard.

stunsail (studding sail): An additional sail that extends beyond the square sails.

Starboard: The right side of a ship.

Steward: Crew member in charge of provisions and meals.

tacking: Changing the direction of a vessel so that one zig-zags towards the wind, thereby making progress without vainly attempting to sail directly into the wind.

tell-tale: Pieces of string or light material hanging from sails or rigging to indicate the direction of the wind.

third mate: Fourth in command. Often responsible for security.

topgallant: The mast or sails higher than the top mast.

topsail schooner: Schooner with square rigged sails on the foremast.

weather deck: The deck exposed to the open air.

wheel: Steering device.

yard: Horizontal beam from which a square sail may be hung.

ABOUT THE AUTHOR

C.S. Houghton studied creative writing at Southern Connecticut State University. He enjoys painting, drawing, old cameras, and gardening. The author lives in Connecticut with his adoring wife and their heterochromic dog.

Made in the USA
San Bernardino, CA
05 July 2013